PLAYLIST FOR VIBES

People Watching – Conan Gray

The Prophecy – Taylor Swift

To Be So Lonely – Harry Styles

Dress – Taylor Swift

Falling – Harry Styles

Just a Friend to You – Meghan Trainor

You Are Enough – Sleeping At Last

Cruel Summer – Taylor Swift

Foolish One – Taylor Swift

Pretty Enough – Amanda Williams

Say Don't Go (Taylor's Version)(From The Vault) –
Taylor Swift

This Love – Taylor Swift

**okay there could have been so many more Taylor Swift
songs but I chose to control myself**

To the girls who dream of an unconditional love, like the ones they read about in books.

You deserve the world.

Never settle for anything less.

I PROMISE I WON'T FALL

EMILY NICOLE

PROLOGUE
Ella

I haven't had sex for a whole year. 12 months. An entire calendar. It's not like I haven't tried, I've been on plenty of dates and approached plenty of men when I've been out with friends. Unfortunately, there's a man drought in this city. I swear, all the good men left Adelaide the minute they turned 25. It's either that, or my standards are too high and I'm being too picky. To top it all off, I've also been single for five years, so I reluctantly downloaded Tinder again a few weeks ago, as part of the vicious, lonely girl cycle of downloading and deleting dating apps. I was feeling alone and in need of validation from strangers—it's not the best way to go about it and is something I should probably bring up with my therapist, but it was the serotonin boost that I needed. It's also what led me to my current situation.

It's a Tuesday afternoon and I'm currently on a date with Jed, my latest Tinder match. Jed appeared completely normal online when we matched two weeks ago. The conversation flowed easily, and the banter was great, so we agreed to meet at one of my favourite pubs, Jimmies. I was feeling hopeful, even though his name starts with 'J' (as all women know, we must be wary of men whose name begins with a 'J'). However, that feeling has dissipated, and we've only been on this date for 15 minutes.

Firstly, I didn't recognise him when I walked in because he had shaved all his hair off, which was the complete opposite to his profile photos. I was looking for a man bun and instead found a buzzcut.

Eventually, I located him at a table in the beer garden, slouching in his seat with the biggest man spread I've ever seen. He'd also already bought himself a beer and was halfway through it. I wasn't even late for the date; I was on time.

Though it really started to go downhill when I approached the table, said hello, and he said, "Aw yeah, g'day Ella, how's it garn? Gonna grab yourself a drink before you sit down or nah?" He then proceeded to look down at his phone, assuming I'd headed straight to the bar. I stood there for a few seconds, feeling dumbfounded, before muttering "sure" and heading back inside.

I'm now at the bar ordering a drink and I know I'm being super rude and ignoring the bartender, but I'm frantically scrolling back over our messages to see what I've missed. This guy spoke so eloquently online, yet my first real impression of him is that he's an 'abrupt bogan'. I make my way back to the table and sit down with a glass of prosecco, hoping it will improve.

I am literally in the middle of telling him about my week—how I'm working at a school as a librarian and how much I'm looking forward to the summer holidays—when he interrupts me. Another red flag, it's not looking good.

"Oi, you look different to your pictures aye. Do ya know that? Your hair is red, and you're like, taller than I thought you would be." As he says this, he eyes me up and down. Normally, I don't mind being perused by a man who I am interested in, especially after a good bout of flirting. However, Jed's perusal of me made me feel like I was a cow being on show at the market.

My profile is as honest as they come. I don't use filters on my photos, I don't like to alter my appearance and give a misleading representation of myself. I want people to see the real me. I have long, strawberry blonde hair, blue-grey eyes, and I'm 5'7". My height is literally listed on my profile, and sure, my hair can look a little blonder in some photos because, you know, lighting. I'm incredibly confused by his comments, and to be honest, I'm a little annoyed.

"I'm sorry but you're one to talk, where did your hair go?" I ask, waving my hand at his now shaved head.

"Shaved it off on the weekend aye, whatchu think? Hot, yeah?" he asks, completely ignoring my other comments.

"Umm…." I don't know what to say. This date is awful. I take a large sip of prosecco to try and avoid answering the question. Turns out he doesn't care for an answer and has already moved onto the next topic.

"So, Ella, have you been on Tinder for long? Do you meet up with many dudes?" He asks, voice raised.

I nearly choke on my drink. *What the actual fuck?* He's asked that question loud enough that every table around us has turned to look at me. I don't think I've ever been so embarrassed before in my life.

"Uh, well, not long, I guess. This is my first date in months," I say, hopefully loud enough for those still listening in to hear, and not think I'm some desperate serial dater. I am so done with this guy. I down the rest of my drink. "Look, I'm sorry to cut this short, but I only really had time for one drink. I have a… uhh… presentation I need to finish before going back to work tomorrow." I stand from the table, and so does he.

"Oh yeah, nah that's chill. I've finished my drink anyway aye. I'll walk you back to your car."

I really want to say no, but he's already trying to lead me through the beer garden and out the door. I walk towards my car, with him standing uncomfortably close the whole time, hand on my lower back as if to say 'I own her'. "Well, this is me," I say as I reach my car and lean out of his reach. "Thanks for a nice time, I'll… uh… be in touch."

"Yeah, for sure. Oi, do ya reckon I could have a cheeky little kiss?" He smirks.

What in the male audacity? I stand there, stunned, and unsure what the hell to say.

"N-no, sorry. I have a 'no kissing on the first date' rule." I try to casually brush him off while subtly moving closer to my car door.

"Nah, c'mon, you wanna kiss me. I can see the signs." As he says this, he leans in closer to me and puts his hand on the roof of my car, over my shoulder. I'm boxed in and I don't know what to do.

"Uh… no… I just… don't…" I stammer as I try to get the words out.

"Excuse me, love, I think you left your jacket in the beer garden."

I look over Jed's shoulder and see the bartender I was ignoring earlier, standing behind him holding a jacket that is definitely not mine. I don't know what brought him outside—maybe he saw how uncomfortable I was walking out of the bar with Jed's hand on me, and now from his perspective, all he can see is a man caging me in against my car. If he heard enough, he would have heard me say no. His demeanour is calm and casual, but his eyes and the white-knuckle grip on the jacket tells me he knows exactly what kind of situation I am in and will intervene if I need him to. I gently push Jed away and step towards the bartender.

"Oh! How silly of me. Thanks for bringing it out," I say, relieved. This man has just saved me from a really, really shitty situation.

"No worries! I'm happy to help." He gives me a look that says 'do you need me to do anything?' I subtly shake my head at him—I really don't want to cause a scene. I unlock my car behind me and open the door. Jed has taken enough steps back to glare at the bartender for interrupting, so I'm able to slide in easily enough. I shut the door before he can reach for me again. I wind down the window far enough for him to hear me speak, but not far enough for him to poke his head in.

"Goodbye, Jed. I'll chat with you later. Thanks again for my jacket, Mr Bartender man." I smile at him. My rescuer.

"You're welcome. Have a good night!" He walks off, knowing that I'm safe, but waits outside the entrance of the bar. I wind the window back up and start my car, giving Jed a wave goodbye as I pull out of the car park. He's standing there looking both annoyed and confused. As I drive past the bartender, I mouth a "thank you" to him. He gives me a nod and a small wave before heading back into the bar. I drive a couple of blocks before I need to pull over. My eyes are burning and my bottom lip is quivering. I feel a tightness in my chest and the overwhelming sense of crushing disappointment. I turn the car off and bury my head in my hands and start to cry.

Why? Why is this my life?

I am so fucking sick of being single.

CHAPTER 1
Ella

"I'm sorry, he asked for what now?"

"A cheeky little kiss," I say with a groan. I'm sitting in the staff room at work, having lunch with my colleague-turned-best-friend, Millie. She's getting the full rundown of my disaster of a date; it's been three days and I finally have the time to tell her all about it. I still can't shake the awful feeling I left the date with.

"And even though you said no, he went in for it anyway? What the fuck!" Millie exclaimed. A few of the older English teachers look our way, frowning at our inappropriateness.

"Yup. Thankfully, one of the bartenders intervened. Came out to give me my jacket, even though I didn't have one. I'm pretty sure it's his, actually."

"Well, thank God he jumped in. I can't imagine what would have happened if he hadn't. I know what you're like, Ella Hart, you would have kissed the guy because you don't like confrontation. What happened after the bartender interrupted?"

"Thankfully I was able to get into my car without any trouble. And then I cried for a bit, felt sorry for myself, and drove home. You know, the usual routine after a date."

"Oh, Ella…"

"What? I wish I was kidding. It's dismal out there, Millie. Dismal. You just wouldn't know. Little miss, I've been happily married for six years." I say, sulking.

"I know, I know. I just hate seeing you like this. Men fucking suck." She once again draws attention from the older English teachers, one of them shaking her head and telling us to shush.

"Preaching to the choir," I mumble.

We both work at Lake View College, a rather conservative secondary school in Adelaide. I've been here for six years, and Millie started working here two years ago as an English teacher. She was quiet and timid at first, until she discovered my bookstagram page and saw the types of books I enjoyed reading. I'll never forget the day she waltzed into the library, sat down at my desk with a pen and paper, and asked me for all my favourite smutty book recommendations. I nearly fell off my chair with laughter, but I gave her a list and sent her on her way. Fast forward two weeks, and we were inseparable. Our lives couldn't look any more different, she's been married for six years to her absolute golden retriever of a husband, Clay. They own a house and are looking at starting a family soon. And then there's me, perpetually single, renting a low-income house and living off of mostly Nutrigrain and pasta. We don't make sense as friends, but somehow, we work beautifully. Plus, we share the same birthday, January 2nd.

"I'm so glad that the bartender noticed what was happening, though. At least you experienced one man showing decency. Did you happen to get his name?" she asks.

"Nope. I have no idea who he is! But I should probably go back to return his jacket and thank him properly."

"I wonder if he's single." She grins and waggles her eyebrows at me.

I groan again. "Ugh, no. I've already had one dating fail this week. I will not set myself up for another one."

Honestly, I don't think my heart could take another failed date. That date I had with Jed was the first one in months, and the only reason I actually went was because of Millie bullying me into it. I don't blame her, he looked so promising, and he seemed so normal online. But once again I've been reminded to never trust the internet. Dating is exhausting. I'm so sick of having to start from the beginning, giving my life story over and over again. I would love nothing more than for the love of my life to be someone I already know, someone who knows me well enough that I don't have to explain myself in such a robotic and rehearsed sort of way. Unfortunately, almost all of the men in my life are either married or gay. So, there isn't much, if any, chance of that ever happening.

"Besides," I say, "I didn't even get a good proper look at him; I was too busy trying to escape my bogan red flag of a date. He could be 19 years old for all I know. I'll go there on Sunday afternoon and hope that he's working. Want to come?"

"Ahh, I can't Sunday. Clay has organised a date night. I have no idea what he's got planned, other than that he told me to wear loose clothing. So, I'm either going to be eating my weight in food, or he wants easy access to what's underneath the loose clothing. Both options would be ideal, but either way, I'm getting stuffed."

I bark out a laugh. That's another thing I love about Millie, she's just as open and positive about sex as I am. It definitely makes working in a conservative school rather difficult at times. Last year, I had to hold Millie back from putting one of our teachers on blast for lecturing some of our female students about modesty and purity. But at least we have each other. My favourite time of the day is recess and lunch where we can chat shit, get it all out of our system before putting our professional hats back on and going our separate ways. Millie to the classroom, me to the library.

"Well, I can't wait to hear all about that! But okay, I'll go alone then. Should be fun." I say. Hopefully the ick feeling I have about Jimmies has disappeared by then. It's one of my favourite pubs, and I'd hate for one guy to ruin it for me.

The school bell rings, signifying the end of lunch. We pack up our things and head out of the staff room, but not before gaining some more judgemental looks from the English teachers again. I just give them my biggest and brightest smile and wish them a happy Friday. There's only a few more hours of work until I can get home to my bed and books for a quiet, uneventful weekend.

I'm lying in bed, scrolling through Instagram. My book is beside me, screaming for me to pick it up. Typical of me, I plan an evening specifically for reading and spend most of the night just staring at my phone. I'm finally about to put it down and pick up my book when I notice a message request. I open it and groan. Somehow, Jed has found my Instagram page.

JED

> Hey Ella, for some reason I can't seem to find you on Tinder, there must have been a glitch or something, so I thought I'd try my luck on here. I really enjoyed spending time with you on Tuesday night, wanna come have a drink at my place this weekend? Perhaps have a bit of
>
> fun too? ;)

"Is he actually joking?" I mutter to myself. This guy must be delusional. How could he possibly think that I would like to see him again? I gave absolutely no signals that I was interested… I mean, I unmatched him on Tinder, and he seems to think that was just an error. Men. Honestly. Also, how is he this coherent online? I'm still blown away by this contrast. I'm tempted to just block the guy so I can put it behind me, but decide to respond. I'm not normally one for confrontation, but he needs to know how uncomfortable he made me feel and learn from it. Plus, I'm a couple of wines deep, alone in bed on a Friday night. I have nothing better to do.

ELLA

> Jed, I don't know what signals you thought I was giving you on Tuesday, but none of them implied that I would want to sleep with you. You cornered me and almost forced yourself on me after I told you I didn't want to kiss you. I felt really uncomfortable. I'm sorry, but it's just not going to happen. Perhaps you should reassess how you approach women, because backing them into a corner is not going to get you laid. Good luck for the future.

I take another sip of wine and wonder about the audacity of this man. Being single in this day and age is a fucking joke. Maybe I'd be better off alone. No one wants me for anything but my body anyway. Well, not even my body lately….

I take a deep breath to refocus. "Ella, stop. You're having those thoughts again," I say to myself, just like my therapist taught me. A trick to use when I start to have sad or negative thoughts that I usually just try to ignore—which never works, FYI. I now acknowledge these thoughts out loud, and if I do it enough, perhaps I'll detach myself and not obsess over them.

My phone vibrates and I open the response from Jed. His message makes me want to laugh, scream, and cry all at once.

JED

Wow, didn't realise you were such a bitch. Why did you lead me on then? I don't need women advice from a stuck-up cow. Whatever, I didn't actually want to fuck you anyway. Enjoy being a lonely slut.

There is nothing more entertaining than a man-baby trying to insult a woman who rejected him. Lonely slut? That's a new one. It's also a pretty good oxymoron, though the man probably has no idea what that means. I wonder about the other women he's dated, and hope that they also had someone to save them from his advances. I should just leave it there, but I *am* a bitch. A petty one.

ELLA

A good man takes advice on the chin. I guess you've just proven yourself to be the opposite of that. Enjoy fucking your hand for the rest of eternity.

I press send, wait until he's seen the message and then block him. I take screenshots, forward them to Millie, and then put down my phone to finish my glass of wine. I pick up my book and settle myself in for a couple of hours of smutty heaven. The best way to escape reality, in my humble opinion.

CHAPTER 2
Ella

It's a blazing hot Sunday afternoon and I can't stop fidgeting with my baby blue sundress. I'm about to catch the train so I can drop this jacket off to the bartender. I loathe parking in the city and am lucky enough to live around the corner from a train station. The only reason I drove into the city for my date with Jed was so I could make a quick escape if I needed it. In hindsight, it was good thinking on my part.

"Why am I fidgeting? This dress is cute, I look great. I'm literally just going to a bar to drop off a jacket. To a stranger, whose face is a blur. Suck it up," I say to myself. I say a lot of things to myself—I've lived alone long enough that it feels normal now. Though to other people, I'm sure I look like a crazy person. I finish my makeup, wearing nothing fancy because again, this is a non-event. I grab my handbag, making sure my Kindle is inside. I never go anywhere without my Kindle. I'm extroverted most of the time, but sometimes a girl needs to escape for a little bit. I rush out the door and head for the train station.

It's only a 20-minute ride into the city, so I arrive in no time. I walk 10 minutes to the pub, and then I'm there. I take a deep breath and head inside. I don't know why I feel so nervous. It's weird, I'm usually a lot more chill and confident than this, but my date with Jed seems to have really shaken that confidence. *Stupid man, I need to fix this.* I walk up to the bar where a young woman is pouring a beer. She's absolutely stunning, with sleek black hair, tanned skin, and gorgeous dark green eyes. I'm momentarily dazed by her beauty, until I realise I am slightly gawking at her. I clear my throat; thankful she didn't notice me staring at her as she was too busy with another customer.

"Um, hi. I was just wondering if there are any men working here tonight?" I say, giving her my friendliest smile.

She looks at me and smiles back. "We have a few men working here, hun. Are you looking for someone in particular or are you just after any man?"

I laugh.

"Oh my God. That came across way worse than I intended. I'm looking for someone, but I don't know his name."

"Hmm. Can you describe him for me?"

"Uhh. He's tall. And has a beard. That's all I got."

She laughs. "Okay, that's not a lot to go on, but it could be Xavier."

I look at her blankly.

"Tall, beard, killer smile, nicest guy ever, bartender extraordinaire… ring any bells?"

"I mean it could be. Whoever it was gave me their jacket the other night when I was in a… uhh.. tricky situation. I'm here to return it." I show her the jacket, it's plaid with dark greens and blues woven through it.

"That definitely looks like something Xavier would wear. I think he's out the back taking stock. Do you want me to get him for you? What's your name?"

"Sure. I'm Ella, though he doesn't know who I am, not really. If you could get him, that would be great. I'll just wait at that table in the corner if that's cool?"

"Yeah sure, I'll send him out," she says, and heads into the back of the bar.

I take a seat and pull out my Kindle as I wait. Might as well read a few pages in the meantime. The pub isn't too busy yet, with just a few groups milling about. Jimmies has been one of my favourite pubs for the last few years. There's nothing particularly special about it—it has a standard mahogany bar with spirit bottles lined up on shelves reaching to the ceiling. The furnishings are old, with green velvet couches, wooden tables, and chairs scattered around. The floors are sticky in the main bar area from years of spillage and the only music they play is old school '80s rock. The best part about this place is the beer garden, which was added only a couple of years ago. It's the main drawcard for people of my age. The place could definitely make do with some upgrades, but it's comfortable and familiar.

Admittedly, I was worried Jed could possibly be here. I don't know what I would do if he was, but thankfully he's nowhere to be seen. I look up from my book to see a man walking over to me and I swear to God, my mouth almost drops open. No way this man is my rescuer. He reaches my table and smiles at me.

"Ella?" he says. I nod.

"Xavier. Nice to meet you properly. I was wondering if I would see you or my jacket again." He laughs.

I'm just looking back at him like an idiot. This guy is definitely not 19—he is all man. At least 6-foot, with thick, dark brown hair that's shoved back messily from his face, showing off deep caramel eyes. A short beard, and a body that screams *I'm not an athlete, but I can chop wood and carry you over my shoulder with ease.* He's wearing ripped jeans and a tight black t-shirt, and I am deceased.

"Ella? You good?"

I snap out of it and scramble for something to say.

"Um, hi, yes… yeah, sorry it took so long to return it, it's been a busy week. Here you go." I practically shove his jacket at him. He takes it in his hands and either doesn't realise how flustered I am, or he doesn't care, because he asks if he can sit down. I nod, and he takes the seat opposite me. I'm mentally trying to compose myself. Generally speaking, he isn't my usual type. I have no idea what is going on, but this man has me in a head spin, and I've been in his presence for only 30 seconds.

"How are you going? I'm sorry if I overstepped the other night. I saw you leaving, and you looked quite uncomfortable. And then when I walked out and saw him cornering you, I had to step in."

"No, don't be sorry at all. I don't know what would have happened if you didn't intervene. I… froze. And was trapped. So thank you, really. I appreciate it more than you know." I smile at him, though it doesn't quite reach my eyes. I really don't want to think about what would have happened if he didn't step in. He seems to notice that.

"Happy to be of assistance. Is it bold of me to assume that it was a date gone wrong?" he asks, tentatively.

"Sure was, first date in fact. Definitely not what I was expecting given his online presence. But no worries, he is out of the picture now. Though he didn't quite comprehend that I wasn't interested and couldn't handle the rejection," I say, rolling my eyes.

"Oh, let me guess, he was one of those guys who resorted to insulting you instead of just accepting it wasn't meant to be?"

"How did you know!" I exclaim. I pull out my phone and show him screenshots of the messages. "He is now blocked and hopefully gone for good."

Xavier reads the messages and throws his head back laughing. His laughter is deep yet warm, the kind that is infectious and makes everyone around him want to laugh as well.

"Wow, what an absolute tosser! Nice comeback, by the way. I hope that man never has a woman in his bed ever again." He hands me back my phone. "Hey, did you want a drink? On the house, given the last time you were here you had a shitty time."

"Actually, that would be nice, thanks! But I'm happy to pay." I reach for my purse.

"Nope, it's on the house. The manager insists."

"Who's the manager?"

"Me. So, what would you like? Cocktail? I can make you whatever you want," he says. He seems like a nice enough guy, and really, I have nothing better to do tonight.

"Oh! Well okay then. I've been really craving an amaretto sour lately, they're my favourite," I say.

"Easily done! I'll be back shortly." He scoots his chair back and walks back over to the bar to make my drink. I get my phone out and pull up my message thread with Millie.

ELLA

OMFG MILLIE. This bartender. I am dead. He's like a metropolitan lumberjack. I am dying. He's so hot. Help.

MILLIE

FUCK YES GET IT GIRL.

ELLA

Um, no. I'm just going to look. I've spent five minutes with the man!

MILLIE

Ella I swear to God. At least find out if he is single. Please.

ELLA

Ugh, okay fine. He's coming back. Gotta go! x

Xavier comes back to the table with two drinks in his hands. "I've actually just finished my shift, so I hope you don't mind if I join you for a knock off drink?" he asks.

"No, not at all! You did rescue me, after all. If anything, I should be buying you a drink to say thank you."

"Well, perhaps if you're not sick of my company after this drink you can buy me the next one. Unless you have somewhere to be?" He hands me my drink.

"Nope, no plans for me tonight."

"Awesome, well… cheers! Here's to calling out dickhead men."

I laugh. "I'll definitely cheers to that! And cheers to decent men who intervene when a woman is in a tricky spot."

We clink glasses and I take a sip. I look over the lip of my glass and make eye contact with him as he does the same. There's something electric about making eye contact with someone when having a drink, and I can definitely feel it with Xavier. The cocktail is delicious, and it takes everything in me to not down the entire thing in one go. But I don't, obviously—I'm a lady.

"So, if you don't mind me asking, how did you meet that guy?" he asks.

I sigh, and then tell him the whole story. He has a look on his face the whole time, but I can't quite pick it. It's a mix between disgust and amusement. Which, realistically, sums up the whole experience perfectly.

"God, I'm really sorry you had to deal with that. The dating world seems like a real shitty place to be." He's shaking his head.

Ah, there you go. The dating world "seems" really shitty, meaning he isn't part of it, meaning he isn't single. That's disappointing, not that I was even going to attempt to go there.

"It sure is, I've been trying to navigate it for a while now. It doesn't get any easier," I say.

"How long?"

"Um… five years?" I say, somewhat embarrassed.

He looks at me, head tilted slightly to the left. He seems to be contemplating something.

"Nope, I don't believe you. There's no way you've been single for five years."

I can feel myself start to blush. That's sweet, though perhaps a little weird, given the man doesn't know me from a bar of soap. I clear my throat.

"Yes, well, it's true. I haven't had a lot of success in that area. Just haven't found my person yet, or whatever."

"Well, that's a damn shame. Probably sounds weird coming from someone you've just met, but you seem pretty great. You give off a really good energy." He smiles at me, and I can see a dimple in his left cheek. Goddamn it, I'm an absolute sucker for dimples.

I'm definitely blushing now. "Thank you. You're right, it is weird." He laughs. "But also, it's sweet." I smile back at him. "So… what about you?"

"What about me?"

"How long have you been with your… partner?" I ask.

"Oh." He blinks. "I don't have a partner. Not anymore. I separated from my long-term girlfriend about… seven months ago now."

"Crap! I'm sorry, I shouldn't have asked." *Shit. Yeah, good work Ella.*

"No, it's fine. It's a very amicable separation. Just wasn't meant to be, you know?"

"Okay, well, I'm still sorry. Like you said, we've just met. This is weird. You're not weird, I mean, I'm weird. I'm going to stop talking. Want another drink? I'll get another drink." I stand up awkwardly and walk towards the bar. I can hear him chuckling behind me as I walk.

My god, I am embarrassing myself. I really need to pull it together. I order us two more cocktails from the gorgeous bartender from earlier.

"So…" she says. "You know Xavier well?"

"No, not at all actually. He, um, saved me from a bad date earlier in the week. I just came back to say thank you," I say.

"Oh you're that girl! We all heard about you. That guy sounded like a complete dick. I'm glad Xavier was there to help. He's one of the good ones, for real."

I groan inwardly. Of course, they all heard about my shitty date. This is so embarrassing. She must be able to tell how I'm feeling, because she reaches out and touches my arm.

"Hey, don't be embarrassed. We've all been there. As a bartender, I've faced many loser men who think they're God's gift to women." I snort. "There's always going to be guys like that out there, but at least you've weeded out another one." She smiles at me. "My name is Lena, by the way. If you're ever in a shitty situation like that again, come see me. I have a few tactics that will make them regret their choices." She hands me my drinks and I pay for them.

"You're right, thank you Lena." I smile at her and return to Xavier, drinks in hand.

"Okay, no more 'relationship talk'. You're clearly flustered…" he says with a knowing grin. Bastard. "Tell me a bit about yourself instead," he says as he takes a sip.

I blow out a breath.

"Well, I'm 30. I grew up in a small, country town but moved here about nine years ago."

"Oh cool, did you move here for uni or something? I've always loved the country lifestyle, but just can't make myself leave the city. I have a property in the Adelaide Hills though, and some chickens. So, close enough."

I laugh.

"Love that! Chickens are the best. Definitely country-esque. But no, I didn't end up going to university. I got a Diploma in Library Studies and am now working as a school librarian."

"That is so cool," he says, genuinely. "I'm guessing you're a pretty big reader then? I didn't even know you could study to be a librarian."

"Yeah, I get that a lot." I chuckle. "But yes, most librarians are qualified in the field. And yep, big reader. Obsessed. Books are my entire life. What about you?"

"Oh yeah, I love to read. Mostly fantasy, but I'll pretty much read anything."

Oh, be still my beating heart. Guys who read are my kryptonite. Not to mention, he's also the first guy I've met to not outright objectify me after I've told them I'm a librarian. Most guys will immediately tell me of their sexy librarian fantasies the moment they find out what I do for work. It's a refreshing change, and

I smile at him.

"Fantasy is one of my favourites, too. Growing up, it was my favourite means of escape. As an only child, books were my greatest company."

"I'm an only child too!" he says. "Another thing we have in common."

"Cheers to the only child club." We raise our glasses again. "Now, tell me about you. Have you always wanted to be a bar manager?"

"Not necessarily a bar manager, but my family actually owns this place." He gestures around him.

"No way! I love Jimmies. That is so cool."

"Thanks. It's been in my family for generations. It's kind of always been my plan to take over once my dad, Arthur, retires. I've worked here ever since I was old enough to load a dishwasher."

"And how old are you now?" I ask.

"I'm 32."

Excellent. Definitely not nineteen then.

"Cool. Can I ask, where did the name Jimmies come from?" I've always wondered.

"Well our family name is James. My great grandad was nicknamed Jimmy and when he opened the place up, that's what he called it." He shrugs.

"Huh. Simple, I like it."

Xavier James. Bar manager. Family legacy. Lumberjack look alike. I'm starting to like this guy.

My stomach starts growling and so we order some food to share. The conversation is so easy—it's flowing and there are no awkward moments of silence. If this was a date, I would say it was going well. But it's not a date. And that, I think, is why this is so easy. It's just two people getting to know each other with no expectations. It's nice.

After I finish telling him about my last overseas holiday to Germany, I check the time. I need to go if I'm going to make the train home.

"Well, I think I need to head off. I do have to prepare for work tomorrow," I say. "Thank you so much for this. You have restored my faith in men, and my love for this pub is no longer tainted."

He laughs and stands up from the table. "It was an absolute pleasure, Ella. Come back for a drink any time. Would you like me to walk you out to your car?" he asks. I pause and he panics, remembering the last time I was here and someone offered to walk me to my car. "Not in a creepy way!" He blurts. "Just to make sure you get out safely."

I just smile. It's kind of cute how he keeps reassuring me he's not a creep like Jed.

"It's fine. Unless you feel like walking me to the train station? I didn't drive in today."

He stops and turns to me. "You're catching the train home, alone, at this hour?"

"This hour being… 9pm? Yes. I always take the train, it's fine. I've only been mugged once."

I wave my hand dismissively and he blanches at the action.

"Oh my God, I'm kidding!" I say, laughing. "I do it all the time, it's a

20-minute train ride and I live around the corner from the station. It's fine." I say again.

"I don't like it," he mumbles. "I can give you a lift home if you'd prefer. I know we've only just met, but I promise I'm not a psychopath."

"That's exactly what a psychopath would say."

He laughs again. "True, true. But seriously, I would like to drive you home. I hate the idea of you catching the train at night by yourself. It goes against all of my morals. I am a gentleman, after all."

To be honest, I really don't feel like catching the train. And the guy seems genuine.

I look over my shoulder and yell over at Lena, who's wiping down the bar. "Hey Lena, if I let Xavier drive me home, will I end up tied up in his boot? Or is he really a gentleman?"

Xavier grins at this and she cracks up laughing. "Nope, definitely a gentleman. You're safe with that one! Trust me."

"Okay, you can drive me home. Lena is my witness. Lead the way!" I say as I look back at Xavier.

He leads me out the back and of course, he drives a ute. My first thought is, *I've always wanted to have sex in the tray of a ute, under the stars.* I hop in the passenger seat, give Xavier directions to my house, and we set off. The drive is mostly quiet, but it's a comfortable silence. No awkwardness.

We're almost at my house when I turn to him.

"Thank you again for tonight. I really needed it. You're an alright kind of guy." I grin.

"And you're an alright kind of girl," he says. "I meant what I said, come have a drink any time. I can give you my number if you'd like. Just shoot us a text and I can let you know when I'll be around."

"Yeah, okay. I'll definitely take you up on that."

I am screaming internally and doing my best to play it cool on the outside. He's giving me his number—willingly. And not in a creepy 'I'm only going to text you at 2am' sort of manner. *Unreal.*

We pull up at my house and exchange phone numbers. I say goodnight, and we have one of those awkward car hugs, hindered by seatbelts and handbrakes. I hop out of the car and close the door.

I turn back and he's wound down the window. "Oh and Ella?" I meet his gaze as he leans a little closer. "That sundress you're wearing looks pretty phenomenal, I just thought you should know that."

I stand there, blush rushing to my cheeks with my jaw hanging open. He winds the window back up, gives me a cheeky smirk, and drives off into the night. I'm on cloud nine as I hop into bed.

I feel giddy.

Shit.

CHAPTER 3
Ella

It has been 12 days since my not-date with Xavier, and I still can't get it out of my head. It has also been six days since I heard from him. The man has only texted me a handful of times; the first time was the night he dropped me off at my house. He texted to let me know he got home safe, and my heart melted a little at the gesture. Other than that, there have just been a few casual texts here and there to check in. I know I could send him a few messages, but I already felt like an awkward mess, and I thought it was best to just leave it and hope he would reach out a bit more. It's fine though, he's probably busy and besides, I have another date lined up for tonight.

I'm not that excited about it—it's a blind date (cue my anxious freak out). A few weeks ago, Clay mentioned to Millie that one of his colleagues is recently single and looking to get back into the dating world. They mentioned I was single and told him a little bit about me, and he was willing to meet up for a drink. I agreed to it but had completely forgotten about it until two days ago when Millie told me she had booked us a table at Jimmies. When I protested her choice in venue since I didn't want Xavier to see me on a date, she said, "I booked it there because at least we know there'll be a good man nearby who can step in for you again if you need it. Plus, you haven't heard from Xavier all week. Might as well remind him of your existence by showing up with another man."

Now, let's be real—this doesn't work. Men don't really care unless they're a possessive alphahole. And possessive alphaholes are only okay in a fictional sense. But I guess she is right, in a way. Though really, Xavier isn't even an option at this point. He gave me one compliment, one I admittedly can't stop thinking about, but he didn't hint at anything else. *Whatever, I should really be focusing on this date.* I'm wearing my blue sundress again, but I've left my hair down and curly tonight. I'm wearing a little more makeup than I usually would, and I'm wearing heels. I'm feeling just a tad insecure, as I've never been on a blind date, and I want to impress.

Clay showed me a picture of the guy and he is the epitome of my 'usual type'. Blond hair, blue eyes, a jawline that could cut you. Probably works in finance or something else that could be described as sensible and boring. I don't know why I tend to go for guys like this, it has never worked for me in the past. But he was attractive, and he was interested in me. The only thing I'm weary about is his age, he's 26. It isn't that big of a deal, I've dated younger guys before, but being 30 years old myself, I want to settle down.

I'll have to figure out a way to bring that up in conversation. I'm a strong believer in asking the big questions straight up when dating. There's no point in spending months getting to know someone and then finding out they don't want kids or have plans to move to Canada in the next three months. Both of these scenarios have happened to me in the past.

Before I head out though, I want to give Xavier a heads up that I'm coming into the pub tonight.

ELLA

> Hey Xavier, I hope you've had a good week! I'm just letting you know I'm meeting someone at Jimmies tonight for a blind date. Terrifying. If I feel like I need rescuing again, I'll give you a signal. That's if you're working tonight. And if you're not, then ignore this message. Bye! x

I grab my purse and once again make my way to the train station. I should drive, so I have another quick escape, but I want to be able to have a couple of drinks tonight and not worry about it. I pick up my kindle on the train, as I was halfway through a particularly steamy scene in the reverse harem novel I was reading. Thankfully, I finish the chapter by the time the train pulls into the city. I put it away and walk to Jimmies, a little more flustered than I was before.

I walk through the doors and I'm relieved to see Lena working behind the bar again. I'm 10 minutes early, so I go up to her and have a quick chat.

"Hello again, Ella!" she begins. "How've you been? Are you looking for Xavier?"

I laugh, awkwardly. "Hey Lena, I've been alright. And no, I'm not. I'm meeting some guy here on a blind date. My best friend set it up so it should be interesting. Is Xavier working tonight? I messaged him to ask, but he didn't reply," I say.

"No, sorry, he's not working tonight, but he might pop in later. I think he's got a family dinner or something. If you need rescuing though, I'm happy to help out in his absence!" she says.

I smile at that, though I am a little disappointed that Xavier isn't here. I was hoping to at least just look at him, or maybe even say hello. "That would be great, Lena. Thank you. If I come to the bar and ask for a Fireball, save me."

She laughs as I make my way over to an empty table. It's busier tonight, being a Saturday. The dinner rush has finished, and the drinks crowd has just started to appear. I check my phone, it's 8pm, right on schedule. I look around the room and I can't see anyone who looks like my date anywhere. It's only just now that I realise Millie never gave me his name.

8:15pm. Still no date.

8:30pm. I've ordered myself a rosé, still no date.

9:00pm. Lena has brought me over a second glass of rosé. I'm sitting at this table reading on my kindle. I definitely haven't been stood up. It's only been an hour. It's fine, he's just late.

9:30pm. I finished my book. I've been stood up. *What. The. Fuck.*

"Hey Ella," Lena appears at my table again, a sad smile on her face. "I'm going to make a guess and say he's not coming?"

"I guess not. Ugh. This is so embarrassing! Just my luck. Who stands someone up these days?!" I bury my head in my hands and groan.

"Nope. No. This isn't on you. That guy is clearly a wanker, who has now missed his shot with an awesome chick. He's not worth it," she says. "Do you want another glass of wine? Or are you done for the night?"

"Nah, I'll have another. I didn't drive in tonight for a reason, so I might as well drink away the shame of yet another failed date." I sigh. *This fucking sucks. I haven't even met the guy and he's decided I'm not worthy enough of his time. What a kick in the gut.* I pick up my phone and send a message to Millie.

ELLA

> This guy is great! I'm having such a great time!

She responds immediately.

MILLIE

> OMG really?!

ELLA

> No. He stood me up. I'm about to have my third glass of wine. Fuck my life, honestly.

MILLIE

> NOOOOOOO! What the fuck! Ella, I'm so, so sorry. Clay said he was a decent guy. God, I feel terrible.

A glass of rosé appears at my table, and I look up to thank Lena for my drink, but instead, I'm looking into the dark caramel eyes of Xavier James, bartender, metro lumberjack, and my constant rescuer.

"Oh, hey. I thought you were Lena," I say and try to plaster a smile on my face.

"Nope. It's me, Mr Bartender Man. Do you mind if I join you?"

"Go ahead. That seat has been cold all night—you might as well warm it up," I say, jokingly. It doesn't help the sting of rejection I'm feeling.

"Yeah, look, Lena texted me and let me know about your... ah... situation? I hope you don't mind her telling me. She just felt bad and thought perhaps I could try and cheer you up."I try to smile, but it doesn't reach my eyes, and it feels forced. I take a big sip of wine, more of a gulp actually. "It's fine, I don't mind. She's so lovely to even think of trying to cheer me up. Though, if I'm being honest, I'm feeling pretty shitty about myself right now. So, I don't know if there's much you can do."

I can feel myself sinking further and further down into the pit of self-loathing I have built. I was already feeling awful after my date with Jed, and then to not hear from Xavier for a week, to now being stood up. How is a girl supposed to feel? Rejection is fucking hard. It's one of the reasons I don't date very much. I wear my heart on my sleeve, I get attached quickly, and the fear of rejection keeps me from completely putting myself out there. I don't want to fall for another guy, just for him to tell me 'sorry, I'm just not looking for anything serious right now' two months in. It's a vicious, never-ending cycle. One that has completely drained me of any hope of finding my person. Nights like tonight just reinforce that feeling.

Xavier is just looking at me now, and I know the look. He's looking at me like I'm a fragile little flower.

I sigh.

"It's fine, Xavier. Really. The feeling will pass, it always does. I'll finish this glass, head home, and find another shitty romance novel to lose myself in. It's a well-practised routine, so I know it works." As well as crying myself to sleep, but I don't tell him that.

"Okay. I have an idea but feel free to say no, because I don't want to overstep. How about this, you finish your wine, then I'll drive you home. You can show me your book collection, and I'll let you pick out the cheesiest, spiciest, or most fucked up romance novel for me to read. Does that sound good to you?" he asks.

I smile and actually perk up a little at that idea. He wants me to pick out a book for him to read. I have so many ideas running through my head already. It's not going to make me forget about tonight, but it'll definitely distract me for the moment. It's actually my perfect style of distraction and I'm more than happy to go along with it.

"You know I actually don't mind the sound of that. Let's do it." I tell him.

"Excellent. Take your time though, you've still got almost a full drink—" he starts to say as I'm downing my drink in one go. Not the best idea, drinking wine like that, but no matter. I'm now buzzed and ready to go.

"Lead the way, Mr Bartender Man." I giggle.

"I wonder if I should get that on a t-shirt."

"Oh my God, please do! I'll make it and sell it to everyone."

He laughs. "Okay, entrepreneur. Let's go. Bye Lena!"

We both turn and wave goodbye and head out the door. Xavier has his hand on my lower back, guiding me. Not in a creepy and possessive way like Jed did, but in the way a gentleman leads his lady.

I don't know if it's the wine or the smut I was reading earlier, probably both, but just that little bit of contact has me so turned on.

I'm sad and horny—what a combination.

CHAPTER 4
Ella

We make it back to my house and the moment we walk through the front door, I suddenly become very self-conscious of my space. I do a quick scan of my living area, thankful that I hadn't left the house too messy. When you live alone, you get accustomed to living in your own mess because you're the only one who has to put up with it. Sometimes I will leave the dishes on the sink until I've run out of forks. It's a terrible habit that I've gotten into, and lord help the next person I end up living with. I'm glad I spent the morning doing a quick tidy though, and I only have one plate left on the sink.

My house—if you can call it that, since it's more like a shoebox—has two small bedrooms with an open living space and teeny tiny back courtyard. I've lived here for three years and despite wanting a bigger home, the rental market is shit and I won't get anything for this price again. I rent it privately through some old guy who never bothers me. It's the perfect set up and really, it has all I need. Well, not everything. A dishwasher would be nice.

Xavier is standing in the middle of the room, taking it all in. "Nice space! It's cute." "Thanks, it's small but comfortable. Do you want a drink? I've got wine or water," I say, opening the fridge and having a look. It's a little bit empty, thank God it's pay day this week.

"Sure, I'll have a glass of wine if you will."

"Oh, I'm definitely having a glass. I got stood up. I am sad. I may even finish the bottle. Who knows! The night is young." I fill up two glasses and hand one to him. I clink my glass against his and take a big sip. He just stands there and looks at me.

"What?" I ask.

"Nothing. I'm just trying to figure out how someone could possibly think standing you up is a good idea," he says and then takes a sip. Once again, I feel myself starting to blush. I've never blushed so much around anyone in my life. Before I can respond to him, he asks me for a tour of the house. I laugh, since he can literally see 80% of it from where we are standing.

"Well… this is most of it. Over here is the bathroom…" I lead him to one of the doors coming off of the living area. One thing I am grateful for, is that despite the size of this place, I do have a bath. I try to have at least one bath a week, because *self-care*. I walk to the next door, which is my bedroom.

"Uh, this is my bedroom. Nothing too exciting, just a wardrobe and a cold, lonely bed. Moving on," I say. He pops his head inside, and again, I am glad I tidied this morning and that I actually made my bed for once.

"Now this room is my favourite room in the whole house. I spend almost all of my time here."

I open the door to my personal library and turn on the lights. In one corner I have my vintage armchair, where I sit for hours on end. I bought it online for an absolute bargain and it's some of the best money I've ever spent. I have a fluffy, baby pink rug placed on the floor in the middle of the room, and of course, my books. One whole wall of the room is covered in floor to ceiling bookshelves. I've lost track of how many books I own, there are books of every genre on my shelves. Along with a few plants and souvenirs from my travels. This room is my happy place, and a direct representation of who I am.

"Oh wow." He steps inside and walks up to the shelves. "When you said home library, I didn't think you meant an actual home library."

"The only thing missing is a rolling ladder. Every bookworm's dream." I sigh. "But yes, I wasn't exaggerating. This is where all of my money goes."

"I mean, you could be spending it on worse things. It could be drugs," he says.

I laugh.

"You're not wrong there. Now, what was it you wanted me to pick out for you again?"

"Whatever you think is the cringiest and smuttiest book on your shelf. Shock me."

I grin at him, then

he smirks back at me. "There's a smile! Though, that one terrifies me a little."

"I am going to have fun with this. Let me have a think." I start to look on my shelves; there are a couple that stand out that I know for a fact would have him squirming. But no, he wants to be shocked, and there is only one book I can think of that would do that.

"Ah ha! Found it. Here you go. I can't wait to hear your thoughts on this one. I think it might change your life." I hand him the book and his jaw goes slack just looking at the title. He sits down on the armchair and opens to the first page and reads.

"Woman, you need Jesus," he says with a laugh.

"Just you wait. I expect live updates and reactions as you read it, please and thank you."

We move back out into the living room and plop ourselves onto my couch. I'm feeling quite tipsy at this point, but not quite enough to distract from the feeling of rejection I got from being stood up. Plus, I'm a little bit antsy. It's weird having Xavier here. Yes, he's hot, but I barely know the guy! But then, I think about some of my friends who will literally invite a man from Tinder into their bed without meeting them first. I wish I had that sort of confidence, but I'm too paranoid and insecure for that shit.

"Is this not a bit weird?" I ask. "You being here right now, I mean. I barely know you, and here you are on a Saturday night trying to cheer up someone you've only just met. Do you not have anything better to do?"

"Could I be out drinking with the boys right now? Yeah, probably. But there was no way I was going to let you go home sad and alone tonight, regardless of how long we've known each other. It's just not in my nature. Are you okay with me being here? I hope I've at least proven myself to not be a complete psychopath."

"I am, actually. You're very easy to be around, and I feel quite comfortable in your presence. I think it just feels a bit strange, it's been a while since I've had someone new in my house." I go to take another sip of wine but realise my glass is empty. I grab the bottle back out of the fridge and refill my glass. Then, I top up Xavier's.

"What do you mean by someone new? I know you said you've been single for five years, but what about one-night stands?" he asks, curiously. I wasn't expecting the conversation to go there. Am I comfortable enough to talk about sex with him? It could be the wine or his comforting presence, but weirdly enough, I think I am. However, it's bad enough that he knows I can't even manage a decent date, let alone admitting that I'm in the longest dry spell of my life.

"You don't have to answer that if you don't want to. But you also described your bed earlier as cold and lonely, so I'm a bit curious," he adds.

"I did, didn't I? Well, let's just say that my sex life is as pathetic as my dating life." I cringe.

"Okay I wouldn't describe your dating life as pathetic. Surely, it's not that bad though?"

"Well, I haven't been penetrated by a man in a year. I'd say that's pretty bad."

He chokes on his wine.

"Okay, I wasn't expecting you to put it like that. But really? You haven't had sex in a year? I don't believe you," he says, wiping droplets of wine from his beard.

"Sorry, I tend to overshare. But I wish I was kidding. It has been a long, long year. Throw in a few shitty dates and it doesn't leave a girl feeling very good about herself." I don't know why I'm telling him this, I don't want him to pity me and again, I barely know this guy. "But it's fine, I'm fine. I probably shouldn't have told you that."

"Why not?"

"Because it's embarrassing. And I don't really talk about this sort of stuff with people I don't know that well."

"Okay, that's fair enough. We can change the topic if you want. But honestly? I wouldn't say it's embarrassing. Not at all—shit happens. Life happens. It's more… surprising."

Oh.

"Is it that hard to believe?" I ask.

"Well, yes. Actually. You're hot. I would have thought you'd have men lining up at your door."

I can't remember the last time I felt butterflies in my stomach. *Xavier thinks I'm hot. Me.*

"Well… thank you. That's uh, kind of you to say." I can't tell if he's flirting with me or if he's just being nice. Plus, I'm a little bit more than tipsy at this point. This gorgeous man has complimented me a few times now, so if he is flirting, then maybe I'm in with a chance. If he isn't and I'm reading it wrong, then I am likely to just embarrass myself even further. I decide to play it safe and assume he's just being nice. There's no point in hoping. I gave up hoping a long time ago.

"You are. Any man would be lucky to spend time with you. I feel lucky just being here, sitting and talking with you," he says with a smile that makes the butterflies in my stomach do backflips. That dimple in his left cheek makes an appearance once again. "I'm really sorry about what happened tonight. Are you okay? Really?" he asks.

"If I'm being honest? No, I'm not okay. Rejection sucks and really, it shouldn't hurt this much. I hadn't even met the guy. But I guess that's the problem, he's made me feel worthless by not showing up. He decided I'm not worthy of his time before he had even met me. I mean, look at this guy." I pull out my phone and show him a photo of who I was supposed to meet with. He frowns but says nothing. "I just don't know why I bother anymore," I say, staring into my glass. "Just another thing to bring up with my therapist I guess."

"Well, I'm sure nothing I say will help change how you feel, and I'll leave the therapy talk for your actual therapist. But I will say, you are not worthless. I know I've only known you a couple of weeks and we've really only met in person two-and-a-bit times. But I can say with certainty that you are worth it. He is an absolute prick for making you feel that way."

I don't know what to say to that. It seems like the bar is so low for men in my life that someone who has come in after knowing me for three weeks tops can treat me better than any man has in years. I can feel the back of my eyes start to burn and I refuse to cry in front of this guy. So, I just say thank you and have another sip of wine.

We sit on my couch for a while, just talking. He is so easy to talk to, and I find myself able to open up to him quite quickly, which could be dangerous. I have my walls up for a reason, and a man like this could definitely smash through them within no time. Then, he tells me a little bit more about his last girlfriend.

"Her name is Jade. We met quite young, and despite there being no real problems within the relationship itself, the spark just wasn't there for me anymore." He sighs.

"The next step for us would have been marriage, and she'd been waiting for it for a while, but I just couldn't do it. We spoke about it, and though she was devastated, she understood. We actually lived together for nearly six months after breaking up, but it got way too difficult."

"Um yeah, I imagine it would have." I can't think of anything worse than living with an ex, but each to their own, and good on them for trying.

"Mmm. So yeah, despite breaking up seven months ago, it's only now that it's really starting to hit me that it's over."

I take all of this in. There's no way he would be looking to date at the moment. Which he confirms when he says how much he is enjoying his new found independence. It seems that all he needs right now is someone to talk to, and I'm happy to oblige. We end up finishing the bottle of wine and it's only then that I remember Xavier drove here.

"Crap, you drove here, and I've just fed you half a bottle of wine. Do you think you'll be okay to drive?" I ask.

"Well, I feel fine, but I probably shouldn't. No worries, I'll just get an Uber home. Shouldn't be too expensive from here." He pulls his phone out and opens the Uber app. I see him type in his address and then frown at the screen. "Ah..." he says.

"Hmm?"

"It's saying it will cost me $87 to get home."

"What?! That's ridiculous! You're not doing that. You'd then have to get back here tomorrow somehow to pick up your car. You can just crash here if you're comfortable? The couch isn't too bad to sleep on." I'm half tempted to offer him my bed, but I'm not drunk enough or dumb enough to do that.

"Are you sure? I don't want to impose."

"I offered, so you're not imposing. You got me home safely the other night, the least I can do is offer up my couch for you to sleep on." I go to the linen cupboard and get out a blanket and a spare pillow.

"Thank you, Ella. I appreciate it. I didn't plan to drink much or stay this late. You're just very easy to talk to, and I guess I lost track of time." He's standing right in front of me now and I look up at him. The way he says my name sends a pulse straight through my core and once again I find myself turned on by the smallest action. I have zero chill with this man.

"It's fine, I feel the same way. It's been really nice; I haven't done anything like this for a while." I smile at him. "If you need anything, just let me know. I'm going to go to my room."

"Sure thing. Goodnight." He goes in for a hug and I don't stop him.

He's quite a bit taller than me, so I wrap my arms around his middle. He is the perfect build for cuddling. Strong arms but still soft around the middle. He wraps his arms around me and rests his chin on the top of my head. I feel a lot of things at that moment. This hug makes me feel safe. Protected. And after an emotionally draining afternoon, it's the comfort I needed. He lightly brushes his thumb against my rib cage, and it sends shivers down my spine. His slight touch is electrifying. I don't know how long we stand there embracing, but it's enough for me to conclude it's one of the best hugs I've ever had. Which is actually kind of sad. It's this thought that has me pulling away from him, ending the moment.

"Thank you, I didn't realise how much I needed that." I say, stepping back.

"I figured you might need one, I hope it helped." He tucks a loose strand of my hair behind my ear, and I almost swoon. "Goodnight, Ella."

"Goodnight Xavier."

I walk towards my room but stop when I get to my door and turn to look back at him. He's still standing, watching me. There's a softness to his eyes, but also something more. Something I can't quite place. I smile at him and give a little wave before stepping into my room and closing the door behind me.

CHAPTER 5
Ella

I wake up the next morning and stare at the ceiling for a while, replaying everything that happened last night. I do have a slight headache from the wine that we drank, but otherwise, I'm feeling okay. Well… at least physically. I'm still feeling the hurt from being stood up, but I am now also feeling confused after what happened with Xavier last night. If it wasn't for him, I probably would have come home and cried myself to sleep, feeling like a sad and unwanted loser. He saved me from that—his distractions worked a charm.

I definitely still need to talk to my therapist about how I'm feeling, and thankfully I have a session with her on Monday. But there's also now some tension between Xavier and I that I can't quite place. He openly admitted to thinking I'm hot. And he gave me the best hug I've had in a long time, but I thought that maybe he would have tried to make a move. Or at least kiss me. So, I can't actually be certain if he's interested in me or not. Am I interested in him? Yes. Unfortunately so. He's shown me more kindness in our few interactions than any man has in the last five years. That shouldn't automatically make me want him, but he's also very attractive. And easy to be around. And smells nice….Okay, I should stop. I should also probably get out of bed and make sure he's okay. I get up and do a once over in the mirror. I'm not looking too much like a trash panda, and my pyjamas are cute enough to be seen in, so I open my door to say good morning. Though, when I look around, I don't see him. The only evidence of him being here is the second wine glass that was left on the sink, and the lingering scent of his cologne. He seems to have packed away the linen from last night. I notice a note on the dining table and read it.

Ella, thanks for letting me stay last night. Sorry I couldn't stick around this morning. I hope you're feeling okay today. Thank you for the book. I'll text you with updates.

Xavier x

"Oh… well I guess that's that then."

I think of the way he hugged me last night, and the feeling of his thumb rubbing circles on my ribs. He was just being friendly, I suppose. It meant nothing if he didn't even want to stick around this morning. Disappointment settles upon me, and I hate myself for it.

CHAPTER 6
Xavier

I felt a little bit guilty about leaving before Ella woke up this morning. I hadn't intended on staying over, but I definitely would have been over the legal limit after the wine we drank. She looked so defeated after being stood up that I couldn't just borrow a book and bail. So, I stayed a little bit longer. Apparently, I needed the company and conversation just as much as she did. I can't remember the last time I just sat with someone and talked. About everything and about nothing all at once. I barely know Ella, and yet it is so easy to open up and be around her. Perhaps it's because I don't know her that well. I don't fear her judgement the same way I do with the people who know me best.

When I broke up with Jade, I hadn't anticipated the reaction I got from some of my friends. They couldn't quite understand why I was "giving up" my life and "starting over" at 32. I tried to explain to them that 32 was still young, and that I wasn't going to force myself to stay in a relationship I wasn't happy in. After a while, they claimed that they understood and that they supported me, but I could tell that they were judging me for it. They were all married themselves, some of them had kids, and half of them were miserable but would never admit to it.

So yeah, that's probably why I ended up staying later and drinking more than intended. Companionship without the side of judgement. If I wasn't meeting up with Jade to talk about house stuff this morning, I would have stayed until Ella woke up, maybe had coffee with her. But that wouldn't have been a good idea. I don't want her to get the wrong impression and think I'm trying to date her. I'm not interested in dating right now. Do I think she's attractive? *Absolutely.* I thought so the moment I saw her. She had come up to the bar on that terrible date she went on, barely even looking at me. She was flustered and obviously anxious. I thought she was beautiful. Strawberry blonde hair, eyes the colour of storm clouds... yeah, she definitely caught my attention. And then when she came to return my jacket, I couldn't walk away without at least getting to know her a little bit. I didn't expect her to be so open, funny, and captivating. I immediately wanted to know more.

Last night she needed a friend, and I found myself wanting to fill that role. But then, the hug. It seemed innocent enough, and she looked like she really needed one. But the moment she wrapped her arms around me and rested her head beneath my chin, something shifted. She fit perfectly in my arms and when I felt her body relax and melt into mine, my attraction to her skyrocketed. It took everything in me to not tilt her head up and kiss her. But I would never do that. She was upset and drunk, and I'm not the type of guy who takes advantage of women in that position. So instead, I just held her tight and let my thumb lazily trace her side. I heard her breath hitch when I did it, so I think it would be a fair assumption that the attraction is mutual. But then she pulled away. I'm not sure why she did—all I know is I immediately wanted her back in my arms.

When she retreated to her room, I lay on the couch and tried to think of anything but her warmth. I tried not to think about following her into her bedroom, holding her, kissing her, breaking her dry spell and giving her the pleasure she deserves. I tried, and ultimately failed, to not think about her lips on mine, my hands fisted in her hair, the little moans that would come out of her mouth... let's just say, I went to sleep horny as fuck and knew I had to be gone before she woke up. She's not interested in one-night stands, or friends with benefits. She's looking for a relationship. And that's just not something I can offer right now. So, with all of that in mind, and that little fantasy still replaying itself in my head, I took off early. I left a note, and I hope she was okay when she woke up this morning. I plan on texting her once I finish up with Jade.

I pull up outside of Jade's new apartment. It's a nice place, exactly the type of house I envisioned her living in. Whilst I've always loved my property, Jade was always a city girl at heart. I enter her apartment number into the intercom and she buzzes me in shortly after. I take the elevator up and knock on her door. This is the first time I've been to her place since she moved out a few weeks ago. I'm feeling… nervous? Which is ridiculous. I was with the woman for five years. There's no drama between us and we're friendly. I still hold a lot of guilt over our breakup, but I couldn't stay in a relationship that had dwindled into something platonic. It was gradual, but eventually I just couldn't keep going the way we were. We lived with each other for six months after the breakup, and it was actually easier than I thought it would be, as we swiftly fell into a housemate type relationship. It worked well for a while—the only rule we had was don't bring someone back to the house if the other person was home. That was purely out of respect. Not that I had to worry about that rule often, I've only slept with one other person since we broke up. Which is another reason why staying at Ella's place last night probably wasn't the best decision. I have a lot of built-up sexual tension. My hand can only do so much.

Jade opens the door and startles me out of my own thoughts. Her smile is calming and familiar, and all feelings of nervousness are gone. She invites me in, gives me a hug and I take in her new living arrangements. It's very her. Modern, chic, with small hints of our past scattered around the place. Mainly, the coffee table that I designed and built for her birthday three years ago.

"So, what do you think of my new place?" she asks.

"It's amazing, it's so perfectly you, Jade. And you got a view, just like you wanted," I say. In Adelaide, you either get a view of the ocean or a view of the hills. She wanted the latter and that's what she got. I'm so happy for her.

"Thank you, I'm really happy here. It took me a while to settle in. I definitely felt homesick." She laughed. "But it's now starting to feel like mine, and I love it."

"I'm glad. Though I have to say, the chickens back home sure do miss you."

She laughs. The chickens most definitely do not miss her. She was never able to bond with them, and she was often chased out of the coop by my biggest hen, Meryl Cheep.

"Mmm yeah, I'm sure Meryl misses me terribly. Tell her I'll come to visit soon."

"I'll be sure to do that. She'll be thrilled to hear it." I smile at her. I have to say, I do miss her. She'd been my best friend for so long and I really hope we don't lose that, now that we aren't together anymore. It's selfish of me to think that, given I'm the one who ended things, but so far, we've been okay.

She walks to her kitchen and starts to make us coffee. We chat as she goes about it, and I catch her up on the house and how things are going at work. I believe Dad will be retiring within the next 12 months, so the handover of the business will hopefully begin soon. I've been ready to take over for years, but he's being stubborn and won't retire. Says he's got plenty left in him, which he probably does. But I can see he's getting tired, and I'm ready to step up. I've worked hard enough; he should see that I'm ready.

"Speaking of the pub…" she says as she puts two mugs down on the kitchen table. "A little birdie told me that you've left work, twice, with a hot little redhead." There's a twinkle in her eye. My stomach does a nervous flip for some reason.

"Oh really? Would that little birdie happen to be my dear pal, Lena?" I ask. She just smiles. "Seems I may need to have a word with her about workplace gossip."

I'm joking, of course, but I do find it a bit uncomfortable that my friend and employee is gossiping about me to my ex-girlfriend, even though she is friends with both of us.

"But before you ask, don't worry, there isn't anything going on. And her name is Ella." I take a sip of coffee.

"Why would I be worried? We're not together anymore, you can see whoever you want," she says, and I know it's true, but I don't really like how easy it is for her to say it.

"Yeah, I know. It's nothing, though. She was in a tight spot, and I helped her out. A couple of times. Nothing has happened."

"It's fine, Xav. You don't have to explain anything to me. I was just being nosy. And, you know, it's okay if something did happen, too. It's been seven months; you could try opening up to the possibility of someone again," she says softly. I know she's being nice, being my friend, but I don't like this topic of discussion. It just feels a bit too strange to be talking about other women with her. I feel guilty.

"I know that. But really, we're just friends. Now… about your half of the house, are you still okay with me buying you out?" I trail off, hoping she drops it and realises that I want to change the conversation. She pauses, like she wants to say something more, but she takes the hint and answers my question.

I think about what she said as she's talking and I begin to wonder, is she encouraging me to start dating other people because *she* wants to date other people? Or is it because she's trying to gauge whether or not I am looking elsewhere? All I know is that it's still too soon to jump headfirst into another relationship. Afterall, my last one was a total failure.

CHAPTER 7
Ella

It's late Sunday afternoon when I receive a text from Xavier. I've spent most of the morning moping about for absolutely no good reason other than my stupid overthinking brain. Of course, I automatically jumped to the conclusion that Xavier wants nothing to do with me after last night and think that's why he bailed. It wasn't until I called Millie to explain what happened that she told me I was overreacting and to do some journaling or something to clear my head. She obviously felt awful about what happened with my blind date, whose name I discovered is Conor, and she has told Clay that he needs to get answers about why this guy just decided to not show up. But then I told her about Xavier, and she pretty much forgot all about Conor.

She actually squealed when I told her he slept over but was promptly disappointed when I said that he slept on the couch and not with me. She still demanded to hear every little detail. I told her about the hug, and she agreed that it was best to not read too much into it. We ended up talking on the phone for an hour, where I cried for a little bit about not feeling wanted and she comforted me. It feels like a routine at this point, and I sort of hate the fact that I'm always crying to my best friend about my love life. Though if she was sick of hearing about it, she hasn't let on. So I did what she said, wrote in my journal, and was halfway through a walk when Xavier's message appeared.

XAVIER

Okay I've read seven chapters of this book
and I'm worried you might be corrupting me. I
like it, but I'm scared.

XAVIER

Sorry for leaving so quickly this morning. I
had to meet Jade to talk about house stuff
and I didn't want to wake you up. How are
you feeling today?

Well, there you go. He had to meet with his ex; he wasn't running away from me. I'm immediately relieved and then angry at myself for once again being so damn dramatic.

"Stupid overthinking brain," I mutter to myself as I'm walking along. Also, damn. Seven chapters? He reads quickly. I type out a reply.

ELLA

Just you wait, it gets soooo much better. And
yeah, all good. I'm feeling fine. Just trying not to
think about it too much, you know? I'm currently
on a walk to clear my head. I'll be okay, thanks for
checking x

ELLA

How has the rest of your day been?

I put my phone back in my pocket and decide to start running instead of walking. This lasts for about 30 seconds before I remember I fucking hate running and have to pause on the footpath to catch my breath. I am ridiculously unfit, and so I make a mental note to try and go for a walk every day to try and fix that.

I get back to my house and am about to jump into the shower when Xavier's reply comes through.

XAVIER

> I can't put it down and I'm slightly disgusted
> in myself. The rest of my day was good,
> after I left Jade's I came home, did a bit of
> housework, and fed the chickens before
> settling down to start this book. I'm about to
> run myself a bath so I can read in comfort. If
> you ever wanna talk, I can lend an ear 😄

A smile spreads across my face as I picture him sitting in a bubble bath reading my book. It's a hot image. His offer to talk is really sweet, too, since I only really have Millie in my life—well, my real life. I have a whole bunch of internet besties too, but it's not quite the same. You can't just show up and vent and cry like you can with real life besties. I have other friends, but I'm not as close with them. Then there are my parents, though I don't tend to talk to them about my love life. They ask too many questions and make comments like, "When are you going to settle down? You're not getting any younger Ella." So, having someone else to talk to is really nice.

ELLA

> Never would have picked you as a bath guy,
> but that sounds perfect! And thank you, I do
> appreciate it. I like talking to you. I'm really glad
> you rescued me on that shitty date. I didn't get a
> boyfriend out of it but I definitely got a new friend,
> and I'm not mad about it!

XAVIER

> I fucking love baths. Have one every Sunday
> if I can! I'm glad I rescued you too. You've
> definitely got a friend in me.

Friend. I can settle for a friend. A hot friend.

I hop into the shower and start washing my hair. The scent of my favourite shampoo, pineapple and coconut, envelops me. I start to picture Xavier in the bath again, and what would happen if I were in there with him. I'd be lying between his legs, my back to his chest. I'd be all soapy, and his hands would be gliding across my skin, starting at my arms. When he reaches my breasts, my nipples would already be peaked, and he would pinch one of them, teasingly. Ever so slowly, he would explore my body, moving his hands down, first reaching my stomach, and then dipping lower, getting closer and closer to my cli….

"Oh fuck!" I'm shaken out of my daydream when shampoo runs into my eyes and I'm temporarily blinded. "Goddamn, that stings." I reach out of the shower for a towel to wipe the shampoo from my face. Serves me right, I guess, for objectifying the man. My *FRIEND*. But shit, that was hot. I don't know how I'm going to be able to look him in the eye the next time I see him. I finish washing my hair, and my body (which is extra sensitive in some areas now), and hop out of the shower. There's another text from Xavier waiting for me.

XAVIER

HE HAS A BARBED DICK?!?!?!?

ELLA

Hahahahahahahahaha

XAVIER

Ella. Honey, are you okay? This is not normal reading lol

I try to ignore the warm fuzzy feeling I get in when he calls me honey.

ELLA

… but it's hot, right?

XAVIER

I refuse to answer that question.

ELLA

🙂

XAVIER

Shut up.

I am still laughing as I make my way to my bedroom. I throw on my pyjamas and plop onto the bed. Suddenly, my phone rings. It's Xavier.

"Hello, Xavier." I answer the phone with a smile on my face.

"Hey. So, I'm calling for two reasons. The first: I'm going to need the number of your therapist after reading this book, because I should not be into this, but I am. Damn you."

"You did want the smuttiest book on my shelf."

"Yes, but I wasn't expecting barbed penises, okay?"

"You're welcome. What's the second reason you called?"

He clears his throat. "Uhhh, well… I kind of, accidentally, maybe dropped your book into the bath. I was quite rattled after he, you know, did the thing with the barb… and it just slipped out of my hands, and I dropped it. I'm so sorry!"

Now normally, as a book lover, I would be absolutely pissed at him for this. I never loan my books to people; it was a miracle I gave one to him in the first place. But for some reason, I don't even feel annoyed. In fact, I find it highly amusing and burst out laughing.

"Oh my God, that's hilarious! It's okay, shit happens. You uh… you weren't reading it one handed, were you?" I ask, wondering if he understands what I mean by that.

"One handed? No, no I was reaching for a glass of wine…." He trails off. "OH. Oh God, no I was not doing… that. God. Ew. Why would you ask that?"

I start laughing again, he sounds so flustered it's comical.

"I'm joking Xavier. But if you were, hey, whatever floats your boat!"

He groans into the phone. It's a hot sound, and for a moment my mind wanders back to the little daydream I had in the shower. "If I had known you would tease me, I wouldn't have bothered calling to tell you," he says. "I do owe you another copy of the book, though. I can salvage this one enough to finish reading it, but I don't want it going mouldy."

"You don't have to, it's fine. I was going to go book shopping at Dymocks next Saturday anyway, so I'll just grab myself another copy."

"What time are you going on Saturday?"

"At about 11am, I think. I was going to take myself out for brunch first."

"Do you want company?" he asks.

"Oh! Um… really? You want to go book shopping with me?"

"Yeah of course. It sounds like a lot of fun. I'll be able to buy you a replacement, and also grab the next book in the series that I'm reading."

"Well, yeah, okay then. Let's lock it in. We can plan where to meet up later in the week."

"Perfect. I'm looking forward to it. Now, if you'll excuse me, I'm off to try and dry this book so I can continue reading this absolute filth you call literature. Have a good night, Ella."

"Actually, it's called cliterature. I hope you manage to salvage enough of it. Goodnight Xavier."

I hang up the phone to his laughter and smile to myself. Book shopping and brunch with Xavier. I'm trying to convince myself that it's not a date. It's just two friends, hanging out. If it was a date, I'm sure he would have said, 'hey, it's a date'. The butterflies in my stomach don't know the difference though, and of course they are now doing somersaults. This is going to be a long week.

CHAPTER 8
Ella

I get through Monday relatively smoothly and now I'm currently sitting in the waiting room of my therapy appointment. I think back to the first time I was waiting in this room; I was so scared and anxious. I never thought therapy would be something I'd do. I always had the mentality of 'I've made it this far on my own, I don't need help'. Well, after a stressful six months at work, as well as my complete lack of a love life, I was feeling incredibly anxious, unwanted, and unworthy. Millie finally convinced me to talk to someone, and I am so glad she did. Though, it did take me a few goes before I found a therapist who I felt comfortable with. I went to three different psychologists, two of them felt super clinical and I didn't connect with them at all, and the other one had a connection to my parents. Despite patient confidentiality, it just didn't sit well with me. Then, I met Jane. I was immediately put at ease when she first walked out to greet me. She's in her mid-fifties and was rocking a pink power suit and stilettos. She was calming and professional but also personable. I didn't feel like I was talking to a clinical robot.

"Ella, come on in." Jane appears in the doorway and I walk in behind her. Another thing I like about Jane is that her office isn't set out with a couch for me to lie down on and cry while she takes notes on a clipboard. She has a desk in one corner and a tea and coffee station in another, with a group of armchairs surrounding a coffee table in the middle of the room. It's full of natural light, plants, and books. I take a seat in my usual chair, and she sits opposite me with my file, does a quick recap of our last session, and then asks me how I've been since we last spoke.

"Well, it has been an interesting few weeks," I start. "The work front is fine at the moment. There's just the usual busyness and shitty attitude from my boss, but the tactics you suggested last month have really helped."

"That's great to hear! So, what else has been happening then if work is going okay?"

"Just my love life creating feelings of unworthiness and ugliness. So, nothing new," I say casually.

"Ah, I see. Tell me all about it."

I dive into the last couple of weeks, starting with my date with Jed, being stood up, and meeting Xavier. I then go on about our blossoming friendship. Saying it all out loud, it hits me with just how chaotic the last few weeks have been—it's no wonder I've felt on edge lately. Jane is writing notes as I talk. She's nodding along with a look of concentration on her face as I finish up.

"Okay, I can see where those feelings are all stemming from. I know how you feel about going on dates, and I know what it takes for you to actually attend them. I'm really proud of you for putting yourself out there, so you should be commending yourself for taking that step. Though, can you explain to me why you're feeling unworthy and ugly? Am I correct in assuming that being stood up elicited these feelings, and not the date with Jed?" she asks.

"I think you're right in that assumption. I mean yeah, I was disappointed that the date sucked, but I got over it pretty quick. Jed cornered me and scared me and made me uncomfortable, but honestly, I've experienced that sort of thing as a woman more times than I can count. I can bounce back easily, which is incredibly sad now that I think about it. It definitely was from being stood up. Knowing that the guy had decided I wasn't even worth meeting, without knowing anything about me or what I look like. From what I heard, he was hot and successful, so I was excited and hopeful at the thought that he must be interested in getting to know me. Especially since he was the one who agreed to the date in the first place. But instead, he decided I wasn't worth his time." I can feel myself starting to tear up already, and she pushes a box of tissues towards me.

"Did you ever find out why he didn't show up?" she asks.

"No. Clay hasn't seen him at work, or so he says, and he isn't responding to any messages, so I can't even ask for a reason."

"Okay. I don't want to tell you that you shouldn't be feeling that way, because you have autonomy over your own feelings and no one can take that away from you. I will ask you, however, to think about what you've just told me, and tell me what parts are factual and true."

"I'm not sure what you mean," I say, confused.

"So, the act of you going on the date is a fact. You getting stood up is a fact. Is him thinking you aren't worth his time, still a fact?" she asks.

I think about all of the things I said, and all of the things I have felt since the date.

"A lot of what you have said to me is based on assumptions you have made about why he didn't show up. There is no evidence, no proof, to suggest he thought you were ugly, or that you weren't worth his time. Until you know these things as facts, you are hurting your own feelings with your own interpretation of what happened."

I sit there for a moment to process what she is saying. It makes sense. Like… a lot of sense. One of my worst habits is to create scenarios in my head and convince myself they are reality, thus causing myself to become anxious over something that doesn't exist. I guess this is like that.

"You're right. I don't know the real reason, and I shouldn't try and come up with my own answers. I just don't know how to change my mindset. I've been on my own for so long that I can't help but feel unwanted. I'm so lonely, and this just added to the pain." The tears slide down my cheek, and I hastily wipe them away.

"Ella. Don't rush your tears. Let them fall, let yourself feel."

She gives me a moment to just sit in my feelings and reflect. I close my eyes and breathe deeply through my nose and out through my mouth. It takes me a moment, but I eventually bring myself back to the present.

"As for how to change your mindset, it takes time. You need to keep working on convincing yourself that you are worthy of love. I can see that you are confident and comfortable within yourself, however that confidence seems to diminish when seeking out a partner."

She gives me some tools to help me with changing from a fixed mindset to a growth mindset. I tell her that journaling has actually been really helpful. I find that writing down how I'm feeling in the moment and then reading back what I've written puts things into perspective, and at times, it shows me how unrealistic I'm being. She told me to keep going, but to try and add in some notes of daily gratitude as well. Every day, I need to write down something that I love about myself at that moment. I then need to say it to myself, out loud, that I am loveable because of what I've written down.

"Now, tell me about Xavier. Is this just a friendship, do you think?" she asks.

"I think so. He's recently single, and other than a few compliments and a hug, he hasn't made any sort of move on me. Do you think it's weird how quickly we've become friends?" It's something I've been wondering about lately, since the ease of which we have become friends just feels surreal.

"Why would it be weird? You and Millie became best friends in a matter of weeks. Why is this different? Because he's a man?"

"Maybe. I don't know."

"Are you attracted to him? Or, more importantly, do you want more than a friendship with him?"

I ponder this for all of five seconds. "Am I attracted to him? Absolutely. Do I want more? I don't know. Maybe. But he's hinted at the fact that he's not interested in dating right now, and the fact he hasn't made a single move is telling me that he's not attracted to—"

She raises a brow at me.

"Oh. I'm doing it again, aren't I? Making assumptions based on my own interpretations. Huh." I've surprised myself by making that realisation so quickly.

"Good to see you're a quick learner." She laughs. "But yes, you are making assumptions. If you're interested in something more, talk to him. If not, then enjoy this friendship for what it is. But don't overthink it like you were just now. Take each interaction for what it is and communicate your feelings when they arise. From what you've told me about him, he seems quite switched on and mature."

"He is. And you're right. It's only been a month and I need to see where this goes. I don't want to push any sort of romantic intentions on him and ruin the friendship that we have created. I'm really enjoying getting to know him."

"That sounds like a good idea. And I'm so glad you've made a new friend. Male friendships can be hard to navigate, especially if there is mutual attraction. So, communicate with him, and write things down. I'll be looking forward to seeing where you are at when I see you next."

We finish up my session and book my next appointment, which isn't until the New Year as Jane is going away for two weeks over the Christmas break. So hopefully, nothing goes wrong in that time. I walk back to my car and reflect on the session, feeling a bit more confident in myself and ready for the rest of the week.

CHAPTER 9
Xavier

This week has been the fucking worst. I walked into work on Monday morning, feeling pretty confident that the meeting I had scheduled with my dad would result in the announcement that he is retiring, and I will take over management of Jimmies. I soon learnt that would not be the case, and the meeting was just to discuss all of the upcoming holiday functions we were hosting. There was absolutely no mention of me taking over and no mention of retirement. The man looked exhausted and kept complaining of back pain throughout the hour we sat in his office. I don't understand why he won't give it up. Stubbornness, most likely. I am beyond ready to take over the business, I've worked my arse off, and I've proven that I am more than capable. I need the challenge. What more do I have to do to prove to him that it's my time?

The rest of the week consisted of one bar fight resulting in a cracked window (on a Tuesday night mind you, the quiz nights here get really competitive), a fox attempting to enter my chicken coop but thankfully not succeeding, some dickhead backing into my car at the supermarket leaving a dent in my passenger door, and a migraine that forced me to take Friday night off of work. The only things that got me through this absolute shitshow of a week were my conversations with Ella. I didn't call her again after our chat on Sunday, but we've been texting every day. I've been giving her chapter updates on the book she lent me, and I somehow managed to finish it despite the water damage. I am ashamed to say, I really enjoyed it. I told her it was okay, a bit of fun, but I think she saw right through me.

She's been updating me on the chaos of her own work week. The school year is wrapping up for her, which means books are being returned in bulk. She's been sending me pictures of all the fun things she's discovered in the books (seven books so far with dick and balls graffiti, chewing gum stuck to pages, a used tissue as a bookmark… they're teenagers, so you get the picture). I've found myself looking forward to receiving her messages throughout the day. On top of work updates, she's also been sending me more book recommendations. My TBR pile is growing with rapid speed and I've only known this girl for like a month. She's become one of my favourite people to talk to, it still shocks me how quickly we've become friends. I'm still conscious to not try and lead her on, but I'm finding the more we talk and the more I get to know her, the more attracted to her I am becoming. Which is fine, as long as I don't act on it. We have to remain friends and friends only.

It's now Saturday morning and I'm currently stuffing my face with bacon and hash browns at Ella's favourite café for brunch. I've never been to this particular spot, but the coffee here revived my tired soul like nothing ever has before, so I will definitely be returning. She's sitting across from me talking animatedly about her book wish list and how she's limiting herself to two books today when we go shopping.

"I honestly have zero self-control when I enter a bookstore so please hold me back if I try and buy more than I need," she says with maple syrup dripping down her chin. She's eating French toast like a fiend and it's oddly endearing. The urge to reach across the table to kiss the syrup from her lips takes me by surprise. I take a sip of water to quench the rising heat in my cheeks as I try and ignore the image that's forming in my head.

"I can definitely restrain you if you need me to. Remember though, you'll be going home with three books after I buy you a replacement copy," I say. She blushes a little and clears her throat at the mention of me restraining her. *Interesting.*

"It's not the same. There's nothing more satisfying than adding new books to your TBR pile."

"Mmm… and how long do they sit on that pile waiting to be read?" I ask with a smirk.

"That is a question I refuse to answer," she says. I know full well that some of her books have been sitting unread for years.

"I thought as much. Don't worry, I promise to not let you overspend today."

"Thank you." She continues eating and talking and I just sit there, listening. She's so passionate about books, I just nod along and take it all in. I smile at her as I listen to her gush about her favourite fandom, something about Bat Boys and wingspans. She notices and she stops talking.

"What?" she asks.

"Nothing, I'm just really enjoying listening to you. You love all of this so much, it's infectious. I could listen to you talk about it all day and not get tired," I say. And I mean it. She's making me want to read more just from her passion alone.

"Oh." She smiles. "Thank you. That's… actually really nice. Most people get sick of hearing about it. But I guess you like reading, so…"

"Not just that. When someone is passionate about something, I like to listen. There's nothing more enchanting than watching someone express their love for something so deeply. You do that."

She just looks at me and blinks. I get the impression that she's been misunderstood by a lot of people, and she doesn't hear this sort of thing often. I make a mental note to encourage her passion as often as I can.

"Anyway," I continue, "are you finished with your breakfast? That last rasher of bacon has my name on it if you're not planning on eating it."

She shakes out of her stupor and chuckles. "I'm so full, it's all yours."

I scoop up the bacon and eat it in one mouthful.

"Classy," she says.

"Always." I reply. "Right, ready to go shopping?" I watch as her eyes light up. We pay the bill and split it, "because this isn't a date" she says. I don't respond, which elicits a small frown from her. I'd love to know what's going on in her head. I even wonder, *does she want this to be a date?*

We walk down the mall, admiring the hustle and bustle of the city on a Saturday morning. We reach Dymocks and walk in, going up the escalators. I look back at Ella as we crest the entrance. She closes her eyes and takes in a deep breath.

"Honey, I'm home!" she exclaims. I laugh, she really is such a book nerd.

The store isn't too busy today, which makes the experience so much more enjoyable. This is definitely one of my favourite book stores. I remember walking in for the first time and being in awe. The high sculpted ceiling, the arches, the new book smell. It was perfect. It's located in an older building, with crown-moulding and a chandelier hanging high in the centre of the room, basking all of the books in a soft glow. It's super easy to navigate, and Ella knows exactly what she wants. She marches straight over to the fantasy section. We spend the next 20 minutes discussing our favourite fantasy authors, pointing out our favourite series and talking about how if a book has dragons in it, it's an immediate yes. I find the book she lent me and grab a copy off the shelf to buy as her replacement. Thankfully, the cover hasn't changed and it's the same size. She probably would have refused it if it didn't match the rest of the series she has at home. After a while, she wanders off towards the romance section as I continue to browse, giving my attention to the sci-fi collection. I spend about 10 minutes browsing, choosing for myself a new Brent Weeks, before joining Ella in the romance aisle. I'm betting on the fact that she has at least four books in her arms that she plans to buy.

I round the corner and find her talking to some random guy. He looks familiar, but I can't figure out why. He's tall, not quite as tall as me, blond, with a chiselled jaw and a cocky expression that seems like it's permanently etched onto his face. I walk up to them and can immediately tell by Ella's body language that she's uncomfortable. I put my arm around her shoulder and pull her into me. I look down as she looks up at me, and our eyes meet. She instantly calms with my presence and relaxes her body into mine.

"Hey, you've only got two books! I'm so proud." I look at the guy. "Oh. Sorry, who are you?" I ask.

"I'm Conor. Who are you?" he asks, his eyes darting between my arm around Ella and her face. I start running my fingers up and down her arm reassuringly, goosebumps appearing on her skin. The way he's looking at her has me feeling all sorts of protective. Conor. *Have I heard that name?* And then it hits me. I've seen his face before, Ella showed me a photo of him. He's the guy who stood her up. Immediately, I see red.

CHAPTER 10
Ella

I've just gotten my hands on the latest romcom by one of my favourite romance authors, which was only released today. I'm standing in the aisle reading the blurb of something that looks deliciously smutty when a man's voice interrupts me.

"Hey, are you Ella?"

I look up and see some blond guy walking over to me.

"Uhhh… yes?" I have no idea who this guy is, though he does look somewhat familiar. He's tall-ish, slim, and muscular, blond-haired with a chiselled jaw, and a smattering of stubble. "I thought it was you. It's me! How are you going?" he says confidently, thinking that I'd recognise him. I just stare at him blankly.

"Sorry, I don't know who you are…" I trail off.

"It's Conor. I work with Clay. We were supposed to meet up for a drink last week."

Immediately the blood drains from my face. I recognise him now from the picture Millie sent me before our date. *What. The. Fuck.*

"Oh. Wow, hi?"

"Sorry I couldn't make it last weekend. Just got busy, you know? No hard feelings I hope. Anyway, what're you up to? Just a bit of shopping? I'm here to get some texts for work, finance guides and whatnot. You look different in person, compared to the photos, I mean," he says, completely oblivious to the fact that I am shrinking inwardly on myself. The way this guy holds himself is so self-assured, so confident.

He got busy. *He. Got. Busy.* I don't think I've ever heard such a pathetic excuse. No respect or even decency to try and get in touch, despite Clay trying to contact him all week. And now he's trying to chat with me as if everything was fine? But also, what photos is he referring to? Millie told me they didn't show him any.

"You got busy. Really? That's the excuse you're going to give? I waited in that bar for an hour and a half. You could have at least had the decency to try and contact me afterwards to apologise. And what photos are you talking about?" I can feel myself starting to get all hot and flustered. My palms are starting to sweat, and my heart is racing.

"Did you really wait for an hour and a half? Why would you wait that long? I was watching cricket with the boys and time got away from me. I didn't have your number, and I figured because it was a blind date I didn't need to reach out. As for the photos, I was a bit hesitant when they said you were a librarian but a couple days ago, I thought I'd look you up and I found your Instagram account. You're definitely not the stereotypical librarian I had in my head." He smirks.

I can't believe he looked me up on Instagram, and is trying to compliment me by saying I don't look "stereotypical". Gross.

"I waited that long just in case you were late. Or had gotten the time wrong. Reaching out would have been the respectful thing to do, given how much of my time you wasted. But never mind, after this interaction, I feel like I should be thanking you for not showing up. You are definitely not my type." I can feel my eyes starting to burn. One of the things I really dislike about myself is the fact that I can't stand up for myself without crying. It drives me insane and makes me look weak in front of the other person.

"Well now, that's a bit harsh. You don't even know me. I'm sorry for not showing up, but we could always get a coffee now if you're free." He puts on what I assume is some sort of smile he uses when trying to get female attention. I think my vagina is shrivelling up at the sight of it.

"Yeah… I don't think so, buddy," I say. Suddenly, a warm body appears next to mine and an arm wraps itself around my shoulders. I immediately know it's Xavier; his smoky scent envelops me and I'm so relieved. Saved by the lumberjack once again. I look up at him and our eyes meet, but there's concern shining in his. I relax under the weight of his arm.

"Hey, you've only got two books! I'm so proud." He starts running his fingers along my shoulder and I immediately break out in goosebumps. The effect is calming and grounding. He must be able to tell I'm uncomfortable. He then looks at Conor.

"Oh, sorry. Who are you?"

"I'm Conor, who are you?"

Xavier frowns for a moment, and then I feel his body stiffen next to me as the realisation hits him. I showed him Conor's photo that night at my house. His arm tightens around me, and when I look up at him again, his eyes are burning into Conor's. *Oh, he's pissed.*

"So, you're Conor." He looks him up and down giving him a thorough perusal. With a sneer, he looks him in the eyes and says, "Yeah, that makes sense. You seem the type."

"What makes sense? What type?" Conor's confusion is evident in the furrow of his brow as he looks between the two of us.

"The type of guy whose ego is bigger than his dick and thinks it's okay to stand up a beautiful woman and not apologise for it." I try to hide my smile but fail.

"What the fuck man? Who even are you? I told her I was sorry. It's not your concern."

"Who I am is irrelevant. You hurt my friend, so that makes it my concern. I think it best if you just walk away. Bye-bye." Xavier starts to turn me away.

"Hang on a second. Ella, can I give you my number at least? I can try and make up for last weekend?"

"No thanks, I'm good." Conor stares at the two of us, realises he isn't getting anywhere, and storms off. Xavier and I stand there watching him go, his arm still around me. Once we see him heading down the escalator, I start to calm down. I didn't realise how tense I was. We walk towards the back of the bookstore to a more secluded corner, where I can recover away from the crowds.

"Oh my God. Why, of all places, did I have to bump into him in a bookstore?" I groan and bury my head in my hands.

"Hey." Xavier pulls my hands away from my face and takes my hands in his. "Are you okay?"

I huff a laugh. "Yeah, I think so. Just pissed off. He's ruined my morning and I was having such a good time."

"What excuse did he give for standing you up?"

"He got busy. Was watching cricket with the boys or something." I mumble.

"That's pathetic." Xavier spits. "He's a piece of shit. Be glad he didn't show up, guys like that are a waste of time."

"Yeah, you're right. Whatever. A guy like that wouldn't be into someone like me anyway."

"What are you on about? Someone like you? What do you mean?"

"I mean… you saw him. He's like, stereotypically hot. And I'm… me. Book nerd, lover of carbs, and a hopeless romantic. There's no way he would have been attracted to me even if he did show up on the date." I can feel a lump forming in my throat and pressure building behind my eyes. I take another deep breath. *I refuse to cry in public over this. It's pathetic.*

Xavier just looks at me like I've sprouted a third ear.

"Ella, stop. Fuck that guy. You are gorgeous."

I shake my head. "You're only saying that to try and make me feel better."

"The fuck I am." He grabs my chin and forces me to look at him. "I'm saying it because it's true. You are intelligent, passionate, and witty. You're beautiful. Any guy would be lucky to go on a date with you. I feel lucky being here with you, in your favourite place." A single tear escapes and slides down my cheek, and he brushes it away with his thumb.

"You don't believe me." It's a statement, not a question. And he's right. But it's so hard to truly believe what he's saying, after being alone and unwanted for so long.

"I want to believe you," I whisper. "But it's hard. Xav, I've been alone for so long. It's hard to believe you when no one wants me—"

Suddenly, I'm cut off, as Xavier's lips crash onto mine. It takes me a second to register what is happening. He's kissing me. *HE'S KISSING ME.* I hesitate for just a moment, but before my overthinking brain can ruin this, I relax into it and kiss him back. His tongue softly brushes against mine, and something inside me ignites. I lose all self-control and kiss him with everything I've got. He grabs the back of my neck and pulls me closer to him. The kiss intensifies, and I let out a soft moan as he nips at my bottom lip. He tastes so sweet. He pulls away and starts to trail soft kisses along my jaw before reaching my neck. Pleasure rocks through my whole body as he kisses the spot behind my ear before his lips find mine again. I don't know how long we kiss for, but eventually he slows, and then stops. He rests his forehead against mine.

"Now… what were you saying, about no one wanting you?" he asks, breathless. We're both panting. "Because this…" He pushes himself against me and I gasp as I feel the evidence of his arousal. "Is me showing you. You are wanted. You are so fucking beautiful, and I don't want to hear any arguments coming out of that mouth of yours. Understand?" He takes a step back and looks at me. I nod.

"Good."

He stares at me for a moment longer, before he clears his throat and runs a hand through his hair nervously, a far cry from the confidence he showed mere seconds ago. It's almost like he can't quite believe what he just did either.

"Now, let's go pay for these books. Shall we?"

I'm still speechless so I just nod again. We walk over to the register and pay. What in the seven circles of hell just happened? Xavier kissed me. I kissed him back. I could feel how hard he was, *for me.* And I can feel the evidence of my own arousal between my legs. I walk out of the store with slightly swollen lips, turned on as hell, but possibly more confused than ever before.

CHAPTER 11
Xavier

"Shit."

I jump back as glass shatters everywhere. This is the third glass I've smashed since my shift started tonight. I'm distracted, clearly, by what happened this morning with Ella. I don't know what came over me. Seeing her so visibly shaken by her encounter with that douchebag Conor, I felt such a fierce need to protect her and to make sure she was okay. Then when she started going on about how she's not beautiful and nobody wants her, I snapped. I'll admit it, the last couple of weeks, my mind has often wandered to what her lips might feel like against mine. But I swore to myself that I would keep our relationship strictly platonic.

All I know is I wanted to prove to her how beautiful and desirable she is. She didn't kiss me back at first, and I was worried that I overstepped. But then she kissed me back with such fervour, I lost all sense of the world around us. It was just Ella and me, living in the moment. She didn't say much on our walk back to our cars—I think she was in shock, because I sure was. She gave me an awkward hug, thanked me for a great morning, made another joke about her hero, Mr Bartender Man, and then hopped in her car and drove off. It felt similar to when I was a teenager and I'd just gone on a first date. Neither of us knew how to act around each other.

"What's up with you tonight, boss?" Lena smirks. "You're in your own head about something, I can tell."

I hate that my feelings are so blatantly obvious, I can never hide things from anyone.

"I know, I'm just distracted. I'll be right. Hand me that broom, would you?" She hands it to me, and I proceed to sweep up the broken glass.

"Would a red headed librarian be the cause of that distraction?" she asks with a knowing grin.

"Maybe," I mumble. I scoop up the glass and toss it into the bin. "Not that I would tell you anything about it, seeing as you'll likely go straight to my ex with the gossip." I lift a brow at her. I haven't had the chance to discuss her conversations with Jade yet. Might as well bring it up now.

She laughs, albeit nervously. "Ah. She dobbed me in. She asked me how you were doing, so I told her. All I said was that you'd made a new friend." She shrugged. "I didn't insinuate anything. Jade's my friend too, you know. I can't not talk to her about things just because you two aren't together anymore."

I sigh. "I know. I just don't appreciate my ex-girlfriend asking me questions about my dating life, based on information she's garnered from you. It's… weird. If I start seeing someone, I want her to hear it from me. Not that I'm seeing Ella, we're just friends. Understand?"

"You got it boss. From now on, I will not talk about you to Jade." She mimics zipping her lips shut. "Now, tell me what's happening with Ella. 'Just friends' my arse."

"Yeah, not gonna happen Lena. I'm not telling you shit." I laugh. "The ladies on table 12 need a refill. I'm going into the office for a while, so call out if you need me."

"Ugh. Such a party pooper. I'll get it out of you eventually Xavier James!"

"Unlikely," I mutter. I head into the office and try to focus on the paperwork in front of me. No matter how hard I try, I can't concentrate. I have so many conflicting feelings in my head. I hope Ella is okay. I haven't heard from her since this morning, so I send off a text just to check in.

XAVIER

Hey. Hope your Saturday night is going well. What are you up to?

I again pick up the invoices I'm supposed to be going over but I'm just skim reading them at this point. All I can think about is the feeling of her lips on mine, the soft moans that came out of her delicious mouth… and despite everything telling me I shouldn't do it again, it's all I want to do. I want to run my hands through her hair, feel her skin on mine. I want to taste every inch of her.

I had a simple one-night stand after Jade and I first split and it wasn't exactly a night of passion. With Ella, I can imagine it would be electric. I'm really not ready for another relationship yet. However, if I could maybe start something casual with Ella, something that would satisfy both of our needs… I should talk to her, make sure she's really okay and possibly hint at the idea of a little bit of extra fun.

Just as I start to think about all the things we could do together, a knock on the door shakes me out of my daydream. I have to adjust myself before telling whoever it is to come in. *Good one Xavier, give yourself a boner at work. What am I, 14 years old?*

Lena pops her head in. "Hey Xav, we need a keg changed."

"Sure, I'll be right out," I grunt.

"You all good?" she asks.

"Yep. I'm perfect."

Then,

my phone dings with a response from Ella.

ELLA

Hey, my night is going great! I'm curled up on the couch reading my new book. Hope you're having fun at work! x

I wish I was curled up on the couch reading, but alas, I have a keg to change. I pocket my phone and get back to work. My daydreams will have to wait until I'm home, *alone*.

CHAPTER 12
Ella

I'm sitting on Millie's couch in her living room, a hot Milo in hand, with Taylor Swift playing in the background. It's Sunday night, and I called an emergency debrief following my book shopping adventure and unexpected kiss with Xavier yesterday.

"Okay, so tell me… what did he taste like? What did he smell like?" Millie asks as she takes a sip.

"Oh my God, Millie, really?"

"What! I want to know everything. Give me all the details."

"It was just one kiss," I say. She just looks at me, waiting.

"Okay fine. Um. He tasted sweet, like maple syrup from our breakfast. There was also the scent of smoke lingering on him, as if from a woodfire." I have no idea where the smoky scent came from, given it's summer and it's fire ban season. But whatever, the combination was delicious.

"That's kinda hot. Sweet and smoky, I like it. Now onto bigger things…" she waggles her eyebrows at me, and I groan.

"Okay, here we go."

"He literally pressed his boner into you to prove how attractive you are. That is so fucking hot, Ella. So, tell me… how big are we talking?"

"I don't know Millie—I only felt it for like a second and I didn't exactly get out a measuring tape to measure his dick in a bookstore."

She laughs and we sit in silence for a moment, taking sips of our drinks.

Hot Milos have become somewhat of a tradition of ours. We start our evenings with a bottle of wine, and then after dinner we switch to a hot beverage. Mostly, it's to counteract the alcohol because one of us always has to drive home.

"Okay, but all jokes and dicks aside, how are you feeling about the kiss?" she asks.

"Honestly, I'm so confused. He's hinted a couple of times before that he thinks I'm attractive, but he's never made a move or made any indication he wants to act on that attraction. And then out of nowhere, he kisses me. And not just your average kiss either… that kiss felt desperate, the type of kiss you give someone when you've been holding it in for a long time."

"Confused is fair. Did you like it?"

"Yes. I get goosebumps every time I think about it."

"And have you spoken to him since it happened?"

"Um. We texted a little bit last night while he was at work. I didn't bring up the kiss, though." I wanted to bring it up, but I didn't know how to approach it. He didn't say anything either, so I settled with ignorance and pretending everything was normal.

"Okay. Get your phone out right now and organise to meet up with him. I know what you're like and your overthinking brain is going to go into overdrive the longer you put off talking to him about the kiss."

"Firstly… I hate that you're right. And second, do I have to? I'm perfectly happy pretending nothing happened." I wasn't, but I didn't want to admit that I had in fact already started spiralling.

"Yeah, I call bullshit on that one. Why did you come over again tonight?"

"Touché."

"I know you too well, Ell. You can't get anything past me. Now. Send. That. Text."

"Okay, okay! So bossy."

"You love it." She blows me a kiss and I roll my eyes. I really do love it, but I won't tell her that.

I pull up my text thread from Xavier last night and type out a new message. I don't know why, but I'm nervous.

ELLA

> Hey. Hope your Sunday was a good one. Are you free to catch up this week at all? No biggie if you can't, nothing urgent or anything. Just let me know when you're free x

"Okay, done." I put my phone down and finish my Milo.

"Good. Now here's another question for you. What do you want to happen with him moving forward? Do you want to kiss him again?" she asks.

I ponder this for a moment. *What* do *I want to happen with Xavier?*

"I mean, I wouldn't say no to another kiss. No one has ever kissed me like that before. As for more? It's been a year since I've had sex, and if that kiss was anything to go by, sex with Xav would be hot."

"Okay, that's good! What's to stop you from doing that?"

"Probably the fact that he isn't looking for a relationship right now, but I am. I've been single long enough, I don't want another one-night stand, and that's what it'll be with him." The idea of another root 'n' boot fills me with literal dread. I couldn't think of anything worse and would rather stay abstinent for another year than hook up with someone just for the sake of breaking my dry spell.

"I understand not wanting a one-night stand. But you don't know if that's what it'll be for Xavier. What about something casual? Would you be up for that?"

"I don't know… maybe? But those types of arrangements never work. Feelings develop and someone always gets hurt." Usually, it's me. I get the feelings. Because I'm hopeless.

"Yeah, but you don't know that for sure."

"Okay but what if—"

"Girl, stop with the what ifs. You need a good dicking, and this may be your opportunity to get some with someone you ACTUALLY like. So go meet with the man, see what he has to say about the kiss. If he regrets it, then forget everything I just said. If he enjoyed it and wants more? Then go for it!"

I take in what she says. I do deserve some good sex. And I do like Xavier, as a friend. If he was up for some casual, no-strings-attached fun, then what would be the harm? It's not like I've known the man my whole life. It's been less than two months since we met, so I don't have too much to lose, despite really enjoying his friendship. Perhaps it's time I push myself out of my comfort zone. Right as I think this, my phone pings with a new message. Millie and I both stare down at it.

"Check it!" she demands. I pick it up and read the message out loud.

XAVIER

Hey, right back. My Sunday has been fine. Nowhere near as good as my Saturday :p I've got a pretty busy week and weekend coming up, but I can probably meet somewhere or come to your place on Thursday night when you get off work? I have the night off.

"Flirt alert. This is a good sign!" Millie says excitedly. She's practically bouncing in her seat over this text.

"Maybe. Good thing I'm free Thursday night, I guess." Immediately, Millie squeals with excitement.

"Jesus Millie, you're making me feel like a teenager all over again! It's a midweek catch up. I doubt anything exciting is going to happen on a Thursday," I say.

ELLA

Thursday works for me! You can come over. I have another book recommendation for you. Come any time from 6pm x

"You never know, Ella. You never know."

CHAPTER 13
Xavier

The week goes by in a blur of invoices, wine spills, and cheeky texts between Ella and I. Ever since I kissed her, our texts have gone from 90 percent platonic but flirty banter to something with a little more spice to it. Nothing explicit has been said, but I can feel the sexual tension within our messages. I can read between the lines, and I've been looking forward to Thursday. Now, it's finally here.

I haven't been able to stop thinking about the kiss. Everything inside me is telling me to do it again. What she wants, though, I have no idea. I'm driving to her house now and the nerves are starting to hit. You would think by my age I wouldn't get nervous when approaching these types of conversations. I'll blame it on being out of the game for so long. I really hope she isn't expecting anything more than something casual. Getting to know her has been great and if we can add a little bit of no strings attached fun to it, I think we'd be in for an amazing time.

I pull up outside of her house and take a moment to collect myself before getting out and walking to her front door. I knock twice and ring the doorbell. She must have been waiting for me because in less than a heartbeat, she opens the door and is smiling shyly at me. I smile back.

"Hey," she says.

"Hey."

"Come in, make yourself at home."I follow her inside. She must have been burning a candle, because the house smells faintly of coconut and lime. It's delicious, just like the sight of her. She's wearing a tight cropped white tee and denim shorts. So basic, yet so hot. She heads to the fridge to get us both a drink and I contemplate where to sit. The dining table feels way too formal, especially if the conversation goes where I hope it does, so I settle for the couch.

"Beer or wine?" she asks. I look over to her and see that she's bent over with her head in the fridge, and from where I'm sitting, I can just see the underside of her arse peeking out from her shorts.

"Beer works for me," I say as I clear my throat. "The last time we drank wine I had to sleep on the couch, remember?"

She stands up and walks over to me with two beers in her hand and a grin on her face.

"How could I forget? I'll always remember that the first man to sleep over in this house, slept on the couch and snuck out the next morning." She's still smiling at me as she uncaps her bottle and takes a sip.

"Hey now, I apologised for sneaking out, not that I *was* actually sneaking out. I had no reason to be sneaky, I just didn't want to wake you." I take a large swig of my drink and it goes down smooth. The girl has great taste in beer.

"I know. I'm only stirring you because it's fun."

"Mhmm. And as for being the first guy to sleep over. Was I really the first? Even platonically?"

"Yep. You were the first. Congratulations!" She salutes me and takes an even bigger sip. She seems nervous.

"Well, I'm sorry that your first male sleepover wasn't very eventful."

"No need to be sorry. You know my backstory, it's kind of how things go for me."

We both sit in silence as her last sentence settles over us. I think back to how she reacted in the bookstore. The lack of self-confidence, the disappointment, the rejection. I know she's thinking about it, too. But I know the moment she starts to think about the kiss because she starts to fidget with the label on her beer bottle, and her cheeks begin to flush.

"So…" she starts. "About the other day. The kiss, I mean."

"Yeah?"

"What was that all about? One minute I'm feeling super depressed and rejected and the next your tongue is in my mouth and you're all hot and heavy up against me." She blurts out. I sit back in my seat. She's so cute when she's flustered.

"Well, it's like I said on the day. I don't want you to ever think or feel like you aren't good enough or attractive enough, so I was proving my point. With my own attraction."

"But you've not shown any interest in me, not like that at least. What changed?" she asks. She's chewing on her bottom lip, so I know that she's definitely nervous.

"I've always found you attractive, Ella. Don't doubt that for a second. But given the way we met? I didn't want to just pursue you straight away, I wanted to give you time, get to know each other a bit. Now that we're friends, and I feel comfortable knowing you don't think I'm some creep, I thought I'd see what happens."

"Okay, I guess that makes sense."

"Did you like it? Would you… do it again?" I ask.

"I mean, I didn't not like it," she says.

I laugh.

"Liar. You loved it."

She leans over and smacks me on the arm.

"Okay! Yes, Xavier, I loved how you kissed me. It's the most action I've gotten in over a year and is probably the hottest kiss I've ever had. I would gladly do it again. Happy?" She slumps back down in her seat.

"Very," I say, smugly. Hottest kiss she's ever had? Yeah, I'll take that.

"So, what now then?" she asks.

"What do you mean?"

"I know you don't want another relationship right now."

"That would be correct."

"But you find me attractive. And you kissed me. Would it be a safe assumption, then, to say that you want to kiss me again?" She doesn't look at me when she asks this, she just keeps picking at the label on the bottle.

"You know picking at labels like that is a sign of sexual frustration." I say.

"No shit, Sherlock, I haven't been fucked in a year. I'm beyond frustrated. Now, answer my question, do you want to kiss me again?"

I stare at her for a moment, impressed with how quickly she went from shy to direct, before answering wholeheartedly.

"Yes. I want to kiss you again. Very, very badly. I want to do more than kiss you. It's all I can think about."

"Well… okay then. Good."

"But— "

"Ahh, there's always a but." She sighs.

"Shush. But before—or if—I do, I think we need to establish some expectations."

"What do you mean? Like, rules or something?" she asks.

"Yeah, sort of. Like you said, I'm not looking for a relationship right now, and I assume that you are." She nods. "You need to release some of that sexual frustration, and whilst I'm not the guy to date you, I can certainly be the guy who can help you with your… needs. If you want me, that is."

She puts on an act of pondering what I've just said very carefully before answering.

"Yeah, I want that. I thought that might have been obvious."

"A guy can never be too sure." *Because really, one can't.*

"Good point. Okay… so, expectations." She takes a moment to think. "For me, I think if we were to do this, I would still need to maintain some distance. I know myself and I know that I get attached easily, so I don't want to end up hurt."

"That's good, the last thing I want to do is hurt you. So how about this: no emotional attachment, a strictly physical relationship. If feelings start to develop, we need to walk away."

"Yeah, I think I can work with that. I think as long as we communicate openly with each other, this could really work." Her eyes are lighting up as she says this. Her cheeks are still flushed, and I bet that if I could feel her pulse right now, it would be fluttering like mad.

"I agree." I put my bottle on the table and stand up from the couch. I hold out my hand, indicating for her to stand, too. She puts down her bottle, now completely label-less, and takes my hand. I pull her towards me and look down into her eyes, but she doesn't break contact like I thought she would. Instead, she's looking at me, eyes twinkling with desire.

"So, Ella… can I kiss you now?"

"Yes." She breathes.

So, I do.

CHAPTER 14
Ella

Xavier holds my face in both hands, brings his lips to mine, and I instantly ignite. He's slow and tender at first, with soft pecks and kisses on the side of my mouth. He's taking his time and just enjoying the moment. But the instant I open my mouth to him and his tongue touches mine, he picks up the tempo. Now, he's kissing me like a man starved. One of his hands moves behind my head as he fists my hair, the other on my cheek as his tongue continues to explore my mouth.

Then, he pulls away and starts to trail kisses up my neck and along my jaw. He pauses for a moment, seeming a little breathless.

"If I keep kissing you like this, I'm just going to end up taking off all of your clothes right here and now, so I can taste every inch of your body. Do you trust me?" he asks, thumb stroking my cheek.

"Yes. I trust you," I whisper.

"Okay? You're sure?" he asks.

"Yes. I want you." I barely get the sentence out before his lips are crashing back onto mine. I'm already feeling weak at the knees.

He walks me back until I'm standing pressed against the wall closest to my bedroom door. His hands are roaming up my body, one hand going to my throat and the other working its way under my shirt and up my stomach. He slips his hand underneath my bra and gently pinches my nipple. He presses into me, and I can feel how hard he is for me.

I wrap my arms around his neck and pull him closer. I press my hips into his, because I want to feel all of him. His hand moves from my chest and slides down to my shorts. He unbuttons them, pulls down the zip, and then slowly takes them off. His hand then slips inside my underwear and his fingers graze the lace covering me. I thought I was turned on before, but the feel of his fingers so close to my most sensitive spot has me unravelling. I want to feel even closer to him, and an idea pops into my head.

"Would you care to join me in the shower?" I ask, breathless, as his hands continue to explore me. He groans. There's nothing more intimate than showering with someone.

"Um, fuck yeah, I'll join you."

"Excellent." I pull his hand from my pants and drag him into the bathroom. I turn on the shower and pretty much rip his shirt off over his head. He does the same to me. Then, he unclips my bra and all I'm left standing in is the black lace G-string I put on in the hopes that he would be the one taking it off.

He stares down at me hungrily, reaching out to gently brush my nipples. They instantly harden at his touch. He squeezes me with both hands and I let out a soft moan. His hands slide down my body and as he reaches my underwear, he slowly peels them off, leaving me bare.

I step into the shower and stare back at him as the water cascades over my naked body. He strips off the rest of his clothes, and I can't look away. He's standing there, naked, and my mouth waters at the sight. He steps into the shower and stands in front of me, most of the water hitting my back, and doesn't hesitate. He wraps a hand around the back of my neck and pulls me to him with just enough force, and then he truly devours me. He kisses along my jaw and down my neck, nipping at the skin as he moves further and further down. He reaches my peaked nipples and kisses me gently before sucking hard and I moan with pleasure. He bites down gently and pulls, my thighs squeezing tight as I can feel myself getting more and more turned on. He continues his trail of kisses and before I know it, he's on his knees before me. "You are stunning," he says as he looks up at me.

This is quite possibly one of the hottest moments of my life. He kisses my belly, then moves from one of my hips, then to the other. As he continues to kiss me lower and lower, I lean back, urging him on. As I do this, the stream of water from the shower hits him right in the face.

He coughs and splutters and I can't help the laughter that bursts out of me.

"Oh my God, I am so sorry!" I'm laughing so hard. This is not how I thought this would go.

He stands back up, luckily with a smile on his face.

"It's okay." His fingers lightly trace the bones of my hips and move closer and closer to my aching centre. I am desperate for his touch at this point.

"I didn't mean to nearly drown you, I promise. Maybe… we should… move to the bed." I'm breathing hard and I can barely get the words out as his fingers graze my clit.

"That's a good idea. Because the only thing I planned on drowning in tonight is you, and I'm done waiting."

Holy shit. I am a fucking puddle at this point. I didn't think this man could possibly turn me on even more and yet, he just said THAT. He turns off the shower, pulls me out, and effortlessly picks me up. I wrap my legs around his waist as I kiss him deeply. I moan into his lips as he carries me to the bedroom, we're both still dripping wet from the shower, and I'm also dripping wet… from him.

He throws me onto the bed, drags me to the edge, and spreads my legs wide. He isn't wasting any more time.

"I've wanted to taste you from the moment I met you," he says. And then, his tongue is on me. He gently parts me, drawing long strokes until his tongue brushes my clit. I gasp and grab his hair in both hands, encouraging him to go harder. He stops and looks up at me.

"Put your arms above your head. Don't let them come down, Ella, or I will stop." Oh. Oh, okay. He wants to give me orders? I'll do whatever the fuck he tells me to at this point. I let go of him and bring my arms above my head. It seems like the man has a plan and I'm not going to complain.

"That's a good girl," he says, and then he dives right back in, pushing his tongue hard against me.

"Oh my God, Xavier." I breathe as he flicks my clit over and over again. He starts sucking as he drives a finger inside of me, instantly finding my g-spot.

This man is a fucking god.

"Oh, holy fuck!" My back arches and my arms come down to grab his hair again. He instantly stops.

"Ella, what did I say?"

"To keep my arms above my head."

"Correct. And you didn't listen, did you?"

I bite my bottom lip and shake my head.

"No, I didn't.""Do you know what happens when you don't follow instructions?"

I shake my head again. In an instant, he has me flipped over and onto my stomach. He draws my knees up so that my arse is in the air. He gently rubs his hand over my left cheek.

"I'm going to spank you now. Is that okay?" he asks.

Oh. My. God.

"Yes. Yes, please," I plead. I don't know what's hotter, the fact that he asked for consent first, or the anticipation of being spanked. I've been spanked before and enjoyed it, but I've found in the past most guys just aren't into it—they either say they are but don't commit to it fully, or they are into it but only for their own pleasure.

He brings his hand down and spanks me, not too hard at first, but enough to bring a tingle up my spine and for a soft moan to slip through my lips. He spanks me again, a little harder, and then flips me back over onto my back.

"Now, I don't want to have to tell you again. Put your arms up and keep them there." And then, he's right back to where he was. He thrusts a finger inside of me and hits the sweet spot. He leans in and lightly flicks his tongue to the rhythm of his finger until, miraculously, I'm close to climaxing.

"Oh my God, yes! I'm so close."

He picks up the pace and presses his tongue down harder on my clit and I come undone. He holds me down as I arch my back, forcing me to ride out the orgasm in its entirety as he continues to gently lick me.

"Ohh fuck," I say breathlessly. I can't remember the last time a man made me come like that. If ever, actually.

He makes his way back up my body, wiping the evidence of my pleasure from his lips.

I pull his face to mine and kiss him. We slide further up onto the bed, until my head hits the pillows. I look down at him and see that he is achingly hard. I take him in my hand and slowly stroke him up and down. His eyes slowly close as he rests his forehead on mine.

"Fuck Ella, that feels so good."

I kiss him again as I pick up my pace, squeezing him as I get to the tip. Our kiss deepens and I'm ready for more. I want this man to fuck me into tomorrow.

"I need you to fuck me now, Xavier."

"Oh, do you? Whatever happened to please?"

I smile at him and bat my eyelashes in a ridiculous fashion.

"Please, Xavier, will you fuck me now?"

"Well, only because you asked so nicely. Condom?"

I point to the bedside table because I'm beyond words at this point. He pulls away from me and opens the drawer to get a condom out. He opens the packet and slides it on. Once he's ready, he pulls my legs open. He is so hard and ready for me, positioning himself at my entrance, slowly teasing me.

"Is this what you want?"

"Yes, please Xavier. I need you." I moan.

He continues to tease me, rubbing himself along my clit which is so sensitive that I could come again just from the friction alone. I'm practically begging at this point. Finally, he slowly enters me. Once he is fully inside, he stops moving, enjoying the feel of me and letting me adjust. Not because he has a super unrealistic massive dick like I read about in all of my romance novels, but because I haven't been fucked in so long, I just need a moment. He leans down and kisses me passionately as he starts to move. He brings his mouth to my ear and whispers,

"I'm going to fuck you until you're screaming my name."

Before I could answer, he pulls out and thrusts into me hard. The sounds that come out of me are barely human. He continues to pull out almost completely before slamming back into me. I drag my fingernails down his back, enough to leave a mark, as he starts to set a pace that has me seeing stars. He lifts my hips up off the bed and props my legs up over his shoulders, so he can get an even better angle, and it works. He's hitting a spot so deep within me and I know that it won't be long before I come again.

He reaches down with one hand to squeeze my breast and pinch my nipple, eliciting an even louder moan from me. I can feel my pleasure building again, only this time it feels like it's coming from deeper within. I've never had an orgasm from penetration before in my life, and I think I'm about to experience it for the first time. A bead of sweat rolls down his face as he continues his punishing rhythm, and I know we are both close to the edge.

"Fuck Ella, you feel so good. I want you to come for me."

He picks up the pace, pounding into me a few more times and I reach my peak, the orgasm rocking through me as I indeed scream his name.

He continues to fuck me through wave after wave of pleasure until he finds his release too, shuddering and groaning in ecstasy. He gently places my shaking legs back onto the bed and bends to kiss me. It's slow, sweet, and sensual. He kisses me on the forehead and gently pulls out of me.

"Holy shit," I mutter to myself. I have never come like that when sleeping with a guy for the first time. *Not ever.* Let alone twice. In fact, I don't recall ever having an orgasm that even comes close to what I just experienced. We're both lying on my bed, completely spent, trying to catch our breath. He pulls the condom off and ties a knot in it before placing it on the bedside table.

Pulling back the sheets, he slides into my bed and motions for me to join him for a cuddle.

"I wouldn't have picked you to be a cuddler," I say with an element of surprise. I don't hesitate though, I'm such a slut for cuddles.

He wraps an arm around me and pulls me in tight. "I fucking love cuddles. How are you feeling?" He plants a small kiss on my lips and smiles at me.

"Consider my tension released. That was incredible, and I'm not just saying that. It's normally quite difficult for me to orgasm the first time I sleep with someone, so for you to get me there twice... Are you a magician or something?"

He laughs deeply.

"Not a magician, I just take great pleasure in giving pleasure. As long as you're satisfied, I'm satisfied."

Incredible. Most of the guys I've slept with in the past haven't given two shits about my pleasure, and have just taken what they need for themselves, leaving me reaching for my vibrator the moment they leave.

"I've never heard a man say anything like that before—that's very selfless of you. Most guys I've encountered were incredibly selfish in the bedroom," I say, stifling a yawn.

"Good thing I'm not most guys. You're tired and it's late. Do you want me to stay?" he asks. "I know you have work in the morning, so if you want me to leave, I will."

"No it's fine, you can stay," I mumble sleepily. "Probably shouldn't make sleepovers a regular occurrence though, don't want to grow attached to these cuddles." As I say that, I snuggle in closer. I can't remember the last time someone held me like this, and I'll be damned if I don't make the most of it.

Sometimes I think to myself that it's not necessarily the sex that I miss, but the intimacy. The hugs, the kisses, the small touches here and there. That's what I crave. I can get myself to orgasm easily enough, but there is nothing out there that can replace the intimacy of another human's touch.

"Good plan, but for now, let's get some sleep. Maybe in the morning I can show you again just how selfless I am."

I smile and look up at him to give him a quick kiss before turning out the light. "Now I definitely won't say no to that."

CHAPTER 15
Ella

He does indeed show me how selfless he is the following morning. Instead of waking up to my alarm, I wake up to him caressing my back and planting little kisses along my spine. He continues to nip and tease me before seating me firmly on his face and having me for breakfast. It's only after I've come three times that he feels satisfied enough to let me get out of bed so I can get ready for work. I have a quick shower to wash off the sex from last night and this morning and rush back into my room to get dressed. Xavier is still in my bed, hands propped behind his head with a cheeky grin. Clearly enjoying how flustered I am.

"Someone's in a good mood this morning," I say as I throw on a floral maxi skirt and loose white t-shirt. My hair is beyond salvageable after having Xavier's hands in it for most of the night, so I throw it in a messy bun and hope for the best.

"I'm in a great mood. I just had a woman sitting on my face, nothing can beat that," he says with a smile.

I throw a pillow at him that must have fallen on the floor during the night.

"Yes, and now I'm rushing to get to work on time."

He smirks and his dimple shows.

"Worth it."

I can't help the smile that spreads across my face. I walk over to him and give him a chaste kiss on the mouth.

"Totally worth it."

I move to my dresser and look at myself in the mirror. My skin is still flushed from the multiple orgasms I've received in the last 12 hours, and my hair looks ridiculous. I put on a bit of mascara to make myself look a bit more alive. To everyone else, it probably just looks like I was running late and got ready really quickly. But to me, and most likely Millie as well, I look like I've had a thoroughly good dicking. I smile to myself.

Yeah… I definitely needed this.

"What are you thinking about?" Xavier asks.

"I'm thinking about how I have no regrets about last night. Or this morning."

"Good. Neither do I. I had a great time and by the sound of you screaming my name multiple times, I'd say you did too."

I laugh. Yeah, I screamed his name—a lot. *My poor neighbour.*

"I had more than a great time. I had multiple great times. We both know this." I walk to my wardrobe and grab out a pair of brown sandals and put them on.

"Oh, I know it. I can still taste you on my tongue."

"Jesus Christ," I mutter. "Stop flirting, I'm going to be late for work!"

He chuckles to himself.

"When do you need to leave?"

I check the time on my phone, then notice there's a bunch of messages from Millie on there. They will be fun to read later.

"I want to get a coffee before work, you know, because someone kept me up all night. I need to leave in 10 minutes. You should probably get out of my bed."

I go back into the bathroom and brush my teeth. I do a final check over of myself before heading back into my room where I come to a screeching halt. Xavier has gotten out of bed and is standing in the middle of the room, completely naked, morning wood standing tall and proud. My mouth waters at the sight of him. I can't stop staring, and I know he knows that.

"You good, Ella?" he says smugly. The bastard knows what he's doing.

"Yep. Just saving that image for later when I'm bored at work. Now, even though I would rather you remain naked in my house, please get changed so I can go. If I don't get my coffee this morning, I'll be grumpy for the rest of the day."

I walk up to him and kiss him deeply, my hand gripping his hardness and sliding up and down a few times before I pull away and walk out of my bedroom, hips swaying slightly as I do.

"Fucking temptress," he says to my back. I look over my shoulder at him and wink.

"You've unleashed me now, Xav. You have no idea."

He follows me out of the room and into the bathroom where his clothes still are. I walk over to my fridge to pull out some leftovers I can have for lunch and throw them in my work bag. I make sure I have everything I need, emotional support water bottle included. One of my students actually got me a sticker that says 'emotional support water bottle' because I literally take it with me everywhere.

Xavier walks out of the bathroom, fully clothed, and pulls me in for a hug. It's reminiscent of our first hug in this room, which feels like forever ago now.

"I'm really glad we did this. I hope you have a great day at work. Oh, and try not to think about me naked too much." I laugh and he kisses me. I pull away and grab my bag, then we both walk out of my front door. He kisses me once more before we get into our separate cars and start our days.

I walk up to the counter of my favourite coffee shop, grateful to have made it with enough time to spare. This place is across the road from school, so I go here pretty much every morning. The baristas don't have to ask for my order anymore. My name is even saved in their work phone with my order, so if I'm running late, I can just call so they immediately know to start making my coffee. I love it here. I place my order, including a drink for Millie, and take a seat. While I wait, I check the messages she's sent me. They're all from last night and this morning.

MILLIE

okay so did he show up?

MILLIE

helloooo is he there? Just tell me yes or no

MILLIE

omg I'm dying here pls.

MILLIE

I'm taking your silence as either he didn't show and you're crying in the shower again, or he is there and he has his tongue down your throat.

MILLIE

bitch tell me. For the love of God.

MILLIE

still no response. He has to be there. GET IT GIRL I HOPE HE FUCKS YOUR BRAINS OUT.

MILLIE

GOOD MORNING HOW WAS THE SEX

MILLIE

ffs you're still ignoring me I am SUFFERING! I need details asap!!!

I'm smiling like an idiot at my phone. *I fucking love Millie.* When she says she needs details, she means *DETAILS.* There's no such thing as too much information with her. My name is called out with my coffee so I shoot off a quick text.

ELLA

Girl you are going to die. I have so much to tell you. I'm coming over after work. No sex talk at school. See you soon x

I walk into the staff room and immediately make eye contact with Millie. She's sitting in our usual spot. The grin on her face is all-knowing, she looks like if the purple grinning devil emoji came to life. I take my seat beside her, and she leans to whisper in my ear.

"Oh, you got dicked HARD last night. You are a mess. I love to see it." She takes her coffee from my hand.

"Shush, Mills! Good lord, we're at work." I smack her on the knee.

"I bet you were praying to the good lord last night. And this morning too, by the looks of you." She winks at me and takes a big drink.

"Oh my God!" I squeal. "You are going to get us into so much shit one day."

I look around but thankfully all the other staff are busy with their own conversations.

"But to be honest, you're not wrong."

She smiles wide at that.

"I'm so proud of you."

A matching grin spreads across my face. I even sit a little taller in my seat.

"I'm proud of me, too."

CHAPTER 16

Xavier

I pull up in my driveway, turn off the car, and sit with the dumbest grin on my face. The whole drive home I spent reliving the events of last night. I had zero expectations or plans going into that conversation with Ella. I just wanted to suss out how she was feeling and get a general vibe of if she was interested in something more. I did not anticipate showering with her, fucking her, and eating her out for breakfast. I can still hear her perfect little moans and her sharp intakes of breath as she nears her climax. I'm getting hard again just thinking about it.

"Down boy. Seriously, did you not get your fill last night?" I talk down at my crotch as I adjust my pants. I then inwardly cringe as I realise I'm literally sitting in my car and talking to my own dick. I sigh at myself and get out of the car. I go inside the house and plug my phone in to charge—it must have gone flat during the night. I head to the bathroom and have a quick shower. I can still smell the faint tropical scent of Ella on my skin, mixed with a hint of sex. It's not a bad smell, but I do have a meeting at lunch time with my dad and I don't want to have even the slightest scent of a woman on me. That's not a conversation I wish to have with my parents today.

I quickly rinse off and hop out, getting dressed into some grey track pants and a black t-shirt. I have a few things to do around the house before I have to meet with dad. First up, feed the chickens. I enter the coop and

Meryl Cheep instantly spots me. Some days, she loves me, and others she will peck the shit out of me. Today, she saunters over, looks up at me, clucks a few times, then pecks my foot before running around in a circle, waiting for her food.

"You are such a weird bird." I laugh as I scatter the food around the coop. Guess today is a good day for Meryl. She's definitely my favourite chicken out of the three that I own. Nuggs may be the best layer and Hen Solo is the most placid, but Meryl has character, and I like that. As they start eating, I freshen up their water and inspect the fence to make sure the fox hasn't made another attempt at getting in. Thankfully, there isn't any evidence of digging. I say goodbye to the girls and make my way back inside the house. I check my phone and notice there is already a message from Ella, as well as a missed call from Lena. I call Lena back and put her on speaker while I open up the message from Ella.

"Hey boss man, what time are you coming into the pub today?" Lena pipes up. She's sounding especially cheery this morning.

"I have a meeting with Dad at midday. Why?" I ask as I read the text from Ella.

ELLA

> I'm in school prayer right now and I can't stop thinking about all the dirty things you did to me last night. And this morning. These are not very Godly thoughts I am having. Pray for me 🙏

I snort with laughter.

"What's so funny?" Lena asks.

"Hmm? Oh, nothing. Just laughing at… the chickens," I say, trying to control my laughter. I can just imagine Ella sitting in some church set up, squirming in her seat thinking about the ways I made her come last night. *Brilliant.*

"Uh huh. Anyway, I might be an hour late arriving to work today. Something's come up. I'm all good but I'm a little behind schedule. Hope that's okay," she says.

"Oh, yeah that's fine. You worked heaps of overtime last week so don't stress. Just update me if you're delayed further." I type out my reply to Ella, only half focussed on what Lena is saying.

XAVIER

You were praying to me plenty this morning as you came on my tongue.

ELLA

FFS. I'm going to ignore you for the rest of the day. K bye.

XAVIER

You can try, but I know you'll be thinking about me 😏

ELLA:

seen

"Xav? Hello?" I remember I'm on the phone with Lena.

"Shit, yeah sorry Lena, what were you saying?"

"I was saying I might need to take next Saturday off, if I can. You all good over there? You seem distracted of sorts," she asks tentatively.

"Yeah, I'm all good, sorry. Late night last night. Um, next Saturday should be okay, but let me double check the roster when I get into the office. I'll let you know for sure when you get in. Okay?"

"Sure, sounds good. I'll see you in a bit then. Bye." She ends the call.

I chuck on a load of washing before making myself a coffee and perching myself on the outdoor couch under the veranda. I have an hour before I need to be at work so I make the most of the beautiful morning. I look out over my property with a sense of pride. Even though Jade and I bought this place together, there was no chance I was moving out of it when we broke up. It's my dream home. I'm surrounded by native bush, with a row of huge gumtrees lining my driveway. I'll often find kangaroos in my yard in the mornings and almost every night I'll spot a possum or two. I really do get the best of both worlds living out here—it's about a 30-minute drive into work on the outskirts of the city, yet I get to live a somewhat country lifestyle. If I'm honest, it's my idea of paradise.

I finish off my coffee and get changed into my work clothes, which more often than not is just a button up with black jeans and R.M. Williams boots. We're a pub, not a law firm, so I refuse to wear a tie even though Dad does. I'm pretty sure I've seen that man in a tie more often than not in my lifetime. I attempt to tame my hair and give my beard a quick tidy before I deem myself work appropriate and head back out to my car. Once again, I'm hoping my conversation with Dad today is about me taking over the business, but I've stopped getting my hopes up.

I get to work and walk through the bar, saying hello to a few members of my team before ducking into my office. I check the roster for Lena and sure enough, we have someone available to cover her for next Saturday. The time has just hit 12 noon, so I make my way into Dad's office. I knock before opening the door and sticking my head in.

"Hey, Dad. You ready for me?" I ask.

"Hey mate, yeah yeah, come on in." He's sitting at his desk, which is an absolute mess as usual. I once pointed it out and got a stern "it's my organised chaos, I know where everything is, so it's not an issue". Since then, I try to ignore it as best as I can.

"How's the week been?" he asks.

"Not too bad." I reply. "Bit quiet early on in the week, but Tuesday quiz night has picked up. We've managed to secure quite a few regulars out of it. This weekend we have two functions on, so it'll be a busy one."

"Good to hear. Seems your new marketing strategy is paying off, with all that Intergram stuff."

"Instagram, Dad."

"Yeah, that's the one. Keep it up!"

"Will do. Anything else you wanted to discuss?" I ask hesitantly. I really can't push him on the handover stuff. I tried once about a year ago and he didn't appreciate it, said I was calling him old and useless and declared I wasn't ready. It was absolutely not the case, all I had said was that some of our practices were a little outdated and could use some modernising, and that I'd be happy to take over. He sulked for a week. Eventually, I was able to convince him of at least some of my ideas—like our marketing strategies—and took some jobs off his hands. It's not enough, though. So, I keep patiently waiting.

"Yeah, actually there is something I wanted to bring up," he says. My heart rate picks up slightly and I sit up a little straighter as he takes a brief moment to pause and focus his train of thought.

"There's a new brewery opening up out west and I was thinking we could stock them on tap, have a monthly special going or something. Whaddya reckon?" he asks.

My heart sinks a little, and I hide my disappointment as best as I can.

"Oh, um… yeah. That sounds good. I'll get in touch and organise a meeting with them next week if that works?"

"Excellent! We can post about it on Instagrid." He beams.

"Dad, it's Instagram. GRAM."

"I know, I'm just teasing. I'm not that old, Jesus." He laughs and so do I. I know for a fact that he is not teasing. Frustrated as I may be, he still makes me laugh.

"Old enough," I say as I stand up and go to leave. "Call me if you need me."

"Will do. Hope the arvo shift goes alright. Catchya mate," he says with a wave.

I head back into my office and sit down at my desk, taking in a deep breath. I'm frustrated, but I sort of get it. I get why he's holding onto this role. It has been his job for 40 years. He's taken this place from a standard everyday pub to a local waterhole, one fit with a state-of-the-art beer garden and function space. Jimmies is essentially his second child. It's all he's ever known. He'll never admit it, but I bet he's afraid of the change retirement will bring. I'm just tired of constantly having to prove myself to him, and feeling like he just doesn't see it.

I give myself a few more minutes to sort out my thoughts, before heading out to the main bar to brief my staff on the functions we need to start setting up for this weekend.

CHAPTER 17
Ella

"WHY IS THIS BOOK STICKY?!" I yell to no one in particular. It's just before lunch time and I'm emptying the library returns box. Honestly, if I had a dollar for every time I said the phrase "why is this book sticky/wet/mouldy?" I'd be a millionaire. Kids are gross.

We are deep into the end-of-year library returns process and I swear some of the books I'm getting back have sat in the bottom of school bags or have been shoved in the back of lockers for the whole year. The absolute state some of these books are in just hurts my soul. We've just had a class of middle schoolers come through and return their maths textbooks, and I shit you not, one of them had burnt a hole in the back of the book. Like, smack bang in the middle of the cover. "I don't like maths," this kid said. I mean, *same*, but don't take it out on the book! That'll be a fun email I have to send to her parents later. And naturally, it's my responsibility because my boss is absolutely useless and is once again nowhere to be seen.

I've just finished wiping the unknown, sticky substance from the book when the lunch bell rings. I'm excited for half a second before remembering I have a social committee meeting. *Damn.*

I quickly heat up my lunch in the staff room and make my way into the meeting room. Millie is already there and has saved me a seat, naturally. We run the committee, by the surprise of many. I remember volunteering for the role when I started and the look on management's face was priceless.

Their image of what a librarian should be has been significantly altered since I started working here. I am loud, sociable, and personable. I will talk to anyone and everyone. Basically, the complete opposite of my boss who hardly says a word unless it's to criticise my entire being. I am slowly breaking down the typical librarian stereotype and by heading this committee, I am at least hoping to guarantee some fun in this suffocating institute they call a school.

We are meeting today to finalise the staff Christmas party which is being held in two weeks. Everything is organised, the menu chosen, and the bar tab has been set (and raised, thanks to yours truly). We just need to go over the final details. Most of the other committee members have filed in, so I open up my laptop to go over my list of items to discuss when I notice a new and unread email from the manager of our venue. I open it and my stomach drops.

"Hi Ms Hart, I'm so sorry to email you with this news, but unfortunately, we are unable to host your Christmas function on the 15th of December. Our kitchen had a fire last night, and thankfully the damage was mostly contained, however it did cause damage to our function space. I apologise for the inconvenience this may cause and offer you a full refund. If you have any other questions, please reach out. Regards, Samantha."

"Oh, you have got to be kidding me!" I shout and the whole room startles.

"What? What's wrong?" Millie asks.

"The venue caught fire last night and so we can't use it."

"Oh shit!" Millie exclaims.

"Language!" One of the older male teachers spits, but we all ignore him.

"What the hell do we do? We only have two weeks left… there's no way we can get a new booking for 60 people with such short notice," I say as I slump back in my chair.

A few ideas get thrown around, including a BBQ lunch at the school (boring), hosting it at Steve the science teacher's house (hell no), cancelling the event and donating the money to charity (lol, good one Jan). I look over at Millie who is frantically typing away at her phone.

"Ah ha! I've found a venue with a big enough function space to fit us, you just need to give them a ring and see if they can book us in at the last minute," she says with a mischievous grin on her face.

"Okay… what's the venue?"

"Jimmies," she says, and I nearly fall off my chair. "You know the manager, don't you Ella? I'm sure you could sweet talk your way into a booking." She sits back and smirks at me as I feel my face going red.

"Um, well yes, I do know the manager. But I'm sure it's too late notice. We can think of something else—" I ramble.

"Oh wow," interrupts Doug, the IT manager, who has looked up Jimmies on Instagram and is now showing everyone the photos. "Their beer garden is epic. We should definitely try and get in here." Everyone nods in agreement.

"That's settled then!" Millie says as she claps her hands together and bounces in her seat. "Ella will get in touch with the manager and see if she can get us booked in. Doug, get in touch with the old venue to organise the refund of our deposit. I'll redesign the invites and poster for the staff room, and once we have the go ahead from Ella, we can announce the change to staff. Sound good?" We all agree, though I'm reluctant, and everyone leaves the meeting room.

I grab Millie's arm and pull her back into her seat.

"Oh my God, Millie, Jimmies? Really?" I groan.

"I think it's a great idea."

"Well duh," I say. "It was your own idea."

"Exactly." She beams. "Come on, it's the perfect venue, and maybe Xavier will be able to give you a cheeky discount. If we can get a booking that is. Call him."

"I can't today."

"Um, why? This is urgent, babe."

"Because I told him I was going to ignore him for the rest of the day because he was getting me too horny at work. Now he will think he won!" I whine. She just laughs at me.

"Aw… too bad, so sad. You need to call him, otherwise, we're screwed. 'Kay?"

"Ugh. Fine. But you need to leave, I won't have you listening in on this conversation," I say, shoving her out of her chair.

"You're boring. Do it now and give me an update after lunch. Byeeeee." She waves as leaves the room, shutting the door behind her.

I pull up our message thread and reread the last message we sent to each other. I really did plan on ignoring him all day, really just to prove to myself that I could. Since he first slept over, I don't think we have actually gone a full day without speaking. Now that he has been inside of me, we have crossed into new territory, and that means me keeping some distance, so I don't get attached.

So far, I have failed, but at least I can blame Millie for this one.

I dial his number and am secretly hoping he's too busy at work to answer the phone, but alas, he answers on the third ring.

"Miss me already, do you?" he says into the phone, and I can practically hear the smirk he is wearing through the speaker.

"You wish. This is a strictly professional phone call. I need a favour."

"A sexual favour?" He asks in an overly dramatic sultry tone.

"Nope. An actual favour. But it will benefit both of us, I hope."

"Sounds like a sexual favour, love." I instantly melt when he calls me love. I'm sure he means it in a 'platonic friend who I just fucked' sort of way, but still.

"Will you shush and let me explain?" He laughs. "The venue we had booked for our work Christmas party has cancelled on us, and we don't have a backup. Millie suggested Jimmies might be available and told me to ask you. So… are you? Available?" I literally cross my fingers.

This event is the biggest one we organise for the year, and it's also my favourite. There's always so much pressure to get it right, too, since everyone always has something to complain about or criticise. If we can't lock something in, we will probably have to cancel, and I really, really don't want to do that.

"Oh, you did mean an actual favour," he says. "Right, well that sucks for you. What date do you need and how many people?"

"December 15th and for 60 people. Lunch or dinner, it doesn't really matter. As long as there is alcohol and good food," I say.

He's silent on the line for a few moments and I can hear a computer mouse and keys clicking in the background.

"Well, it really is your lucky day, we have a dinner spot available in either the function room or the beer garden. What would you prefer?"

"Oh my God, yay! Um.. uhh... I'm not sure. The beer garden? There's plenty of seating and stuff, yeah? That'll be nice, a bit more relaxed than a formal sit-down dinner. What food and drink packages do you have?"

We chat for another 15 minutes, negotiating on food and drink options, finally settling on something that actually costs us a few thousand dollars less than our previous venue. Finance will be happy with that.

"I'll have the deposit paid to you ASAP and then the rest we will pay afterwards," I say.

"Excellent, sounds good. I'm rostered on to work that night as well—should be fun," he says.

"Thank you so, so much, Xav. Honestly, you're a lifesaver." Despite my initial hesitations on asking him for help, I'm actually feeling really good about it. Hopefully the event goes off without a hitch from now on.

"It's no problem. You know, you can actually pay me back in sexual favours."

"Oh my… seriously! You and your sex brain need to have a cold shower. But thank you, again. You are the best."

He chuckles.

"You are very welcome. I gotta go, enjoy the rest of your day. Try not to think about me too much."

"Oh Xavier, I don't think about you at all." Lies. Such lies. And he knows it. "Have a good afternoon. Bye!"

I hang up and do a little fist pump in the air. I'm feeling good. The flirting helps, but really, I love planning these events. After my initial panic reading the email earlier, I'm feeling relieved and excited again.

I type out a quick text to Mille—she's supervising a study lesson at the moment so she can't answer a call.

ELLA

> Jimmies is locked in for dinner in the beer garden. You were right, it was a good idea. Will fill you in on the details tonight. Get keen!

She replies almost immediately.

MILLIE

> FUCK YEAH LET'S GOOOOOO. It is on. Told you it'd be worth calling! Talk tonight xoxo

I laugh out loud at her response. Millie is just so animated all the time. I don't know how she keeps it up. I pull up my emails on my laptop and compose a new email to the social committee, updating them on our plans.

CHAPTER 18
Xavier

A week goes by pretty quickly after my phone call with Ella. I didn't admit this to her, but I was actually working the lunch shift that day, and I swapped with Lena. Being able to watch her get drunk among her conservative colleagues? Yeah, I wasn't going to miss that one.

With Christmas fast approaching, the bar is booked out with work functions and family events, I've barely had time to think for myself. I know Ella is in the same boat, but thankfully for her, today was the last student day for the school year. It's almost five o'clock on this balmy Friday afternoon, and I've almost finished the lunch shift. I haven't heard much from Ella today. We talk every day, *all day*. What started out as just messaging has now turned into sending funny videos to each other as well. She also added me on snapchat last week, and let's just say, we've been having fun. The first snap I opened from her had me hard within seconds. I am now very wary when opening messages from her when I'm at work.

It's great and I'm enjoying it all, but sometimes I worry it's too much, given we are supposed to be just friends. Plus, she said she wanted to keep some distance. Every day we get to know each other better, and she has become a really good friend in such a short amount of time. I just don't want to hurt her or ruin that. But we are having sex now, and the risk is far greater. It's not that I regret it, I just have to be careful.

When my phone rings in the car on the way home, I'm surprised to see

Ella's name lighting up the screen.

"Hey, how's it going?" I say.

"Hey, um alright. Had a pretty average day at work, so I just felt like calling you. I hope that's okay?" Her voice sounds small, as if she's been crying.

"Yeah of course, what happened?"

"Just my boss, she's the worst. Always finds a way to make me feel incompetent or useless. It's nothing new, and I don't normally let it get to me, but it did today." She sighs.

"Well, that's a bit shit. After what you've told me, you pretty much run the place," I say. "Is there anything I can do to help?"

"I dunno. I'm just feeling a bit down, might start a new book or something to distract me. Maybe a gin, too. I was going to hang out with Millie, but she told me tonight is baby making night, so I'm out." She laughs sadly. I remember her telling me that Millie and Clay were trying. I also know she finds it hard because she wants a family, too. She's excited for them, but there's a longing for her that isn't being fulfilled.

"Well, if it's a distraction you're after, perhaps I can come over tonight and assist with that? I have a few techniques that I think will help," I say, lowering my voice into a tone that I know will have her blushing. There's a slight pause, and I worry that wasn't the right thing to say, but when she responds, there is a hint of curiosity in her tone.

"Mmm… what do you have in mind?"

"If you're interested, you'll have to wait to find out. I have dinner plans but I can come over afterwards. I need dessert," I say, and I can just picture her face right now. Her cheeks would be rosy and her mouth would be popped open. I smile to myself at the image. She giggles, and it does something to me.

"Yeah, okay, I suppose you can come over. Just message me when you're on your way," she says.

"Perfect, I promise it won't be too late. It's just dinner with the boys and they all have kids, so I'll probably be at yours by around nine-ish. I'll be in touch."

"Okay, sounds good. Have a good night."

She hangs up, just as I'm arriving home. Now to start plotting the perfect distraction. I wonder how she feels about restraints…

Jake, Dale, and Ben have booked us in at 7pm at this fancy Italian restaurant that charges you $32 for a pizza, and to be honest, I think that's a criminal offence. No one should be paying that much money for a pizza, not in this economy. I go with the cheapest option on the menu, pepperoni, and am halfway through my third slice when Jake, my oldest friend, turns my way.

"So, mate, how's the love life?"

I snort.

"Ha. Yeah, non-existent man. Jade and I only broke up, what, nine months ago? I'm not ready for anything serious yet, so I haven't really been looking."

There's no way I'm bringing up Ella to the guys. I'm definitely not ready to explain the concept of friends with benefits to them. Most of them have been with their wives since high school or uni. None of them have been single in the last 10 years—they don't understand anything about the modern dating world. Hell, neither do I, to be fair. It's probably why I haven't put any effort into it. It just seems too fucking hard.

"Ahh, come on. Surely you've at least been having some fun. And nine months is plenty of time my friend, at least for something casual," he says.

"I mean, yeah there's been a couple of casual hook ups, but nothing exciting. Really, I'm just focusing on work right now."

Dale pipes up at this—he and his wife Mel have been married for eight years and they have two kids, with another on the way. He's one of the guys who has wanted out of his marriage for years but will never admit it.

"Boring! Nah seriously man, you're the single one of the group. We were all hoping to be living vicariously through you as you embraced your new-found bachelor status." He raises his beer at me, as if to cheers in solidarity. All I can think in my head is these guys have no idea.

"Sorry to disappoint you Dale, single life isn't all it's made out to be."

"Probably because you're not making the most of it," he says, putting his drink down after I didn't 'cheers' him back. He actually seems annoyed at me that I'm not out there fucking my way through town and telling them all about it.

"What's to make the most of? Meaningless sex with strangers? Coming home to an empty house every day?"

"Yes, exactly that." He scoffs, as if I'm pointing out the obvious perks.

"What's the issue man? Sorry I'm not living the single life to your expectations. But it's my life," I say. I'm getting quite frustrated now. The others are all sitting there, awkwardly eating. Jake clears his throat.

"Dale, relax mate. He can do what he wants. Sorry Xav, I didn't mean anything by it. I was just curious is all. You do you."

Dale slumps back in his seat and I nod my appreciation at Jake. He and I have known each other the longest and are probably the closest within the group. He is the only one who, as far as I'm aware, is still actually happy in his marriage. The other two, not so much. We have definitely drifted apart a little in the last couple of years, especially after his daughter was born. But that happens. Adult friendships change as you get older, and that's life. It's just a bit hard for me now—they're all so far ahead, and I feel like there isn't a whole lot that we have in common anymore.

"Thanks, Jake. It's all good. Ben, how's the family?" I ask, mostly to shift the focus off of me.

We spend the rest of the meal just talking about family stuff and work. Thankfully, the topic of my love life and break up doesn't come up again. I finish my overpriced pizza, making sure to eat every last morsel. We drain the rest of our glasses and as expected, the guys need to get home to the wives and kids. We pay our bill and head outside. Dale is awkward as he gives me one of those 'bro hugs', mumbles an apology, and walks to his car. I shake Ben's hand and give Jake an actual hug. I'm thankful at least one of my friends isn't afraid to show some form of normal affection.

"You could download a dating app or something; no harm in seeing what's out there. At least then you'll be prepared for when you are ready," he says with a wink.

"I'll think about it. See you, Jake." We go our separate ways, promising to catch up again in the new year. I will consider it. I've been putting it off, but he's right, there's no harm in looking. But then I think of a particular red head who is currently waiting for me.

I get in my car and head towards Ella's house. The anticipation is building, and I'm excited.

CHAPTER 19
Ella

It's just after 9pm. I'm in my robe, my hair has been washed, my legs are shaved, and I've done a full skin care routine. I fully committed to an *everything* shower tonight. I spent all of it trying not to think about what happened at work today. I'm practically shaking with anticipation when my doorbell rings. I rush over to the door but compose myself before opening it. I can't appear too eager, gotta be cool. Calm. Casual. I open the door and Xavier is—I kid you fucking not—leaning in the doorway. He's got both arms crossed and he's just standing there with a smug grin on his face, one that tells me he knows exactly what a door lean would do for me. The man is screaming book boyfriend to the point that it'd be comical if I wasn't turned on by the sight of him.

"Well, hello," I say, returning his grin.

"Hi. Mind if I come in?" he says.

I step out of the doorway and gesture for him to come inside. He walks in and instantly pulls me over for a big hug. I was expecting to get straight down to business, for him to grab me by the back of the neck and kiss me so thoroughly I go weak at the knees. I don't know how, but in that moment, I realise he knew this is what I needed. He knew I needed a little bit of comfort. The distraction can come after, but first, I wrap my arms around him and hold tight.

"Thank you for coming," I mumble into his shirt.

"Of course, happy to be here." He places a kiss on the top of my head, and we stand there for a while, not saying anything, just simply embracing.

"Now, here's what we're going to do," he says.

"First, I'm going to steal some mouthwash because I have pepperoni breath from dinner." I laugh.

"Then, you're going to sit and tell me what happened today, because I feel like you need to vent. And then finally, I'm going to distract you so hard that you forget why you were feeling sad in the first place. How does that sound?"

The laughter dies in my throat at that because, yeah, that does sound good.

"I like this plan."I walk over to the couch as he pops into my bathroom to freshen himself up. He walks back in and takes a seat on the opposite end. He pulls me closer to him and drapes my legs across his lap and rests his hands on my thigh.

"So," he begins, "what happened?"

I take a deep breath.

"Well, as I've said before, my boss doesn't actually contribute much at work. We are so busy right now and I was hoping this year would be different and she would, you know, actually do her job. But *no*. Today we had a huge line up of about 60 kids in the library, and instead of getting on her computer and helping, she just stood there chit-chatting with the teachers. I asked her to please assist, and in front of everyone she turns around and says, 'Assist? That's your job.' And then she just continued her conversation. Eventually I got through the line and once the students and teachers left, she had the nerve to tell me that I was working too slow, that I took too long dealing with the students, and that I needed to improve my work ethic if I wanted more hours next year."

Xavier is listening intently, rubbing his thumb reassuringly on my thigh.

"Then, I overheard her complaining about me to management, saying that I was trying to boss her around and that I needed to remember my place. I interrupted the conversation, which is so unlike me because I hate confrontation, and said all I had asked was for her to help out. She then 'explained' to management that the job was below her pay grade and that it wasn't her responsibility, and that if I can't handle a task on my own then I should reassess whether this job is right for me. I just wanted her to help so we could get the job done quicker, not because I wasn't capable."

"Wow. What a piece of work," he says. "So she's trying to make you look bad in front of management, despite the fact that you're the one doing everything. Sounds to me like she's trying to cover her own lazy ass by throwing you under the bus.""Yeah, pretty much. I think her issue is that unlike her, I'm well-liked by the students. That probably sounds vain, but it's true. They don't go to her for anything anymore and half of them think that I run the library because of how much work I do. She's threatened by me, so she belittles me to make herself feel better, probably in the hopes that eventually I will leave."

Honestly, I would leave, but the thought of leaving my students and not seeing Millie every day makes me want to cry. Not to mention the fact that finding permanent work in a library is incredibly rare. So, despite being made to feel miserable most days, it's better the devil you know.

"I'm not surprised they like you more, what's not to like? But yeah, she sounds incredibly jealous. I'm sorry you have to put up with that sort of toxic work environment." He gives my leg a small squeeze. His hand has drifted a little higher up on my thigh.

"Thanks," I say. "Like I said on the phone, I've gotten better at ignoring her bullshit. But when she belittles me in front of other people, it really affects me. I'm already very insecure and I hate the idea of other people believing that I'm incompetent. Especially management, who don't even understand my job that well." His hand drifts a little bit higher and my heart starts beating a little bit faster.

"Yeah, I can understand that. Is there anything that can be done? Put in a complaint?" he asks.

"I wish. I've reported it to management so many times but they don't do anything about it. They basically just tell me that she's the boss, and what she says goes. Short of quitting, the best thing I can do is ignore it and not let it get to me." He's lightly stroking the inside of my thigh now and it's causing goosebumps to spread all over my body. A sensual shiver starts to run down my spine.

"Well, that's bullshit. She's bullying you and they should be taking that seriously," he says as he slowly spreads my legs a little further apart, causing my breath to hitch.

"Mhmm, I agree." It's about all I can respond with because he has started trailing his fingers even higher up my thigh and along the seam of my underwear.

"You work so hard, Ella. You don't deserve to be made to feel useless. You are so good at what you do," he murmurs. "Let me take care of you tonight, I promise to make you feel better." He picks up my leg and places a kiss just behind my knee, and it tickles in the most delicious way.

"Okay." I breathe.

The next thing I know, he picks me up off the couch and places me on his lap, so that I'm straddling him. He grabs a fistful of my hair and brings his mouth to mine, exactly how I thought he would when he first got here. His kiss is punishing, and I can't get enough. He bites down on my bottom lip and I can't tell if he's drawn blood or not, and at this point I don't care. I rock my hips against him and I can feel how hard he is beneath me. He groans into my mouth, so I do it again.

"Bed, now." He growls.

Suddenly he's standing up and carrying me into the bedroom. The way this man picks me up as if I weigh nothing is so fucking hot. He drops me on the bed and the movement has opened up my robe. Fortunately, it appears that he is quite pleased with what I'm wearing underneath. I thought I'd dress up a little for him, so I'm wearing some of my favourite lingerie, a lilac lace bra and thong set. It makes me feel incredibly sweet and sexy at the same time.

"Fuck Ella. You look so fucking beautiful, you know that?"

The way calls me beautiful has me actually wanting to believe him. He crawls onto the bed and slowly pulls my robe aside to reveal more of what's underneath.

"Now… what am I going to do with you tonight?" he asks, slowly stroking my nipples over the lace. I don't respond, instead I just arch into his touch.

"Take off your robe," he commands. His tone is gentle but demanding, and I love it. I take it off and he grabs it from me, pulling the belt from the loops, and my mouth goes dry when I realise what he's going to do with it.

"How do you feel about being tied up?" he asks.

"I'm all for it," I say, breathless.

"Good. Now put your arms above your head." I do what he says and he comes over to me, looping the satin around my wrists a couple of times and then tying me to the bed head. "How is that? Not too tight?" he asks.

"Nope, it's fine," I say as I test my bindings. My circulation isn't being cut off but it's tight enough that I know I won't be getting out of it any time soon.

"Perfect, now let me look at you." He stands up off of the bed. His gaze burns into me as his eyes slowly roam all over my body.

"I am going to devour you," he says and an involuntary whimper escapes me.

He climbs back onto the bed and hovers over me, going in to kiss me, then pulling away just before our lips could meet. He kisses my neck, then my shoulder, then goes in for another kiss before pulling away again. He does this twice more, before I'm pulling against my restraint because all I want is his lips on mine.

"Hey!" I say.

"Hmm? Do you want something?" He's kissing along my collarbone as his fingers pull down the lace of my bra to free my nipple. He kisses it gently.

"Kiss me, Xavier." I gasp, as he takes my nipple in his mouth and sucks, *hard*. He then releases it, but begins sucking on my breast, hard enough that when he pulls away, he's left a dark red mark. I groan, not from the pain but because it's so fucking hot.

"Aw," he says. "It's cute that you think you can make demands right now." He releases my other nipple from the lace and does the same thing. Now I'm *really* squirming. "Plus, you didn't say the magic word."

I have no idea what the magic word is but my argument dissolves on my tongue because he's kissing his way down my stomach. I look down at him as he reaches my underwear and he looks up at me. He keeps his eyes locked on mine as he pulls them all the way down with his teeth.

Fuck me right now please.

Once I am bare to him, he pushes my legs further apart and stares at me with intense hunger. He leans in closer to me and I can feel the warmth of his breath on my clit. I am pulsing with need by this point. He kisses me gently on the inside of my left thigh, and then moves to do the same on my right, only instead, he bites me. I yelp and lift my hips off of the bed, but as the pain hits me, it is replaced with pleasure because his tongue is suddenly right where I want it.

He flicks his tongue at a steady pace that has my climax slowly building. He inserts one finger inside of me and it feels so damn good. I'm writhing beneath him, moaning loudly. Then, he sucks hard on my clit and my climax almost reaches its peak. I'm about to come when all of a sudden, he stops. I groan and look down at him, and he looks me in the eye with a wicked grin.

"You thought I was going to let you come that easily?" he says.

I wriggle my hips and moan.

"Xavier…"

Then his mouth is back on me and his finger is moving inside me once more. Again, I can feel the orgasm building, and just as I'm about to fall over the edge, he stops.

"Fuck!" I scream.

He chuckles deeply.

"Have you ever been edged before, love?"

I haven't.

"No. This is torture!" I groan. He laughs again and then he resumes his tongue and finger combination. He brings me to the edge three more times before I'm screaming his name.

"Say the magic word and I'll let you come," he whispers. My whole body is shaking at this point and I am so desperate to come. I don't know the magic word. I can't think straight, all I can think of is the pulsing need between my legs.

"Please," I beg.

"Please what?" he says between licks.

"Please, can I come?" I'm panting now.

"That's my girl. That wasn't so hard was it?"

He sucks me into his mouth hard and pumps his finger in a punishing rhythm and now I'm really screaming. His teeth lightly graze my clit and I come undone. The orgasm that rocks through me is like nothing I've ever felt before. My whole body is convulsing, and Xavier keeps licking me and finger-fucking me throughout it. Slowly, it begins to subside. He withdraws his finger and sits up on his knees. His face is glistening with my arousal and it's then I feel the wet patch on my sheets.

"Holy fuck." I breathe. "Did I just…."

"Yep." He smiles proudly. "You nearly drowned me."

A dazed smile spreads across my face.

"That's never happened before," I say.

"Well, I am honoured to be the first." He says.

I look down at the bulge in his shorts. He catches me staring and laughs.

"I want you inside me." I breathe. He just arches an eyebrow at me.

"Please. Please can I have you inside me, Xavier?"

He smiles as he bends down to finally kiss me. His tongue swirls against mine and I can feel his hands move to my wrists. He undoes the binding in seconds and then my hands are in his hair, pulling him closer to me.

"Get naked, now." I demand.

CHAPTER 20
Xavier

I look her in the eyes as I rip my shirt off and unbutton my shorts. I pull the zipper down slowly and she tells me to hurry the fuck up. I laugh. *She's so desperate for me.* I pull my shorts and underwear down and she unashamedly stares at me in all my naked glory. I've never felt super confident with my body, but the look in her eyes makes me forget any insecurities I may have.

I'm about to get back on the bed when she launches off and gets on her knees before me. I suck in a breath as she licks up the length of me, tantalisingly slow.

"Holy fuck, Ella." I groan. I wasn't expecting this.

"Sorry." She says, stifling a moan of her own. "I couldn't help myself, I needed to taste you."

Then, she takes me in her mouth, and I see stars.

I take a fistful of her hair and hold her as she fucks me with her mouth. I don't push her, I let her control the pace. She uses one hand to pump me as she sucks me hard and her tongue swirls around my tip.

"I'm going to come if you keep doing that," I admit. She moans around me, and the vibration just intensifies the feeling.

"Okay, enough." I demand. She releases me and I pick her up and toss her back onto the bed. I climb on next to her and go to position myself on top when she stops me.

"No. I want to ride you," she says. *No complaints here.* I lie down on the bed as she gets a condom out of the drawer and rolls it on. She leans down and kisses me with fervour, then she straddles me. She slides herself up and down the length of me, teasing. She's still so wet from her orgasm. Then, she lifts her hips up slightly, before ever so slowly lowering herself onto me. The feeling is heaven.

"*Fuck.*" She shudders.

She leans back slightly as I'm buried in her to the hilt. She rocks gently and I see her nipples instantly harden.

"It's never felt this good on top before." She moans.

She starts rocking back and forth and her eyes roll into the back of her head. I try to match her pace, but honestly, I'm letting her take control with this one. She picks up speed and I can feel her start to clench around me.

"Fuck, Xavier, I think I'm going to come. Oh my God."

She rocks harder and I can feel her pulsing around me as her orgasm takes hold. She's moaning and whimpering as she comes down from her climax. She leans down to kiss me as she starts bouncing. I don't know what it is about this angle, *but holy shit*, it is divine. She bites down on my lower lip and I thrust my hips up to meet her as we work out the most delicious rhythm. I can feel my own climax start to build.

"Yes, Ella. Just like that—*fuck.*"

She kisses me again as my orgasm hits and I moan into her mouth. She squeezes around me, drawing out my climax as much as she can. She rests her forehead against mine as she lies on top of me, both of us sweaty, panting, and completely spent. I can feel her heart beating against my chest as I slowly rub my hands down her back.

"Wow." She sighs.

"I'll say." I reach down and give her arse a small slap and she laughs.

She slides off of me and I pull off the condom. I get up to dispose of it before getting back into the bed next to her and pulling her in for a cuddle. We look at each other before breaking into matching grins. I put my hand up for a high five.

"We fuck good." She laughs and slaps her hand against mine.

"Yeah, we do," I say. "I didn't think we'd be able to top the last time, but somehow we did."

"Well, you gave me two firsts tonight."

"Oh? What was the second one?"

"I've never enjoyed being on top before. I don't know why; it just never felt good for me. So, to enjoy it and orgasm is actually… insane." She interlaces her fingers with mine.

"Do I get a medal?" I reply cheekily.

"Ha ha," she replies.

We lie in bed for a while longer, cuddling and talking. I really should get up and go home. We said no more sleepovers. But as I look down at her, I can see she's slowly drifting off in my arms. And as much as I should, I really don't want to leave.

"Ella?"

"Mmm."

"I'm going to stay."

"Mmm-kay." She mumbles sleepily.

"Just promise to not fall in love with me if I do." I say, and I'm only half joking.

She's quiet for a moment and then she whispers.

"I promise. I won't fall."

CHAPTER 21
Ella

I wake up to soft snores and an arm draped over me, holding me tight. A warmth settles in my belly, and for a few moments, I am so content. I could really get used to this—to waking up next to someone and having them hold me in a way that makes me think they never want to let me go. Except, I can't. Because it's Xavier. And we are just friends. Well, friends who fuck. But still, just friends. He wasn't supposed to sleep over, but once again he's still here.

Memories of our conversation as I drifted off to sleep last night come back to me. He made me promise not to fall in love with him, and I did. I made the promise. But right in this moment with his arm around me, listening to his slow and deep breaths, I can see myself falling if I'm not careful.

Everything with Xavier is just… easy. The conversation, the sex, the comfort. I can be myself around him so easily, he's making me feel safe enough to fall. But at the same time, he's the one who doesn't want a relationship, so why is he making it so easy?

Xavier begins to stir next to me, slowly waking up. His arm tightens around me and he pulls me in even closer. I close my eyes and inhale deeply, enjoying the moment a little longer. I place my arm on top of his and lace our fingers together. He kisses me on the shoulder, and I sigh.

"Good morning." I whisper.

"Good morning," he replies. His voice is still sleepy, giving it a deep and raspy sound. *It's sexy.*

"You slept over again," I said. I roll over so that we are facing each other. He still has his eyes closed as he struggles to wake up fully.

"I know. I wasn't going to, but you were falling asleep in my arms and I didn't want to wake you. I'm sorry if I overstepped."

"No, it's fine. It's just… we agreed, no sleepovers. And so far, we've had two." *And if we keep doing this, it's almost a guarantee that I will fall for you.* I don't say that part out loud, of course.

"Yeah, it seems we aren't very good at sticking to our own rules." He chuckles, opening his eyes and looking at me, dopily. "We can stop doing this, if that's what you prefer."

"Yeah. I mean, no. I mean… I don't know. I like sleeping next to you," I admit.

"I like sleeping next to you, too," he says with a smile.

And yet you're the one wanting to keep this platonic, I want to say.

"Let's just play it by ear. If we stay up really late or there's alcohol involved, then we can make an exception. But if it's just a daytime hook up or quick booty call, then we stick to the rules," I suggest.

"Yeah, I think that'll work. But just remember to be honest and if it starts to become too much—if you think you're getting attached—you need to tell me, and we will stop," he says.

If *I'm* getting attached. Not him, me. Because obviously he won't get attached, he won't develop feelings and overthink and analyse every little moment between us, wondering if things will change. Hoping it could lead to more. No, that will only happen to me.

"Yeah, I will." *I probably won't.*

"Are you feeling any better?" he asks.

"I am. I think you distracted me enough." I smile. At least that much is true. What we did last night completely wiped my brain of any bullshit to do with work. I couldn't think of anything else but him.

"Perfect. I'm glad I could help."

I close my eyes and we both just lie there, embracing the morning silence. I don't have anything planned today, so there's no rush to get out of bed. I open my eyes slightly and see Xavier has closed his again. I watch him for a while, taking in all of his gorgeous features. His enviable long lashes, the different coloured hairs smattered throuhout his beard, his perfect lips that are parted slightly as he breathes deeply. He has a few freckles across his nose and a scar just above his left eyebrow. I get butterflies just looking at him—I've never felt this level of attraction or comfort with any man in my life.

"Ella," he murmurs, eyes still closed.

"Yeah?"

"I can feel you staring at me. Why are you being a creep?" His eyes flutter open and yep, I'm still staring. We both laugh.

"I can't help myself." I say. "You're just so…"

"Perfectly handsome and sexy?" He smirks.

"Wow, so humble." I smile. He's not wrong though. "I was going to say you look so content."

"The humblest of humble. But yeah, I feel pretty content. Your bed is just so comfy. You're okay too, I guess," he jokes.

I go to smack him on the arm but he catches my hand and brings it to his lips, placing a quick kiss on my palm. He then pulls me in and kisses me slow and deep—the type of kiss that steals the breath right out of your lungs. There's no intent in the kiss. There's no rush, no adrenaline. We make out lazily, hands trailing each other's bodies, his tongue slowly sweeping in and out of my mouth, exploring. We continue to do this, for how long I'm not sure. He kisses my cheek, then my nose, then both of my eyelids, and then finally my forehead. He rests there for a while, holding me close.

"What time is it?" he whispers.

"I don't know. I can check, but you'd have to let me go," I whisper back. He chuckles and pulls away from me, reaching for his phone on the bedside table. He checks the time and swears under his breath.

"Shit. It's 10:30. I have to go; I start work at 12." He untangles himself from me and the sheets that were wrapped around us, then he climbs out of bed. Immediately, all of the warm, cosy, and content feelings disappear. *So much for not having to rush for anything this morning.*

"Oh yeah, hospitality workers work weekends. I forgot," I say. I'm trying to not act disappointed that he has to leave. I'm not allowed to feel disappointed.

"I'm sorry, I'd like nothing more than to just laze around in bed with you all day." He finds his clothes on the floor that were discarded during last night's tryst, pulls on his shorts, and throws on his t-shirt. "Have you got much planned for the weekend?" he asks.

"Not really," I reply. "Just reading and life admin. It's getting close to Christmas, and my birthday, so I've got some things to plan."

He cocks his head. "When is your birthday?" he asks.

"January 2nd. Millie and I share a birthday, so we need to plan our party. If you're nice, you might get invited," I tease.

"I can play nice. Wouldn't want to miss it." He smirks. "I've gotta go, I'm glad you're feeling better." He leans down and gives me a final kiss before walking out of my room. I scramble out of bed, still completely naked, and catch him just before he reaches the front door. I quickly pull him into a goodbye hug.

"Thank you, again. Just for being there," I say. He squeezes me tighter, kisses the top of my head, and then pulls away.

"Anytime. I'll talk to you later." He winks, opens the door and heads out.

I watch him drive off from the front window, feeling completely satisfied and yet incomplete at the same time. Maybe even a little empty. I head off into the shower, and as I let the hot water wash away the night before, I repeat to myself, "Do not catch feelings. Do not catch feelings. Do not catch feelings."

Perhaps, if I say it enough, I'll convince myself that it's possible.

CHAPTER 22
Xavier

"She's just a friend."

"Uh huh. Keep saying that Xav, and you might convince yourself it's true." Lena rolls her eyes.

We're sitting in my office after the madness of the lunch rush, having a beer before preparing ourselves for the Saturday night revelry. By the time I got home from Ella's house, quickly showered, then got dressed, I was ten minutes late for work. Dad gave me a scolding for "rushing in like a mad idiot" and is now probably less likely to hand over the baton. Not ideal, and another reason why I probably shouldn't have slept over last night. The way she chased after me to give me one final hug goodbye this morning has me worried she's getting attached and not telling me. Lena saw how flustered I was when I got in, so she came to her own conclusions as to why I was late. I told her to leave it and we'd talk about it later. *Later is now, it seems.*

"It's true, Lena. Yes, we're sleeping together, okay? But that's it. She's a friend, we're fucking. There are no feelings involved, no emotional attachments. I'm enjoying spending time with her and keeping things casual. I'm not ready for more than that." I'm not, and while I know that my words are probably coming out a bit harsh, at least it's true.

Lena fidgets with her bottle cap as I'm saying all of this. She looks guilty, like she knows she probably shouldn't have brought it up.

"Please don't talk to Jade about this," I say. "We had a deal. I know you're still friends, but I really don't need my ex knowing all the details about my current sex life."

"Yeah, sure. Just… be careful Xavier. You might not want more, but that doesn't mean she's on the same page. You're a good guy and I'd hate to see you in a position where you have to reject someone and hurt them like that. I also really like Ella, so don't fuck it up," she says.

"Okay, you've met her twice, but sure. Plus, she and I have spoken about this. She promised if she develops feelings she will tell me and I'll back off," I say.

"Oh, Xav. You clearly don't understand women all that well if you think she will just tell you when she develops feelings. Knowing you will walk away if she does? Do you really think she will admit that when she knows she would lose all of you?" She says in a way that's almost patronising.

Ella wouldn't do that—at least I don't think she would. She would tell me.

"We could still be friends, just without the sex." I reply.

"Ooh boy. Yeah, okay. Good luck with that." She scoffs and rolls her eyes again. "I need to get back to work." She gets up and leaves my office.

"Where did that attitude come from?" I mutter to myself. Lena has been so hot and cold lately. I wonder if she's looking for another job. She just seems so on edge, and almost nervous at times. I can never pick what mood she's in, but today it seems she's easily irritable.

Whatever, she's wrong. It's not a problem. Ella and I are just friends who have great sex and have a lot in common. We have fun and… yeah. But it's fine, it won't go any further. It can't. It's not the right time.

I take a deep breath and do a long exhale out of my nose. I have too many other things to worry about at the moment, I need to focus. I have some major sucking up to do with my dad. I down the rest of my beer and am about to leave the office when my phone buzzes. It's a photo from Ella with the caption:

ELLA

LOOK WHAT YOU DID!

She's sent me a photo of the inside of her thigh, decorated with a bite mark that has started to bruise beautifully. Seeing my mark on her, along with the lacey trim of her underwear which I'm sure was a coincidental choice on her part, has me growing hard once again.

"So much for fucking focus," I mutter as I adjust myself in my pants. She sends me another message.

ELLA

I like having your mark on me ;)

"Fuck." I breathe. This woman is going to make work very difficult for me this evening, I just know it.

XAVIER

I enjoyed leaving my mark on you. Keep sending me pictures like that and you're going to get me in trouble for having a hard on at work.

ELLA

Oh? Well, what about pictures like this?

My phone lights up with a glorious photo of her bent over in a lacy black thong, her perfect arse in the air just begging to be spanked. I am in so much trouble with this one, but I just can't seem to help myself.

XAVIER

Fuck, Ella. You're going to destroy me. I'm so fucking hard and all I want to do is drive straight back to your house, spank that perfect arse of yours, and bury myself inside you.

ELLA

Hmm. Too bad you're at work, then. Have a good night, Xavier!

XAVIER

Girl, you are the devil. I will get you back for this.

ELLA

I look forward to it xoxo

I'm now sporting a major boner and need to sort my shit out so I can go and be the responsible manager that I appear to be. I think of every unattractive thing I can think of, and when I am finally down to only a semi that I can tuck away, I leave my office. The dinner crowd has started filing in and it's soon busy enough that images of Ella's perfect arse are replaced by cocktail orders and spilt beers. By the time I knock off, it's almost midnight. I didn't hear from Ella again, but a plan did form in my head on how to get her back for turning me on at work. I just need to wait for her Christmas party to implement it.

CHAPTER 23
Ella

"It's school holidays, bitch!" Millie yells from across the library as she comes running over to me. Thankfully, my boss isn't here and it's just me. Not that it would have stopped Millie, but I would've copped it for the inappropriateness.

"Jesus, Millie, say it any louder, why don't you?" I laugh as she plonks down on my desk.

"IT'S SCHOOL HOL— *hmph.*" I slap my hand over her mouth to shut her up.

"You're gonna get me in trouble, so shush!" I say.

She licks my hand to make me let go.

"Ew! You're so fucking weird." I laugh.

"I can't help it. It's last day of the year, and I'm so fucking excited to not have to step foot in this place for six weeks!"

"Amen to that," I say. I'm so glad the year is over. It has been a very stressful year and I'll be glad to not have to see my boss for a while. My little anxious brain will get some time to recover a bit before starting all over again after the break.

"I am so excited for this Christmas party," Millie exclaims, her eyes lighting up with mischief. "We are gonna get so fucked up."

"Oh, are we? I thought you weren't drinking as much these days, with the whole baby making thing." It's been so long since Millie and I had more than a glass of wine or two together. No binge drinking allowed during baby making season, she told me.

She slumps her shoulders, and for a second, her sparkle is dimmed.

"Yes well, it's been almost a year and we have had zero luck. I'm tired. I just need a break from thinking about ovulation and pregnancy tests and those stupid little pink lines. I need a proper night out, you know?"

I grab her hand and squeeze.

"Whatever you need to do, I am here, and I will support you. Even if that means shots." I tell her.

She laughs.

"Plus, I get to finally meet Xavier."

"Please do not embarrass me. And play it cool. We're just friends, remember? I don't need anyone on staff talking shit about me. Plus, I'm pretty sure Xavier wants to keep this 'situation' between us, so keep it subtle," I say. I can't think of anything more mortifying than the conservative old farts on staff thinking I'm sleeping with the bar manager for perks. Sleeping with the bar manager *IS* the perk, but they don't need to know that.

"Okay, okay. So I just need to subtly tell him that if he fucks with you, he has to deal with me. Got it." She winks.

"Millie…"

She sighs. "Fine, I'll behave. But I can't make any promises once I'm 10 drinks deep. I apologise in advance for my behaviour."

"Thank you. And same, I have no idea what tonight is going to bring, but I'm so excited to drink away the shit show that was this year with you. Tonight is our night!" I say.

"Fuck yeah. We just have to get through a full day of boring speeches and training." We both groan. Because the party was moved from lunch to dinner, school management decided to throw in some extra professional development to get us through the day. On the sanctity of religion, of all things.

"Want to make things interesting and get a head start on the party?" Millie says as she opens her bag and shows me her flask. I laugh. Millie is probably the most chaotic person I know, so it shouldn't surprise me that she has a flask hidden in her bag.

"Yeah, fuck it. Why not? I'll need something to get us through three hours of religious education." We sneak around the corner and each take a few sips from the flask. I nearly choke on the first mouthful.

"Okay, I wasn't expecting tequila. That'll probably do me until we head off to the party or I'll be slut dropping to the lord's prayer during chapel," I say.

Millie snorts so hard tequila comes out of her nose. I start laughing so hard my stomach cramps.

"Oh my God, Ell, I would pay to see that. The image I'm conjuring up will live rent free in my brain for the rest of my life," she says, wiping tequila from her face.

"Seeing tequila come out of your nose just now was probably the best thing I've ever seen. This day is starting off much better than I thought it would."

She cleans herself up and we give each other a pep talk to behave as best as we can before the dinner. We have five hours to go. We can do this.

We only *just* got through the day without being kicked out. We sat in the back row and kept laughing and chatting like naughty middle school kids. The snooty English teachers very predictably kept judging us and shushing us, and we did get a stern word from the deputy principal after lunch to behave ourselves and "save the shenanigans for later". We plan to take that literally.

Finally, we are on our way to Jimmies for the party. I've been looking forward to this night for so long. Xavier came over on Wednesday night to confirm all of the details of the event. He could have done it over the phone, but after the photo I sent him on Saturday, he couldn't resist confirming it in person. One thing obviously led to another and he did exactly what he said he would do the next time he saw me—he spanked me and buried himself deep inside me. I could still feel his hand prints on my arse the next day, and it made sitting at my desk a fun challenge. He did say, though, that it wasn't the revenge he promised to give me and to stay on my toes. I'm equal parts excited and scared as to what he has in store for tonight.

"I am so excited to meet Xavier," Millie says. She's pretty much bouncing in her seat in the Uber. "I'm keen to see if he's as hot as you say he is."

"He is. *To me.* I won't hear any other opinions." So, we might have had more tequila throughout the day, and I'm already a little bit buzzed. "I don't know if he's your type though. He's not even my type, or what I would normally go for, anyway."

"You mean he's not boring."

"Ouch, Mills."

"You know I'm right."

"I mean, a little bit…" I say.

We pull up to the front of Jimmies and I'm suddenly nervous. So far, this thing with Xavier has just been between us—our own little secret bubble of fuckery, if you will. Millie knows every single detail of our friendship, but for her to actually meet him in person is a whole different story. Especially given how confusing our relationship actually is. I don't really understand why I'm nervous. It feels like when you introduce your boyfriend to your family, only he's not my boyfriend. And Millie is Millie. *I need another drink.*

We walk into the bar and head out the back to the beer garden. This time of year, it is set up with fairy lights and Christmas garlands, including a few cheeky sprigs of mistletoe (fake of course, this is Australia). The place looks gorgeous and is exactly the kind of vibe I was hoping for. I look around but can't see Xavier yet, so I figure he must still be in his office. Lena also isn't working. Millie and I walk up to the bar, and we order a sparkling wine each.

"Cheers to another year over," I say.

"Thank fuck for that," Millie replies. We raise our glasses and take a drink.

"Excuse me," I say to the young guy behind the bar. "Is Xavier around?"

He doesn't respond, just looks over my shoulder and nods. I turn around and there he is. I don't know if it's the alcohol enhancing my senses, but damn does he look mighty fine tonight. He's standing not too far away, with the principal, probably going over the plans for the evening. He must sense that I'm looking because he peers over in my direction. Our eyes meet, and pleasure floods my body. He's still talking to the principal, who is completely oblivious, as his eyes roam up and down my outfit, taking everything in.

I decided to go for a fun and flirty look tonight. I'm wearing a white sundress with puffed sleeves that sit just off my shoulders. My hair is curled, and I decided to put on a red lip. I don't know what it is about red lipstick, but it makes me feel so bold and confident. Sexy too. Three virtues I don't normally have but wanted to have tonight. When I looked in the mirror before I left the house, I felt so fucking good.

Once Xavier finishes his perusal of my body, his eyes meet mine again and I go weak at the knees. His eyes have darkened, and he looks simply ravenous.

"Ella... helloooo?" Mille is tapping me on the shoulder, breaking me free from Xavier's gaze. "What are you staring—oh. Is that him?"

"Yep," I say, looking back at Xav. He hasn't stopped staring at me, but now he has a smirk plastered on his face, his dimple making an appearance.

"Jesus Christ, Ella. The man might as well be fucking you with his eyes," Millie says as she looks between the two of us.

"Yeah." I breathe. I am completely under this man's spell.

"Okay... let's go get a seat. He can come find us later." She grabs my arm, breaking my stupor and drags me over to one of the tables in the corner. One of the wait staff comes past with a tray full of arancini and suddenly I'm no longer hungry for Xavier, but for deep fried rice balls.

"Yeah, you better eat a few of those if you're going to be downing drinks like you did with that prosecco," Millie adds, putting a few on a plate and pushing them towards me. I don't hesitate.

"You're not wrong," I say around a mouthful of rice. These are bloody delicious. She is right though. I've barely eaten today, and I really need to fill my stomach with something other than booze.

"So, what was that all about just now?" she asks.

"What do you mean?"

"I mean, the way Xavier was looking at you just now—it didn't exactly scream 'we're just friends'. That was pure want in his eyes."

"It's… complicated."

"Explain." She demands.

I sigh.

"We are just friends. But our physical chemistry is beyond anything I've experienced. The man does things to me, Mills. What you saw was him giving me horny eyes, that's all. I've told you everything there is to know. He wants my body, I want his. It's a mutual wanting."

What I haven't told her is how every time I see him, my walls start to crack just a little bit more.

"Okay, just be careful. I know you, remember? He better not fuck you over, or I'll ruin him," she says, glaring in his direction.

"Oh my God, stop. Down girl." I laugh and swat at her. I look over and Xavier is heading our way with two more drinks in hand.

"Hello, ladies," he drawls. "I had one of my guys whip up a cocktail for the two of you, seeing as you planned this whole event. I hope you like it." He hands Millie and I a cocktail that looks something like a margarita. I take a sip and yep, watermelon margarita. *Delicious.*

"Well damn, at least these guys recognise our efforts. Thanks! I'm Millie by the way." Millie puts her hand out to shake Xavier's, which he gladly takes.

"Xavier. Nice to finally meet you." He looks at me and I blush like an imbecile. "Having fun yet?"

"Oh. So much fun." Millie smirks at me.

"Yep, loads of fun." I pipe up. "Do you want to sit with us? Or do you have to go be a boss?"

"As much as I would love to sit here and chat with you both, I'm on the clock, and my dad is still here. So, I should probably do some work. But if you need anything, just come find me. I'll look after you." He looks at me as he says this, and I might as well just melt into a fucking puddle at his feet.

"Thanks. We will. Have a fun shift!" Millie kicks me under the table and breaks me out of whatever trance I was in.

"Ouch! I mean, yeah. Have fun. I'll talk to you later." I rub my shin.

"Perfect." He walks away with a smile on his face.

"You're fucking hopeless, Ella." Millie laughs.

"Oh, I know. I'm royally fucked."

"Is he taking you home tonight?"

"Not sure, I haven't asked. He will probably offer to drive me back, though. He's a gentleman like that."

My phone buzzes with a message and I look down to check it.

XAVIER

You look so hot today. That dress?
Big yes from me.

I smile at my phone as blush rushes to my cheeks once again. Looking up, I see him watching me from the bar. He winks at me, and my smile widens even further.

"Yeah, you really are royally fucked." Millie laughs.

As the evening goes on, I gorge myself on an array of cocktail foods and prosecco. Xavier manages to slip us one more margarita each, but the principal kept eyeing us suspiciously, so we stuck to what was on the bar tab after that. Everyone is having a great time and I'm so relieved. This event is so different to our usual formal sit-down lunch, but it seems as though a more casual approach is working well. I'm definitely feeling a little bit drunk, but a good, fun drunk. Not a gross messy drunk. I ask Xavier if we can play some music and so he puts on a classic 80s playlist. Soon enough, the beer garden is full of drunk and dancing school staff. It's a blast.

I've just finished an incredible rendition of 'Living on a Prayer' when I find Millie sitting in the corner, hoovering down another slice of pizza. I hand her a fresh drink and we tap glasses again.

"Fuck, we're good," I say.

"Yeah, we are," she replies, mouth full of pizza. I laugh. I take a big drink when my phone buzzes again. I look down and open the message and it takes me so off guard that the prosecco comes spraying out of my mouth and all over Millie. She squeals and then laughs. I apologise and tell her the drink went down the wrong way. I help clean her up and then excuse myself from the table.

I find a quiet corner inside to open the message again and yep, there it is. Xavier has decided now was the time to get back at me for sending him that photo of me in a thong, by sending me a nude. He's standing in front of the mirror, gloriously naked, gloriously hard. I look around the room until I find him behind the bar, and of course he's watching me with the smuggest look on his face. He picks up his phone and sends another message.

XAVIER

I told you I'd get you back. This is what you do to me.

ELLA

That was so, so cruel.

XAVIER

Now you know how I felt ;)

I don't know if it's the alcohol, the red lipstick, or just some newfound confidence I've picked up, but a plan starts forming in my head. I plaster on a serious face, because I know he is probably still looking at me, then I send a message.

ELLA

Can we meet in your office? I need to talk to you about something.

I look up and he is still looking at me. His smirk is gone, and his face is etched with concern. I put on a mask of uncertainty, just to throw him off even further. I'm such a good actress.

XAVIER

Everything okay? I'll take my break in 10 minutes, so meet me by the bar.

ELLA

> Everything's fine. I just need to talk to you and not have any of my colleagues being snoopy. See you soon.

I head back outside to Millie and finish off my drink. She wants to dance, but I tell her I need to go to the bathroom, and I'll join her when I get back. She doesn't argue and joins the small crowd on the makeshift dance floor.

I head back inside and find Xavier leaning up against the bar, looking sexy as hell. He sees me coming and stands up straight.

"Hi Xavier, are we able to go over the final invoices for the event before I go home?" I ask.

He looks at me, confused as hell. I just look at him, urging him to play along. The last thing I want is for my colleagues to see me sneaking off into his office, so I need a good cover.

"Um, sure. Why don't you come into my office, and we'll get them sorted."

He leads the way, past the bar and down a short hallway, into a small room. There's not much in it, other than a large mahogany desk and black leather chair, a bookshelf crammed full of old books and knickknacks, a brown suede couch, and some filing cabinets. Once we are in, I close the door behind me.

"Does this lock work?" I ask.

"Yes," he responds, wearily.

"Good."

I turn the lock on the door and pull on the handle, just to make sure. I don't want anyone interrupting what I'm about to do. I turn and face him.

"Are you sure you're okay?" he asks me. I can tell he's nervous by the way he's furrowing his brow.

"Absolutely sure," I say. I saunter over to him and grab a fistful of his shirt and pull his mouth down to mine. He's stunned at first, but then relaxes into it and kisses me back. I walk us back until we hit the wall, and then my hand starts to wander. I slowly trail it down his stomach until I get to his belt.

"You thought you were getting revenge, did you?" I breathe. Time to show him exactly what he does to me, as well.

CHAPTER 24
Xavier

"Ella."

I groan into her mouth. Her fingers reach my belt, and she undoes the buckle, pulling it free. She moves onto the button and zip of my pants.

"What was it that I do to you, Xavier?" she breathes. She grabs my pants by the waist and pulls them down. Then, she's on her knees in front of me. I've never seen a more beautiful sight. When she walked into the bar this afternoon, I nearly tripped. She looked so gorgeous, and I couldn't help but stare.

She palms me through my underwear, and I hiss through my teeth. Of course, I'm already hard for her—aching for her. Her fingers slip beneath the band and slowly she pulls my underwear down, releasing me. I have no idea who this woman kneeling in front of me is. I don't know where that insecure girl has gone. Here is this sexy and confident woman, on her knees in my office of all places. We really, really shouldn't be doing this.

"Ella… we shouldn't…" My dad is literally in the office next door, and if he finds out…

"So stop me." She licks my tip, already glistening.

"Fuck." I moan. She does it again.

"If you want me to stop Xav, just say the word." She licks me from base to tip. My heart is pounding so hard I can almost hear it. I look down at her, and she looks up at me. Her eyes are full of lust, full of confidence. She keeps her eyes on mine as she takes me in her mouth. Those cherry red lips wrapped around me are my undoing.

"Don't stop." I growl.

She unleashes. She takes me down her throat until she can't go any further and bobs her head up and down. Her tongue swirls around me as she sucks hard, her hands gripping the base of me and squeezing up and down in a torturous rhythm. I go to grab a fistful of her hair when she pulls off of me, making a pop with her lips.

"No touching. You'll mess up my hair," she orders. I chuckle.

"Yes ma'am." And then she takes me down her throat again and I lose all sense of thought.

It's not long until I can feel my orgasm starting to build. She's working me expertly with her mouth and I know I'm not going to last very long. Someone knocks on the door and my head jerks up. Ella doesn't even react.

Through the door, one of my staff is asking me about someone on the phone enquiring about booking a function after Christmas. They try the handle, but it's locked. *Thank fuck.*

"I'll call them back. I'm just… in a meeting," I somehow manage to yell out. Ella picks up her pace and thankfully, the person on the other side of the door seems to have walked off.

"Fuck babe, you take me so well." She moans in delight at the praise and takes me even further into her mouth.

"If you keep going like that, I'm going to come," I say between gritted teeth. She doesn't stop, just keeps licking and sucking and groaning. I look down and it's only now I notice that she's playing with herself under her dress.

"Fuck, Ella, I'm going to come. If you don't want me to come in your mouth, stop now." She doesn't stop. She goes even harder and moans even louder as she inserts two fingers inside herself. She's whimpering around me now; I look at her and she looks up at me from beneath her lashes, with her red lips pumping up and down my length and I come undone. I thrust into her one more time and spill into her mouth, moaning her name. She takes it all, waiting until I've completely emptied before releasing me. She gives the tip one last little lick, which sends shivers up my spine, before rising back up.

All I can do is stand there, slack jawed and spent, stunned at what just happened. She has the biggest grin on her face. I pull her in for a kiss and let my hands wander under the hem of her dress. They graze the lace of her underwear, and I can feel how wet she is, but then she pulls away.

"Nope, this was my turn. If you want me, you can have me later." She kisses me one last time before turning towards the door. It's only now I remember that my pants are still down at my feet, and I bend down to pull them back on.

"Who are you and what have you done with Ella Hart?" I ask.

"Honestly, I have no idea. I saw that photo of you, and I knew I needed to have you. You're welcome." She blows me a kiss, unlocks the door, and strolls out, sashaying her hips like the fucking tease she is. I do up my belt buckle and check myself in the mirror. I'm looking exactly how I thought I would, flustered and confused, and extremely turned on.

"What the fuck just happened?" I ask myself. I take a deep breath and head back out to the bar.

I look outside and Ella is back with Millie, who is sitting there looking completely gobsmacked as I imagine Ella has just told her what she did. *Women.* They can't *not* tell each other everything. She's looking so smug, so proud of herself. Honestly, I'm proud of her too. There was no sign of the insecure girl from the bookstore who was crying because she was unwanted. This was something else entirely, and I enjoyed it way, way too much.

I hear Millie absolutely cracking up and when I look over, she's beaming at me and gives me two thumbs up. I roll my eyes and laugh.

This thing with Ella, it's exhilarating and it's exciting. The worst part is, I can feel the cracks appearing in my resolve to remain just friends. She's clawing her way in, and I don't know if I should stop or ride it out.

The night continues on, and Ella and Millie get more and more drunk. Most of the party have left by now and it's just the two of them dancing around outside. They've changed the playlist to only Taylor Swift. Our other patrons aren't too happy about it, but they're just too cute to stop. Eventually though, the night dies down and once my shift ends, I make my way to the girls. They're sitting at a table, nursing cups of water and laughing at each other.

"Would you ladies like a ride home?" I ask.

"My husband is coming to get me, but I know Ella wants to ride. I mean… wants a ride," Millie says with a wink.

Ella giggles. "Oh my God, shh!"

I smile. She's drunk and it's adorable.

"Okay, Ella. I'll drive you home once Millie has been picked up. Sound good?"

"Sounds good, Mr Bartender Man." They both break out in fits of laughter.

"God spare me," I mutter, laughing as I walk away.

She's definitely too drunk for sex tonight, but I'll have my way with her in the morning to repay her for what we did in my office.

Tonight is a night I will remember for a long, long while.

CHAPTER 25
Ella

Christmas and New Year's Eve fly by in a blur of food, alcohol, family events, and festive chaos. I barely managed to get through the usual onslaught of questions from my extended family. "When are you going to find a boyfriend?" "The clock is ticking, don't you know." "You should really be married by now; you're not getting any younger." Not exactly fun topics of conversation when you're trying to navigate a situationship with a hot bar manager. I brushed it off as always and laughed along with them, saving my frustrated tears for my pillow when I got home.

I haven't been able to see much of Xavier since my Christmas party. He drove me home and stayed the night, just to make sure I was okay, he said. It was sweet, given how much I'd had to drink. I appreciated it. The next morning, he had his way with me as promised. We caught up quickly the day after Christmas, but this is the craziest time of year for him at work, so he's been too busy. We talk every day though. I had a whinge to him about my family, and he complained about how many staff he had taking sick days, when he knew they were just too hungover for work.

New Year's Eve was uneventful; I spent it with Millie and Clay and all of their couple friends. It was fun, but I was the token single friend. It stung a bit, especially at the stroke of midnight. It's not so fun being the only one not getting a New Year's kiss. Xavier was working, but he did send me a virtual kiss—a smoochy selfie five minutes after midnight. It did make me feel a little bit better. I guess this time of year always hits different when you're single. I only get a slight reprieve in January, and then the next thing I know it's Valentine's Day and I'm depressed again.

Not to matter though, because today I am trying to be more positive. It's January 2nd, my birthday. I'm 31 today, and while it seems like the whole '30s are the best years of your life' thing hasn't exactly rung true, I have a good feeling about 31. My phone rings and I already know who it is before checking the caller ID.

"HAPPY BIRTHDAY, LOVERRRRRRRR!" Millie screams into the phone.

"HAPPY BIRTHDAY, BITCH!" I scream back. Sharing a birthday with your best friend is so fun.

"I'm so excited for this afternoon. Send me photos of what you're wearing, please," she demands.

"I have no idea what to wear. I will send you multiple photos. But to help narrow it down, are we thinking casual but slutty, or a little bit fancy?" I ask.

"Casual but slutty, for sure. I'll send you photos, too." She pauses. "Is Xavier still coming?"

"As far as I know, yes. He told me he took the day off to be my birthday date. Unless a work emergency comes up, he is coming."

"Awesome. No sneaking off for secret blow jobs though, save that for when you get home."

I laugh. "No promises."

"Alright, I gotta go. Clay has cooked brunch. Message me throughout the day and I'll see you soon. Love you!"

"Love you more. Bye!"

I'm getting ready for brunch with my family before we head to a rooftop bar in the city for an afternoon of cocktails and tapas. We've booked a booth and invited a bunch of mutual friends. No set times, it's just a come and go type situation. Everyone is always so busy this time of year and we don't like to put pressure on people to attend events. Just popping in for one drink means a lot.

The only annoying thing about today is that my period arrived early. So unfortunately, no birthday sex. Xavier said he didn't mind, but I don't think we are there yet. I've told him he can still stay over tonight if he wants, as I'll settle for a birthday kiss and a cuddle, it's more than I've gotten in years, anyway.

As if he knows I'm thinking about him, a new message from Xavier pops up.

XAVIER

> Happy Birthday love. Can't wait for tonight. I'll get dropped off at your place so we can head into the city together x

I smile at my phone like a fucking idiot. He's called me love a few times now, and I know I shouldn't read into it, but surely that means… something. Or I'm just being ridiculous, which is the likely scenario. Whatever, I'm just happy he's coming.

XAVIER

> I'll also give you your birthday present before we head in.

I squeal. I love presents. I hate buying them, but I love receiving them. Selfish I know, but I can't help it. I wasn't expecting a present from him, and I spend the rest of the morning trying to figure out what he could possibly have gotten me.

Family lunch was lovely, my dear old nan brought me a handmade library bag which was super sweet, and my parents got me gift cards for all of my favourite bookstores. They know what I want. I'm probably the easiest person to buy presents for. If it's bookish, I'll love it no matter what.

Now, I'm at home putting together the final pieces of my birthday outfit, sending pictures to Millie as I go. It's not very hot today, despite being the middle of summer, so I've decided on ripped blue jeans, with a white top that is technically lingerie, but safe enough to wear in public. I'm feeling quite sexy, despite the period bloat.

As I'm finishing up with my lipstick, there's a knock on my door. I race out of the bathroom to open it, and there's Xavier, looking fine as ever. He's also holding a gorgeous bunch of flowers and a small package wrapped in pink birthday paper.

"Happy birthday!" He walks into the house and sweeps me up into a massive hug, swinging me around the room. He puts me down and gives me a massive smooch on the lips. He's so joyous it's contagious.

"Thank you!" I say. "Are these for me?" I gesture to the flowers.

"Nah, they're for me. Of course they are for you, you goose." He laughs and hands them over. They're the most gorgeous flowers I've ever received. A mix of peonies, poppies, and greenery.

"They're perfect. Thank you, I absolutely love them." I kiss him on the cheek, leaving a big kiss mark, then I head into the kitchen to find a vase.

"Do you want your present before or after your party?" he asks from behind me, as I stand at the sink filling a vase with water.

"Um… now, please. I'm impatient and excited." I finish arranging the flowers and place them in the middle of my dining table. They really are beautiful.

He laughs.

"Okay, it's not that deep, but here you go." He hands over the small package and I not-so-delicately rip into it. It's a wooden box, and when I open the lid to see what's inside, I am enamoured and want to cry.

"It's a personalised book stamp," he explains. "I tried to customise it with a few of your favourite books…" He trails off. The cursive writing says, 'From the Library of Ella Hart' and it surrounds a mountain with three stars at its peak, a crescent moon, a small dragon, and some pine trees. It is absolutely… me.

"Xavier… this is amazing. Honestly, I love it. I love it so much." I whisper.

This is truly one of the most beautiful and thoughtful gifts anyone has ever given me. It may be small, but it's so personal. No other man in my life has ever really cared or supported my book habits, but he does. The walls around my heart have crumbled even further, and that little voice in my head has started whispering, *"What if…?"*

"I'm glad you like it. I was so stressed I would get it wrong."

I rise up on my tiptoes and give him a kiss.

"It's perfect. Thank you."

"You're welcome."

I rush into my book room and find the perfect spot for it on my shelf. My bookstagram friends are going to die when I show them. I walk back into the living room and Xavier is doing a thorough appraisal of my outfit. The twinkle in his eyes tells me he approves.

"You look good, birthday girl. Are you ready to go?" he asks.

"Yep! Oh, but one more quick thing." I wrap my arms around his neck and pull him in for one more kiss. He pulls me in close and kisses me slowly, lazily trailing his hand along my upper back. We end the kiss, and I take a step back from him, grinning. He smiles back at me.

"What was that for?" he asks.

I shrug my shoulders.

"Because I could."

He smirks at me, his dimple showing slightly.

"Now let's go, I can't be late for my own party!"

CHAPTER 26
Xavier

We arrive at the rooftop bar just after Millie and Clay, walking over to the group of tables they've reserved. There are the typical squeals of delight from the women as they gush over each other's outfits and wish each other a happy birthday. It's quite adorable to watch, actually. They're too busy fussing over each other that introductions are skipped, so I reach my hand out to introduce myself to Clay.

"I'm guessing this is a regular interaction between the two of them?" I ask, pointing to Ella and Millie.

He laughs. "Yeah, pretty much. They see each other every day at work, yet they still scream and hug whenever they hang out. You get used to it." He smiles at his wife lovingly.

"Yeah." I laugh. It is quite endearing to watch. Female friendships are something else entirely, almost sacred.

"Hey, birthday girls!" I call out. Both women stop their chattering to look over at me. "What do you want to drink? My shout." They both ask for a gin and tonic and grab a seat at one of the tables.

I walk over to the bar and place my order, getting a beer for myself and Clay. This is the first time I've been on the other side of the bar for a while, socially at least. It's nice. Once I take over from Dad, I'll be able to set myself up with a regular schedule. No more shift work and night duties, and

I'll probably be able to have a proper social life again. Once he eventually retires, of course.

I pay for the drinks and walk back to the group, taking the seat next to Ella. There's not a lot of space, and our legs are very much pressed up against one another. As she's talking, Ella reaches under the table and casually places her hand on my leg. Such a simple movement, not sexual in any way, and yet it surprises me. So much so, I don't react or acknowledge that she's done it. After a while, she squeezes my leg gently, as if to remind me her hand is on my thigh, and I still don't react or reach for her hand. What Ella and I do in private is definitely more than what a normal friendship would entail, but it's exactly that, private. We've never even hugged each other in a public space in front of other people. I don't know how I feel or what to do about this incredibly casual but familiar gesture. It's very… couple-y. And the most confusing part is that I don't hate it. In fact, it feels nice.

A few more minutes pass without my acknowledging her hand and, eventually, she pulls it back. I can see out of the corner of my eye that her shoulders slump slightly. *Is she disappointed I didn't hold her hand?* There's a knot of uncertainty forming in my gut. She knows what this is, but holding hands is such a couple's thing to do, and we're not a couple. Still, I liked it, and I don't know what to make of that.

Thankfully, a small group of people show up for a drink and so, for a while, I'm thrown out of my thought spiral and am distracted by new faces and introductions. We all chat for a bit, mostly roasting the birthday girls and making fun of them. Nothing like some gentle bullying for your birthday. Someone buys us all a round of shots, and two for the girls. It's all good fun.

Ella finishes her drink and I ask if she wants another. She says yes, so I get up from the table to get another round. I place the order, and then feel a hand on the small of my back as Ella appears at my side. She looks up at me and smiles.

"Having fun?" she asks.

"Yeah, definitely," I say. Her hand is still on my back and she's leaning into me slightly. Her gesture is so comfortable that to anyone else, it would look like we are together. I quickly look around the bar, no one is paying us any attention.

"Are you having fun? It is your birthday." I ask.

"Yeah, it's good. I'm glad a few others have shown up. They probably won't stick around for long though, so I don't imagine tonight will be overly big. Plus, Millie has already started giving Clay 'fuck me' eyes, so I give them another two hours maximum before they're heading home." She looks over at her friend with a smile. I follow her line of sight and yep, Millie is definitely giving Clay 'fuck me' eyes, and he is definitely reciprocating.

"Damn," I whisper. "I almost feel like I'm intruding on a private moment between them."

Ella snorts. "Oh, I know. I've never met a married couple with more sexual chemistry than those two. It's insane. It's even more awkward when it's just the three of us. I end those nights quickly." She shudders. Seems like this is a regular occurrence.

"So, you hang out with them together as a couple fairly often then?"

"Yeah, a bit. They joke that I am their adopted child. It will be interesting to see if things change once they actually start a family," she says with a slight nervous tilt to her voice.

"I'm sure it'll be fine. You'll just slip into the Auntie Ella role instead, the friendship won't change." I reassure her, and she just nods. "Have they been trying for long?" I know when we first started hanging out, Ella said that Millie and Clay had started trying for a baby, but I hadn't asked how long they'd been trying.

"A year. Millie has endometriosis, so the doctors said it could take a bit longer for them to fall pregnant. She told me they will try for a year before looking into fertility and IVF stuff, so they're starting that process soon."

"Ah, okay. Well… by the looks they are giving each other, it seems they have the… uh… act of procreating perfected. It's in the hands of biology now."

"Mmm… and God's." She closes her eyes and nods.

I quirk a brow at her. She opens her eyes and laughs at the expression on my face.

"Kidding. Obviously." Our drinks are placed on the bar, and I pick up my beer.

"You know you almost had me, for like, half a second," I say as I have a drink. She leans in and whispers in my ear.

"The only time I pray to God is when I'm screaming his name as you're buried inside of me."

I choke a little on my drink as it goes down the wrong hole. She takes a step back from me, biting her bottom lip playfully as I try to recover myself.

"Well, that was unexpected." I laugh.

"You're welcome!" She giggles. "Thanks for the drink, babe." She blows me a kiss as she walks away. I follow her back to the table, a stupid grin on my face and shaking my head. As I sit down, Ella looks at me and smiles. I smile back at her.

Our fingers are slightly brushing under the table. She leans into me, and as she does, she quickly glances down to my mouth. She wants a kiss. I want to. I really, really want to kiss her. But I can't. *Not here.* Not in front of people where questions will be asked, and assumptions will be made. I dip my head slightly and with a small smile, I shake my head, just a little, to indicate that we can't kiss here. The light in her eyes dims and she withdraws from me slightly. She nods, seeming disappointed yet understanding. Her fingers drift away from mine, though lingering slightly, before she pulls away completely. She closes her eyes and takes a quick deep breath before opening them again and joining the conversation with her friends.

I watch her for a little while. The way she is so animated when she speaks, using her whole body when she tells a story. The slight wheeze she does when she starts laughing. The way she shows every emotion on her face and can't hide what she's thinking at all. But I can also see now the slight tension in her shoulders, the excessive fiddling with whatever item she has in front of her, the shifting in her seat. She's overthinking, and I know I'm the reason why.

I hate that I make her feel like this. I wish it was different. Because the more I try to deny it, the more I'm lying to myself. I'm falling for this girl, and I know that if given the chance, whatever this thing is between us could be really wonderful. But I just can't right now. I've thought about it over and over and it just doesn't sit right. I'm still overwhelmed by the pressure I'm facing from Dad to step up and prove myself, and the fact I am only just getting over my last relationship. I want to be respectful to Jade, and jumping into something new, no matter how great it feels, just feels like I'm hurting her all over again and shitting on the last five years we had together.

The smile slowly falls from my face as I sit there in my own thoughts, watching Ella interacting with her friends. I can feel someone's eyes on me, and I look over and see Millie watching me. She looks between the two of us and eyes me suspiciously. I give her a smile and a single nod, hoping to reassure her. She glares at me, using two fingers to point to her own eyes before turning them on me. She's silently saying, "I'm watching you." I give her a wink and she scoffs playfully, rolling her eyes before turning back to whatever conversation is happening around her.

Ella does her best for the rest of the night to ensure our legs don't brush against each other and our hands don't touch. I hate feeling like she has to avoid me, but I also appreciate her respecting my wish to keep what we are doing private for now. But it's her fucking birthday, so I'm obviously being a dick. I'll have to make up for it somehow.

The night continues on and just under two hours later, yep, she called it, Millie and Clay announce they're heading home. I'm genuinely surprised they lasted this long, between the looks they've shared and the PDA, I didn't think they would still be here. It seems that everyone else is ready to call it a night too, including Ella, so we all say our goodbyes. The girls hug each other like it's the last time they'll see each other for a year, when really, I know Ella is going over to Millie's for dinner in two days. It's beautiful.

I order an Uber and we stand together on the street. A few of the others are doing the same.

"You don't think they'll gossip about the fact that we're getting in an Uber together tonight?" I ask jokingly. She laughs but it doesn't quite reach her eyes.

"Probably. But I don't really care. They can think whatever they want about it."

"Oh yeah, I don't care either." I pause. I do a little, but I try not to think about it too much. "Did you have a good birthday?" I ask. I really hope I haven't ruined it.

I already feel bad for rejecting her affection.

"I did! I'm glad everyone else stayed quite a while, I haven't seen some of them in months, so it was great to catch up. Plus, I got a free drink from the bartender, so that's a win." She smiles.

"Oh? You didn't mention that earlier," I say. *When did that happen?*

"You were in the bathroom I think, I must have forgotten. I went up to get another drink and he asked what we were celebrating. I told him it was my birthday, and he gave me a drink on the house. He was really sweet, actually." The one time I didn't buy her drink for her and the bartender hits on her.

"I'm sure he was," I mutter under my breath.

"What was that?" Ella asks.

"I said that's really nice of him," I say. I remember seeing some young blond guy serving us, but I didn't get a good look at him. He must have been getting a good look at Ella though, by the sounds of it.

"Right. Yeah anyway, we talked for a little bit and then I came back to the table. Millie told me to give him my number." She's fidgeting with the strap on her bag as she says this. Is she serious? Or is she baiting me? Because it's fucking working. The idea of her giving some other guy her number sparks something possessive within me. I don't like it. *What the hell, Millie?*

"And did you?" *Please say no.*

"No. He was nice, but he was only 25. Too young," she says. I'm relieved, but I know I'm being ridiculous. She's still looking for a relationship, so I should be encouraging her to put herself out there more.

"Yeah, fair enough. You know you can, though. Put yourself out there and talk to other people." The idea of it makes me feel sick to my stomach, and I have no right to feel this way.

"Yeah, I know." She smiles sadly. "I talk to people here and there, but I'm just not the kind of person who puts herself out there for the sake of it.

It gets pretty tiring after a while, you know? Unless of course I really want something." I nod, thinking of all the ways she's put herself out there for me. The photos, the lingerie, my office… damn, my office…

"Are you?" she asks, pulling me out of memory lane.

"Am I what?"

"Putting yourself out there, meeting people?" she elaborates nervously, not quite looking me in the eye.

"Not really. One of my best mates told me to download a few apps. I've had a look on there, have matched with a few people, and had conversations, but it just didn't feel right, so I haven't really been on them."

"Oh, okay. Well, the apps suck anyway. So good luck, you know, if you want them to work."

"Oh?"

"Five years of failure over here." She points to herself.

"Not a failure, you just haven't met anyone worthy of you yet." I tell her.

She smiles. A proper smile this time, thankfully.

"Yeah, you're right. I like that approach much better." The Uber pulls up and I open the door for her to slide in first. With a final wave to her friends, who are indeed watching us get in together, we head off back to her house. I hold her hand the whole ride home.

CHAPTER 27
Ella

I really did have a good birthday. It was so good to see some of my friends that I haven't seen in a long time. And it did make me feel good to have the bartender hitting on me a little bit. If he was older, maybe I would have given him my number, though it'd most likely be out of petty spite to annoy Xavier. Any time I so much as touched the man tonight, he acted as if I was dry humping him in public, rather than resting my hand on his knee under the goddamn table.

I'm starting to really feel confused as to what we are. We're friends. And we have sex. But there's more, too. The kisses and hugs, the small gestures, the sleepovers when we agreed on no sleepovers. Even holding my hand on the way home tonight, despite ignoring every single touch when we were out. When we're together in private, I don't feel like just his friend. The lines are blurring just too much, and my poor little heart doesn't know that the man she's falling for doesn't want anything more.

When we get home, he makes me drink a big glass of water before having a shower. I take my time and when I finally get out, I'm feeling fresh and ready to snuggle down into bed. I walk into my bedroom and there he is, wearing nothing but his boxer briefs. My heart flutters at the casual way he's just lying there. I realise this is the first time he's sleeping over without us having sex. It feels different and I feel almost guilty, which is ridiculous.

"Feeling good?" he asks as he pulls the covers back for me to slide in. I climb into bed, and he pulls me into him and starts giving me back tickles.

"Yeah, I'm feeling great. I didn't drink very much, so I'm all good."

"Glad to hear it."

We lie there in comfortable silence for a while as he continues tickling my back. I could so very easily fall asleep in his arms if he keeps going.

"I'm sorry if I upset you tonight."

That catches me off guard. I look up at him.

"What do you mean?" I ask.

"When I didn't, like, show any affection back to you tonight. While we were out. I'm sorry if that upset you."

Oh. I wasn't expecting him to acknowledge it or talk about it. But he's right, I felt awful when he completely ignored any sort of physical interaction while we were out.

"It's fine."

"It's not," he says back. "I could tell I upset you, and I apologise." He places a kiss on the tip of my nose.

"Okay, I did feel a bit… rejected, and embarrassed. Though I thought I hid it well. How could you tell?" I ask out of curiosity.

"Your body language. I can see the signs when you're anxious. I hate knowing I made you feel that way, especially on your birthday." He's holding my hand now, stroking the back of my hand with his thumb.

"It's fine. I'm a big girl and I'll get over it." *After a good cry tomorrow when you're gone.* "I shouldn't have done the whole PDA thing, that was an overstep on my part."

"No, it's not an overstep. I guess we've never really talked about those kinds of boundaries before. I know we're quite affectionate when we're alone, we've just not really been in public together, socially."

"And… you don't want any sort of affection in public? Or sorry, I should say you're not comfortable with public affection?" I ask.

"Sort of. I don't mind public displays of affection generally. It's just…"

"We're just friends," I say for him. He looks at me with a small smile.

"Yeah," he says. "I know Millie and Clay know a bit about us and our arrangement, but I kind of want to keep it private from everyone else, if that's okay. People always ask too many questions when two people who aren't together act like they're together, and I don't want to have to explain myself to anyone."

Right. He wants to keep whatever this thing is between us a secret and keep up the façade that we're *just* friends.. My poor lonely heart is starting to race, and I can feel myself wanting to put up the walls that he so easily knocked down. I don't really know how to feel. Should I keep doing this? Or should I step back? I don't want to lose him. I know if he knew I had feelings, he'd probably want to stop this, and I don't know if I can go back to being just platonic friends after knowing how good our physical connection is.

"That's fine," I say, though I'm pretty quiet. "We should have spoken about it first. Now I know, so you won't have to worry." I'm feeling very, very small.

"Thanks. I know it probably isn't what you want to hear." *It's not.* "But it's all I can give you right now. I'm still just not ready for anything more."

And yet, you act like we're together, I want to say. I wish he understood how fucking confusing this is.

"I know. It's fine, really. I know what the boundaries are now."

He's quiet for a little bit.

"We can slow down a bit, if you think this is becoming too much."

Do I want that? The logical part of my brain is telling me very fucking clearly *yes, you should stop this, Ella.* I know exactly where this path is leading. It's a one-way ticket to heartbreak. But the romantic hopeful in me says to stay. Maybe in time, he will change his mind. He might be ready in a month or two, and then everything will be fine.

"No. I don't want to slow down. I'm good, really. I told you I'd let you know if it got too much, or I started getting attached. We're okay, I promise."

"Okay." I don't know how much he believes me. "As long as you're sure. I care too much about you, so I don't want you getting hurt."

I really hate how he talks as if I'm the one who is going to end up getting hurt, like he's a complete robot and this situation won't affect him at all.

"I'm sure. I promise, I'll tell you."

"Thank you."

I reach up and give him a quick kiss.

"Can you reach over and turn off the lamp? I'm falling asleep." I ask. He reaches over and flips the switch, plunging us into darkness. He pulls me in his arms and holds me tight.

In the safety of the darkness, I can feel his body start to relax against mine.

"You know…" he whispers. "I'm really glad I met you."

"I'm glad I met you too." I whisper back. I can feel my eyes start to sting and I force myself to breathe slowly so I don't start crying. *Why does it have to be like this?*

"Goodnight, Xavier."

He squeezes me tighter.

"Goodnight, Ella. Happy birthday."

CHAPTER 28
Ella

My appointment with my therapist is a week after my birthday. *Thank God.*

I knew that I had to speak to someone after saying goodbye to Xavier the morning after my birthday party. Someone who wasn't Millie, to be exact. A best friend is great to lean on but sometimes you just need an outsider's perspective, and a professional's opinion. It has been a while since my last appointment, since I tend to not need them as often when I'm on holidays. But this situation and all of these feelings? I need an outlet.

I'm sitting in the waiting room reading over the journal entry I wrote last night. I'll admit, I wasn't in the best head space when I wrote what I did, but Jane told me to reflect on what I've written when I'm feeling a bit clearer headed. I'm not exactly feeling super clear headed today, but I'm feeling better than I did last night, and I want to be able to explain to Jane how I'm feeling with full comprehension. I'm not sure how well I'll be able to do it, if I'm honest, because most of what I scribbled down are variations of WHY WON'T HE LOVE ME and I'M GOING TO BE ALONE FOREVER. I was clearly feeling a little melodramatic among last night's tears. Good to know I'm self-aware, at least.

The door opens and Jane welcomes me into her office with a smile. I take a seat, and when she asks me how I've been since we last spoke, I launch into it. It has been well over a month, and a lot has happened. She sits there and notes it all down, sliding me the box of tissues when I inevitably start to tear up because of how overwhelmingly confused I am feeling. The thing I love about Jane is that she will let me vent and say what I need to, and only then will she ask questions. She never interrupts unless she needs me to clarify something. I finish my story by explaining to her that I feel like a lovesick teenager in a 31-year old's body, and that really, deep down, I'm scared, anxious, and don't know what to do.

"Well, things definitely have progressed since we last spoke." She smiles. "And by the sounds of what you've told me, you and Xavier have quite a strong friendship. Have you told him how you feel?"

"No." I groan. "I can't. If he knows how much I like him, he will want to stop what we're doing, and I don't want to stop."

She merely nods slowly and writes again on her notepad. After another beat of her saying nothing, I blurt out, "It's pathetic, right? I know I need to tell him. But if I do, I'll lose what we have. And some part of me I think believes that if I keep my feelings a secret, eventually he will feel the same way. And if he confesses his feelings first, I'll be able to reciprocate, and I won't have to worry about being rejected."

"How long do you really think you'll be able to keep your feelings hidden?" she asks. I think about my birthday, and how he asked if I wanted to slow down or stop.

"Realistically, not long," I mumble. "I think he already suspects I'm keeping my feelings from him. I'm really good at pretending though." Jane doesn't buy it.

"Ella, can I ask, if one of your girlfriends came to you and said she had been seeing this guy who didn't have feelings for her, but was waiting to see if he would change his mind, what would you say to her?"

I know exactly what I would say to her. That she was being delusional and that he wasn't worth her wasting her time. And I know that if I told Millie how I really felt about Xavier, she would tell me the exact same thing. That if he wanted to be with me, he would be. But he isn't. He's still holding me at arm's length.

"I just…" I swallow the lump forming in my throat. "The idea of being rejected again, I can't. I'm so sick of putting myself out there and getting nothing back. This is the closest I've come in five years to something more than an emotionless hook-up. I don't want to lose it. I don't want to lose him." The tears slowly trickle down my cheek, and I press a tissue to my face to catch them as they fall.

"I understand, Ella." Jane's voice is gentle, with no hint of condescension. "I know you've been hurt in the past. I know how much you want to love and be loved." I nod and more tears fall. "I really think that you need to tell him how you are feeling. The more you keep it in, the harder you will fall and the harder it is going to be. You're telling me he has continued to make it clear that he just wants to be friends. I'm not saying that he won't ever change his mind, but I am saying that you deserve someone who knows for sure that you are it. How long do you think you can wait?"

I take a moment to think. How long can I wait? I have been waiting, not necessarily just for Xavier, but for someone. I've never really been in love, not seriously, anyway. I have so much love to give, so how long do I want to waste on someone who won't allow me to express that love? I want someone who shows me off to the world, someone who loves me unashamedly. Jane is right, I need to face this.

"I don't want to wait. I don't want to be hurt again, but I don't want to wait around in the hopes that he will eventually love me back. Not that I'm currently in love with him," I correct myself. I don't love him. It's way too soon for that. It's just like. A lot of like. Deep like. Not love.

Jane smiles. "You can have love for someone without being in love with them. You have love for Xavier. He is your friend, your comfort, and someone you care deeply about. Love has many variables; this is just one of them."

Of course, I might have *some* love for Xavier. And I know in my heart and soul that I will fall in love with him if I keep doing this. I need to tell him. I blow out a breath.

"You're right. I have to talk to him. I can't avoid it, and it will be worse if I wait longer. I just, I don't know how to cope with the rejection. I don't know how to come back again from feeling wanted to feeling discarded."

"I think no matter what, there will be feelings of rejection. What will matter though, is your mindset going into it. You know he likes you and enjoys your company. You know that the reason he doesn't want a relationship has nothing to do with you, and everything to do with where he is in his life. You just have to remind yourself that it isn't you. It's not your fault. It's just not the right time. In saying all of this, he could also reciprocate the feelings. You won't know until you talk to him."

Everything she says makes so much sense. It sounds so simple. I feel almost silly for getting so worked up over something so trivial.

"Thanks, Jane. I feel a bit ridiculous for getting anxious over stuff like this, but you've…" I pause to think of the right word. "You've calmed my chaotic mind. I have an idea of what to do now."

"It's my pleasure. There's no need to feel ridiculous, anxiety is a fickle thing. But at least we know some of your triggers, we just have to find out how to navigate our way through when we can't avoid those triggers."

I simply nod.

She's right. Fear of rejection, fear of letting people down, fear of being alone forever… at least I know. And I have her to help me through it.

"Well, that's our time up for today. Let's book you in for the usual time next month, but if you feel like you need to bring the appointment forward, just give me a call and I'll try and fit you in."

"Sounds good, thanks again," I say.

"You've got this, Ella." She gives me a bright smile. I'll do my best to believe her.

I check my phone as I'm walking out to my car and find a message from Xavier.

XAVIER

> I've got next weekend off work. Do you want to come over to my place and stay Saturday night? I have a spa. And chickens. And I'll cook you pasta for dinner? Let me know

I let out a small laugh and allow myself a glimmer of excitement. He's never invited me to his house before, so of course I want to go. Maybe telling him how I feel in his own home and comfort zone is the best place to do it. I start to formulate a plan in my head and type out my response.

ELLA

I'd love to. You sold me with pasta x

CHAPTER 29
Xavier

I made a promise to myself that I would make it up to Ella for upsetting her on her birthday. I decided it was time to invite her to my house for the weekend. I've spent plenty of nights with her at her place, after all. I've been a bit hesitant to invite her here, mainly because it's the house Jade and I bought together, and I've never invited another woman over. I was worried that Ella might not want to come to the house either, but she's never said anything, so I thought I might as well ask. Her immediate yes had my heart warming.

I've done a lot of thinking since her birthday, and the more I think, the more I feel like an even bigger arsehole for upsetting her. She tried to hide her hurt feelings that night when we were cuddled up in bed, but I could feel her tension in the way she held herself. Her breathing was ragged like she was trying to hold back tears, and she didn't melt into me like she normally does when I hold her. She felt 'rejected and embarrassed', she'd said. It makes sense she couldn't relax around me after that.

We really should have talked about the public affection stuff before. I understand why she's feeling confused, because I'm confused, too. I know I'm falling for her. But I know I'm not ready and I know I don't want others gossiping about the two of us. I just wish there was a way for me to tell Ella how I feel without it sounding like I'm the biggest fuck boy she's ever been with who's wasting her time. I know she deserves so much better, someone who can show her off to the world.

I haven't seen her since her birthday, a whole two-and-a-bit weeks. It's the longest we've gone without seeing each other since we met. I figured she probably wanted the space. I know I did—I needed time to think and figure out the absolute shit show that's happening inside of my head. We spoke everyday though, and I called her a couple of times to check in. She had therapy last week and she told me that it was a good session and that it gave her a lot of clarity. I don't know why I felt a little uneasy about that. I know she probably talks about me, about us, at therapy, but I wonder what her therapist thinks about our arrangement. Probably that I'm an arse.

Saturday rolls around and it's my first full weekend off in months. Well, I did work Friday night, but still. I haven't had a Saturday and Sunday off in a long time. I've been putting in countless extra hours to show Dad just how much I want this gig, and I still can't get a gauge on whether I'm doing enough. He's giving me nothing, and I feel like I'm bending over backwards with no results.

Out of frustration, I spent my morning tidying the house. The house wasn't terrible, as I'm not a messy guy—far from it. But I am a single man who works in hospitality and sometimes I can get a bit behind on the chores, so I cleaned the things I would normally put off. I've also been to the shops and bought groceries for dinner and a bottle of wine. The spa is set to the perfect summer temperature. Everything is ready to go. I'm surprised to find myself feeling a bit nervous for Ella's arrival.

I'm sitting at my outdoor dining table, browsing on my phone when I hear the crunch of tyres on gravel as Ella pulls into my driveway. I walk towards where she's parked and she hops out of the car, smiling as she sees me coming. I almost trip on a large rock because I'm not paying attention to where I'm walking, my eyes are solely focused on her, and how beautiful she looks. She hasn't dressed up, hasn't done anything special. She's wearing a plain white t-shirt and light blue cut-off denim shorts with Birks. Her strawberry blonde hair is down and wavy, framing her gorgeous face that she has left free of makeup for the weekend. She's stunning. I feel pulled to her like the earth is pulled to the sun and it hits me right in that moment exactly how much I feel for this girl, and how much I hate myself for not being able to give her what she deserves.

"Hi, you." She's beaming as I reach her.

"Hi, back," I say and pull her into a tight hug.

"I missed you." Her voice is muffled by my t-shirt because I'm squeezing her so tight she can't pull away. I kiss the top of her head.

"So dramatic, it's only been two weeks!" I say. She grumbles and gives me a light smack. I laugh. "I'm joking!"

I let go and she steps back enough to look up at me with a pout. I give her my best smirk, the one that shows my dimple that I know makes her weak at the knees, and the pout is replaced by a blushing smile. I kiss her then, bringing my hand up to cup the back of her neck. God, I've missed her soft lips on mine. She balls her fists in my shirt and sweeps her tongue into my mouth. A small moan slips out of me, and I deepen the kiss a little before gently pulling away.

"Yeah, I've missed you too," I say and kiss the tip of her nose. She bites her lip playfully. "But save that for later, you'll need it." I wink and she giggles. "Do you want me to show you around?"

Once again, her face lights up.

"Um, yes please! I've been dying to see your place." She turns from me and goes to get her bag from the boot of her car. She grabs another item and I quirk a brow.

"Ell, you do know I'm not a 20-year-old man child? I do have a full set of pillows on my bed. You didn't need to bring your own," I say.

"Well, I couldn't be sure. You are a bachelor, after all. Better to be safe than sorry." She smirks at me as I roll my eyes. "Kidding! I sleep better with my own pillow. It's been a while since I've slept in a bed that isn't my own."

"Fair enough," I say in response. I grab her bag from her and lead the way into the house. We walk in through the back yard and enter the house through the open French doors that lead into the open plan living space. The house is old and not overly big, but I've touched it up over the years and it has modern features throughout to make the space functional and comfortable. I show her the spare bedroom and bathroom and take her to my bedroom for her to put her stuff down. I show her the ensuite, and she was so excited to see my clawfoot bathtub that she actually squealed.

"I can so vividly picture you in here with bubbles and candles. You're like that episode of *Friends* where Chandler and Monica are in the bath and Joey barges in…"

"I'm familiar with the episode," I say. She's biting her bottom lip to keep herself from smiling too hard. "Except it's normally a beer in place of champagne." She tips her head back and laughs.

"Oh, it's too cute, that image will now live rent free in my brain forever."

"Okay, moving on," I say, poking her ribs to get her moving out of the bathroom and back into the living space. I'm about to lead her back outside to show her the garden when she points to the closed door across from my spare bedroom and asks what's inside.

"That's my office, I'll show you that room after dinner," I say casually.

"Ooh… have you got some Fifty-Shades-style red room thing going on in there?" she teases.

"Does your head always live in the smut gutter?"

"Yes," she replies, unashamedly.

"No, I don't have a sex room hidden in there." I laugh. She grins at me wickedly, and something delicious stirs inside of me with that look. "It's just my office, very basic, but I do want to wait until after dinner to show you. You'll find out why."

"Very cryptic, Xav, but I'm a patient girl. I'll wait."

"Good, now, the garden."

I take her hand and lead her back through the French doors, pointing out the BBQ area and the spa, leading her to what I think is my favourite part of my property, my lawn.

"Xavier James." My full name on her lips has me weak at the knees. "You never told me you were a lawn guy."

"Didn't I? Hmm. Well, I am. I love my lawn. She's my pride and joy."

"Cute," she says. I frown.

"It's not cute. It's manly."

She laughs. "Oh yes, of course. Very manly." She looks at me. "Oh my

God, are you pouting now?"

I school my features into neutrality.

"No."

"I'm just teasing. It's a great lawn, babe. Sexy, even."

"You're still making fun of me."

"I promise I'm not! It's one of the best lawns I've ever seen."

"Mmm." I don't give her a moment for another response before I sweep her up off her feet and throw her over my shoulder. She shrieks and starts swatting at me to put her down. I step onto the lawn and gently lay her down on it. She's flustered and laughing, and I lean down and kiss her. Wrapping her arms around my neck, I can feel her smile into the kiss. I pull back, simply wanting to admire her in this moment. She looks so happy.

"What?" she asks.

"Nothing. Just… you're really great. You know that?"

She dramatically flips her hair. "Oh, I know."

"Smart arse." I tickle her again, this time until she's screaming and begging me to stop. Eventually I do, getting up and offering her my hand to help pull her up. Once she's standing and has brushed the grass off her clothes, I take her hand again and show her the rest of the yard. We get to the back corner where the chicken coop is.

"Chickens!" she shouts.

"Yes, chickens." I laugh. "Want to help me feed them?"

"Yes, please."

I open the gate and gesture for her to go inside.

"The white one there is Nuggs, she's my best layer. The black one there is Hen Solo, she's the most placid and will eat right from the palm of my hand. And the brown one…" I point to Meryl, who is eyeing us suspiciously. "That is Meryl Cheep. She's the most judgemental and temperamental. If she doesn't like you, don't feel sad, she doesn't like anyone."

"Okay. Firstly, best chicken names ever," she says.

"Thank you." *I am quite proud of their names.*

"Second. Why is Meryl looking at me like that, and should I be worried?"

I look back at Meryl who has her head cocked while she stares at Ella. I haven't seen her assess anyone so intensely before.

"Um. Good question."

Meryl straightens her head and slowly makes her way over to us. I brace myself to have to step in if she starts attacking, but she instead stops at Ella's feet and clucks.

"What the…" I breathe.

Meryl lightly pecks Ella's shoes and continues to happily cluck and circle her feet. There's no screeching, no vicious pecking, no evil to be seen.

"I am in shock," I say to Ella as she reaches down to pat Meryl, and she *ACTUALLY LETS HER.*

"Never has she ever let me pat her. What the fuck?"

Ella laughs. "I guess she can also sense just how great I am."

I bend down to pat Meryl, and she squawks, snaps her beak at me, and runs away dramatically.

"See that right there, that's her normal reaction." I grab the chicken feed and start scattering it around. Ella holds some in her hand for Hen Solo to eat. She then holds her hand out for Meryl, and I almost fall over because she also eats out of Ella's hand.

"The fuck, Meryl?" I moan.

Despite my shock, I have the biggest grin on my face. My heart warms at the sight. That chicken hates everyone. Even me most of the time. And yet Ella… she loves Ella. It's like in the movies when the main character introduces his new girlfriend to his dog and says, "oh he doesn't like new people," and then the dog sits in her lap and loves her, and then that guy is in awe of the woman and thinks damn she must be pretty amazing.

It's me. I'm that guy right now. But with a chicken.

Ella notices me staring at her and smiles so wide it crinkles the corners of her eyes. I smile back.

We finish feeding the chickens and head back out to the veranda. I tell Ella to take a seat at the outdoor dining table as I get a bottle of wine out of the fridge. I pour us a glass each and sit next to her, toasting "to a beautiful weekend off work, with even more beautiful company."

She rolls her eyes.

"So, how's it all going with your dad? Any progress yet on the job?"

"Not yet. I honestly don't know what more I could possibly do to make him see me."

"Maybe it's not about whether he thinks you're ready, but more about whether he wants to give it up?" she suggests.

"It could definitely be that, but he puts pressure on me all the time to be at my best and putting the pub first, telling me to think of new ideas but then barely implementing them when I present them. The thing is, he's not mean or nasty about it, I never feel like I'm letting him down, only that I could do a little bit more. I love my dad, and we have a great relationship. It's just exhausting, trying to live up to expectations when I don't have a clear idea on what they actually are."

"Yeah, that's rough. I can't say I've experienced that myself, but I can empathise," she says.

"Thanks. It's all I've ever wanted to do, and I'm so close. I just have to keep my focus and work a little harder, and hopefully soon he will see my efforts."

"Hopefully."

We sit outside for a couple of hours, finishing off the bottle of wine and enjoying the warm summer breeze. Once it gets to around dinner time, I tell her to sit back and relax as I cook dinner. She comes in and sits at my kitchen island bench, chatting to me about books as I cook. I plate up and head back outside, eating in comfortable silence.

Once our bowls are empty and our stomachs are full, I take the dishes and dump them in the sink and walk back outside and stand behind her.

"So, are you ready to see inside my office?" I ask her, bracing my hands on top of the chair she's sitting in.

"Dumb question. Yes. I need to know why you're being so cryptic!"

She gets up and I walk her to the door leading to my office. I stand there with my hand on the doorknob, acting like I'm bracing myself, which makes her jittery with anticipation.

"Oh my God, just open the door!" she demands. So, I do. She stands in the doorway, and I turn on the lights.

My office is pretty simple. There's a big window overlooking the backyard and in front of it is my desk. It's an old vintage desk, one that belonged to my grandad that I refurbished. The walls are painted a dark forest green, and I have plants scattered around the room. Ella takes a few steps inside the room, taking in the space in front of her and appreciating the greenery.

"It's gorgeous, Xav. I love the colour and the room feels so calm and cosy. It's very you. But why did you wait to show me?" she asks.

"Turn around."

She does, and her eyes light up as soon as she sees what was hidden behind the open door.

"Yay, books!" she exclaims. "Wait what is…"

She takes two steps to the bookshelf and pulls a book off the shelf. The one book that I knew she would notice straight away.

CHAPTER 30
Ella

My heart is racing.

"Why are these books on your shelf? I thought you said you'd never heard of them?" I ask. I spotted them as soon as I turned around and saw his bookshelf. I'd recognise these covers anywhere; I've read the series five times.

"I hadn't." He shrugs.

"So, you… bought it?"

"Yeah. You talked about it enough that I figured I'd give it a go. I have to say though, I think I'm definitely a Cassian stan. I know Rhys is your favourite but there's just something about Cassian…"

My jaw drops to the floor.

"You've read it." I breathe. "My favourite series of all time, you've read it."

"I thought I could at least try it, and it turns out I really enjoyed it," he says as if it's no big deal.

My mouth is opening and closing like I'm a fish out of water, my eyes moving between the book in my hands and the rest of the series on his bookshelf. He's heard me talk about these books so often, he bought them and read them—he even *enjoyed* them. All because they're my favourite.

My eyes are lined with tears as I look up at him. And it is in this moment, I know.

Looking into his eyes, all of my defences come crumbling down. I've fallen for this man. It's not just like. I've fallen in love with him. I'd been resisting it for so long, holding back my feelings to try and protect myself from the heartbreak, but this…

"You okay?" he asks. He's looking at me contemplatively, head tilted to the side.

I realise I haven't spoken for a while and have just been standing there staring at him as my realisations come crashing down upon me. I love him. There's no doubt about it. No one has ever done anything like this. It may seem ridiculous or no big deal to some people, but I've always dreamed of the type of relationship where someone will try something simply because I love it. And that's exactly what he did. *Especially* when it comes to books. I've been teased and picked on my whole life for loving books, and he has never once made fun. By doing all of this, he's knocked down all the remaining walls I had built around my heart.

Fuck.

"Yeah, I'm fine I—I can't believe you read it." My voice comes out as a whisper, and I have to clear my throat to try and suppress the emotions building there.

He smiles at me softly and again shrugs his shoulders.

"I wanted to know why you loved it so much that you have five copies of it. Let alone the fact that you've read it a billion times."

I laugh. I have no words. All I know is that I definitely can't keep my feelings a secret much longer. I had planned to talk about it tonight, but this has just made me feel even more anxious. And stupidly, it has also made me hopeful. Surely, him doing something like this means he cares… means he might want more. I can only dream.

"I hope you can see why I'm so obsessed with them. These books are like home for me," I say, cradling the book to my chest.

"I totally get it. Though I don't think I need four more copies of each. One will do for me." He smirks. I shake my head and chuckle.

"Do you want to go in the spa?" he asks.

"Yes," I say, and put the book back on the shelf, lovingly and creepily stroking the spine as I walk away. "Oh wait, I forgot my bathers."

He snorts. "If you'd packed bathers, I would have stripped you out of them within minutes, anyway."

A wicked grin spreads across my face. *Well, if that's the case…*

"Alright then."

I'm so anxious talking about my feelings and being vulnerable, and I want to feel bold and confident in any way I can. So, I look him in the eye as I strip my clothes off right there in his office.

He bites his bottom lip as he looks me up and down and doesn't stop me as I saunter past him, heading towards the back doors and outside to the spa. The water is steaming but thankfully it's not too hot, as it is still a warm night. I climb in and after a heartbeat, Xavier walks outside, now completely naked. I not so subtly check him out as thoroughly as he did me, and he climbs in and sits opposite me.

We sit there for a while in silence while just looking at each other, or the swirling water, or the garden beyond. Just enjoying the warmth and the quiet of the late summer night. My stomach is a twist of knots as I try and figure out how I'm going to tell him. *Do I tell him I love him? Or just that I have feelings? What happens if he says he doesn't feel anything for me, should I end it or just pretend?* I'm thinking so many things all at once that it's starting to make my head spin.

Just do it. Just suck it up and do it, then face whatever happens next. I close my eyes and take a deep steadying breath. When I open them, he's watching me. *It's now or never.*

I float across to him, not breaking eye contact, small waves lap at the edge of the spa as I straddle him and wrap my arms around his neck. He wraps his arms around my middle, squeezing me gently. We're staring at each other, and then he brings his lips to mine in a soft kiss. I sigh into it, savouring it. I gently end the kiss and rest my forehead against his.

"You okay?" he asks again.

Keeping my eyes closed, I whisper,

"I don't know."

"Talk to me."

I pause, I genuinely feel like I'm going to be sick. I take another slow and deep breath.

"I think… I think I'm falling for you. Hard."

And there it is. My confession, my heart on the line, coming out as a soft whisper. My eyes are still closed, our foreheads still pressed together so I don't have to see his face when he turns me down. He's quiet for a moment, thinking.

"I think…" he whispers back, "I'm falling for you, too."

I go still. He pulls his head back from mine to look me in the eyes again. Blood rushes through my veins and I'm suddenly feeling too warm for the spa.

"But…" he adds.

Ah. There it is.

"I know I'm falling for you. I know I've got feelings, strong ones. Stronger than I realised if I'm being completely honest. But I just… I just don't know, Ella. I don't know what to do." He pauses, trying to find the right words. I swallow hard. "There's so much going on in my life right now, and I just think it's too soon."

I lower my eyes and I slump down a bit.

"It's been almost a year, Xav." I say.

"I know."

"And that's not long enough? Who determines how long you have to wait?"

"No one determines. I'm the one who broke Jade's heart and ruined her chance of a happy ending. I can't do that to you too. Not to mention the pressure I'm facing at work and from my dad… I'm just not ready, Ell. I care about you so much and I want you in my life. These feelings came out of nowhere. I really thought I'd be able to just keep things physical and it was all so unexpected. But I know I don't want to lose you. I'm just… lost."

And there it is: 'I'm just not ready for a relationship'. I have heard that phrase so many times in my adult life you'd think I'd be used to it by now. Frustration takes hold, and I can feel myself getting worked up. I go to slide off of him, but he holds me in place.

"So, then what do you want?" I ask. "You don't want to lose me, but you don't want to be with me. Is that what you're telling me?"

"It's not that I don't want to be with you. The timing just isn't right."

"Timing…" I shake my head and scoff. *Fuck timing.* "You know what, it's fine. I'm used to this."

"Used to what?"

"This sort of situation. For years, I've been the woman who is fuckable but not dateable. So, it's fine, I'm used to it." A single tear slides down my cheek and he brushes it away with his thumb.

"Ella…"

"What?"

"That's not what this is, and you know it. You know you mean more to me than just sex."

"Just not enough," I say. He doesn't respond.

My head is swimming, and I can't wrap my head around a single thought.

"So, where does that leave us?" I ask.

He sighs and thinks for a moment.

"I don't want to lose you. But I know it's fucking selfish of me to want to keep you around when I'm not ready to give you what you want and what you deserve."

I don't respond. I just sit there looking at the water, another tear sliding down my face and falling into the water, causing the tiniest of ripples.

"Ella, look at me, please." He begs. I don't look up straight away, so he grabs my chin between his thumb and forefinger and tilts my head up so we're eye to eye. He must see the confusion and the pain in my eyes because his face drops.

"I'm sorry," he whispers and pulls me into a hug, tightening his arms around me. I wrap my arms around him tighter and breathe him in.

What do I do? I know the logical answer. Walk away. Why continue spending time with a man only to fall for him further, knowing it will never go anywhere?

He kisses my bare shoulder and buries his head in the crook of my neck.

"Maybe just give me a little bit of time," he murmurs. "Let me figure a few things out. Just, give me a little time. Please." His voice breaks on that last word. "I don't want to lose you," he says again, voice cracking.

I'm an idiot. I know this, because despite every logical part of me that's screaming to walk away and move on...

I can't walk away, not yet. He has feelings for me, strong ones. The small and idiotically optimistic part of me is still thinking there is a sliver of hope that there might be the possibility of us, if I just wait a little bit longer.

"You're not going to lose me," I say, resting my cheek on his shoulder. "I can wait. I don't know how long, Xavier, but I can wait, just a bit longer. You mean too much for me to just walk away now."

I physically feel his body relax and he squeezes me even tighter. *I can wait.* We are too good together to throw it all away just yet. And once sorts his life out and realises he can move on and be happy and successful, then we can be together, and everything will be okay.

"I'll figure it out, I promise." He breathes.

Yeah, just like I promised I wouldn't fall for him. And we promised we wouldn't have sleepovers. And we promised we would keep this purely physical. I'm taking this promise with a grain of salt.

So, I nod. And then I kiss him. The kiss is sweet and slow, his fingers trailing up and down my back. I know this kiss is different. Something has shifted between us and now that we have revealed our feelings, this kiss feels like more. It's a declaration of sorts.

He deepens the kiss but keeps it slow and steady. My fingers are tangled in his hair, and I grip onto him, pulling him closer to me. I can feel him hardening beneath me as I slowly grind myself on his lap. I've never felt closer to him than in this moment, both vulnerable and unsure of what's to come.

We break apart from the kiss and without speaking, he stands and seats me on the edge of the spa. He gets out and I wrap my legs around his waist as he carries me over to the lawn and gently lowers me to the ground. The night is still warm, and the slight breeze is pleasantly cool on my skin as he lies on top of me and kisses me again. Deep and slow and sensual. I am surrounded by him, and I forget everything but the feel of his skin on mine, and our bodies fitting together so perfectly.

CHAPTER 31
Xavier

"I think I'm falling for you. Hard."

Ella's words from last night are playing on repeat in my head. I'm lying in bed, and she's curled up facing away from me, cuddling a pillow like she always does. I'm watching her shoulders rise and fall as she sleeps peacefully whilst I lie here contemplating my entire existence.

Last night was big. I wasn't prepared for what was said and what was confessed. I had a feeling—no, I knew that she had feelings for me. It was obvious, and she didn't say how long she'd been feeling that way, but I could guess it's been a long while. Just like I had buried my feelings and kept them from her.

Hearing her whisper those words and knowing just how scared she was to voice them broke me, and I couldn't keep her in the dark. But I also can't fill her with false hope. I feel like such a fucking arsehole because I can't give her what she wants. I know I should let her go, I don't know when I'll be ready to fully commit to someone again, but I'm being selfish. And when she offered to wait for me, I didn't tell her no. I should. I know I should. But I can't lose her. I don't know if she would be happy just being friends—I want her in my life any way I can, but I don't think she could do it. I want her to be happy, I want to be the one to make her happy, but I have too much shit to sort out first.

She starts to move around a little and I know she's waking up. Before she can turn over, I slide over to her side of the bed to spoon her. I place a hand flat on her stomach and pull her closer towards me. She's so warm from being wrapped up in the blankets, and her hair still smells slightly of chlorine from the spa last night.

She sighs contently and places her hand over mine, interlacing our fingers.

"Good morning," she murmurs.

I kiss her shoulder.

"Good morning. Did you sleep well?"

"Surprisingly, yes. I was out like a light. I guess after last night I was pretty exhausted."

Last night, after we had sex on the grass under the stars. I call it sex, but it felt like more. I've never felt anything more real than that moment. In fact, that was probably the most romantic moment of my life. Ella looked so beautiful, illuminated only by the moon and the stars, and when she came with a soft moan of my name on her lips, I'd never heard anything sweeter.

"Yeah, I'm not surprised, you could barely walk back to the bedroom after..." I trail off, I can't say after we fucked because that is far from what it was.

"Mhmm. I probably should have had you carry me back."

"I would have if you asked me too."

"I know." She laughs softly.

"How are you feeling, after last night?" I ask.

She's quiet, probably replaying every detail of last night, every touch, every kiss, every word that was said.

"I don't really know," she confesses. "I feel relieved that everything is out in the open now. But honestly, I think I'm just scared."

"I'm sorry."

"You don't have to be sorry, Xav." She rolls over so she can look at me. "Neither of us expected this. I mean, maybe I expected it for myself because I'm a hopeless romantic at heart, and as soon as I started to get to know you better, I knew I was screwed. But then you just had to go ahead and read my favourite books, that's when I knew I was royally fucked."

I laugh. "I should have known it was the books that would do it. But in all seriousness, I am sorry. I'm sorry I can't give you more than what I'm able to right now."

I can't fail her like I failed Jade, and I know if I try and commit to her now, it'll likely end in heartbreak again. I don't know what the future holds. I'm busting my arse at work to please my dad; I spend more hours at that pub than I do at home. I want nothing more than to continue his legacy and make Jimmies the best pub in all of Adelaide. I won't be able to give her the time or focus that is required in a relationship. We could try, but I know she'll just end up resenting me. Better to hold off now than hurt her even more when she's grown more attached.

"It's fine. When I said I could wait I meant it, but not for long. I want to live my life. This is the closest thing I've had to a relationship in over five years. I'm willing to give it some more time, but I can't wait around forever."

"I know. I wish I could give you some sort of indication. I just have a lot of shit to figure out first."

She nods. "Let's just take it day by day."

"Do you want to slow things down in the meantime? Like less sleepovers and romance-y stuff?"

"I guess we probably should. But we made that rule right from the start and never stuck to it. Maybe just seeing each other in person a bit less frequently? And no more sleepovers. Cuddles equal feelings in my eyes," she says. I know she hates the idea because her nose scrunches up a little.

"We can cut back on seeing each other. You'll be back at work soon too, so we probably won't be talking as much or have as much free time."

"True. Okay. Less time together and less talking. The rest we'll figure it out as it comes."

We spend the next hour lazing about in bed, exploring each other. This is our last sleepover now for a while, so I'm making the most of having her in my bed for the morning. I cook us breakfast as she has a shower, and we sit outside again to eat. The rest of the day is spent talking and enjoying each other's company. She helps me with the chickens, with Meryl being a fucking traitor again and greeting her happily at the gate. We have a cheese platter for lunch, and before I know it, it's time for her to go home. She packs her bag and loads it into her car, and then we both just stand there awkwardly.

"Okay, I don't know why this feels so weird. I'm probably going to see you in a week or so," she says. I smile. It's true, I don't know why this feels weird.

"Probably. I'll check my schedule and let you know. When do you start work again?"

"I have a week left of holidays and then I'm right back into it."

"Okay, we will try and catch up before it gets too busy for you then."

"Sounds good."

She wraps her arms around me, and I rest my chin on the top of her head. We stay there for a while, before I place a kiss on the top of her head, and we finally break apart. I pull her back to me and I kiss her once, twice, three times.

"Bye," she whispers.

"Bye. Talk soon," I say back. She smiles sweetly and gets in her car. I stand at the edge of the driveway and watch her go. She gives me a little wave before she drives out of sight.

I walk back inside the house and suddenly the whole place just feels empty. She's spent less than 48 hours here and already her presence is missed. I flop down on my couch and stare at my ceiling, going over our conversations, trying figure out what the fuck I'm supposed to do next. I'm overwhelmed, and I have absolutely no clue how to navigate this.

CHAPTER 32
Ella

It's been two weeks since my weekend at Xavier's house, and two weeks since we've seen each other. We're still talking every day, though a little less than before. It turned out he was too busy to see me last weekend, so we've scheduled a visit this Sunday afternoon. He only has a couple of hours, but I'll take what I can get.

I've been back at work for a week, and it has been a welcome distraction from the chaos that is my brain right now. Thankfully my boss didn't start this week, so I didn't have to worry about her watching me and criticising me. I've got too much on my plate as it is without her stirring up my anxiety.

I'm sitting on Millie's couch, Milo in hand. It's Friday night after the first week back and she's been whining all night about how she's already tired and the school year hasn't even properly started yet. I'm yet to tell her about everything that happened at Xavier's; part of me is nervous as to what she will say. I know she's going to think I'm an idiot for sticking around but I hope she can just be supportive.

"So," she starts. "Are you seeing Xavier this weekend?"

"Yeah, he's got a couple hours spare on Sunday afternoon so he's gonna come over before the dinner shift."

She doesn't say anything, just nods slowly.

"What?" I ask.

"Something's happened. I can tell."

"How can you tell?"

"Bestie intuition. You've been off all week!" she explains.

I huff out a laugh and then bite the bullet, telling her everything that happened two weeks ago. The realisation that I am in love with him after he read my favourite books, the spa, and the confession of feelings from both of us; how he still isn't ready, but I said I could wait; sex under the stars… all of it.

She doesn't say much throughout, and she's still quiet when I finish talking. I can't read her face and have no idea what she's thinking. She blows out a breath and looks at me.

"Firstly, are you okay?" she asks.

I start to cry.

"I thought as much," she says, and she pulls me in for a hug. I hug her back and let the tears fall freely. I hadn't realised how much I needed someone to ask me that question, and I really don't have an answer. After a while she pulls back and takes one of my hands in hers.

"I don't know how to feel," I say. "It's all so complicated."

"I know, babe. Do you want advice right now or just a sounding board?"

"Advice, please. I have no fucking idea what I'm doing."

She laughs.

"Okay. My first question, do you see yourself with him long term? Marriage, babies, the whole thing. Can you see it?"

"Yes." My answer comes quickly. "I know we haven't known each other that long, but it's so easy with him, Mills. I don't have to pretend to be anyone but myself. He makes me feel safe, and secure, not just with him but within myself. If that makes any sense at all."

"It does. I've seen the two of you together and you look happy. I haven't seen you like that before. It was so obvious you two had feelings for each other, even if neither of you wanted to admit it. But waiting for a man, Ell?"

I groan. "I know, I know."

"I get that you don't want to lose him. But you should never have to wait for a man to want you. Why do you have to wait around and waste time while he figures himself out? He's a grown arse man! What if even after all of this he decides he doesn't want you? How long are you willing to wait?" she asks.

"Trust me, everything you've said I have told myself a thousand times. I know I'm worthy of more and I deserve better. But I just can't let him go, not yet. It might be stupid, but I just feel like it's worth waiting for."

"I know you want advice, but really, you know I will support you no matter what you decide to do. I can tell you to leave or stay, but it doesn't matter because it's up to you. If you want to wait, I'll be there for you. If you want to walk away, I'll be there and do what I can to help you move on. It's your decision."

"Thank you." Tears well in my eyes again.

"I will say this though, not to be one of those people but… I know how much you want to settle down and start a family. If you have to wait around for him to decide if he wants to be with you, you should probably take that sort of stuff into consideration."

With every fibre in my being, I hate that this is something I even have to consider. She's right though, I've always wanted a family. So much so I've started doing research into freezing my eggs and coming to terms with the idea of having children on my own.

"I know. Don't worry I've thought about it, and I'm looking into ways to protect my future in that regard. But I did tell him I can't wait for long, the whole 'my egg supply is drying up because I'm getting older' thing is partly why," I tell her. I didn't tell him that though, I can't even say the word 'relationship' without him freaking out, let alone the word 'baby'.

"How long are you prepared to wait?" she asks.

"A few months maybe? He's super stressed at work and doesn't know when he's getting this promotion. His dad's putting the pressure on him, and I know he's feeling overwhelmed. I know he needs to talk to Jade and settle the house. Honestly, I think he's scared of hurting me like he believes he hurt her. So yeah, I'll give him a few months. And then we'll see."

"Okay," she says, as simply as that. "Just keep me updated, and make sure you're taking care of yourself along the way. This man does not get to ruin you, you got it?"

"Yes, ma'am," I say, giving her a salute.

"Good." She squeezes my hand one last time before picking up her milo and having a sip. "So, there's something I kind of wanna talk to you about, while you're here."

"Oh?" I ask.

"Do you have any plans for early September?"

I think for a moment.

"Off the top of my head, nope, I don't have any plans for that time of year. Why? Are we going on a holiday?"

"I wish! No, I'm going to be in hospital for a few days, so I might need your help around the house." She almost sounds nervous.

"Oh. Yeah, of course. Is everything okay?"

"Yeah, everything's fine! Fantastic, actually."

"Okay… I'm confused," I tell her.

"Let's just say that when I come home from the hospital, you'll have a new title."

"Huh? What the fuck are you on about, woman? Stop being cryptic." I smack her on the leg, and she laughs.

"You'll be Auntie Ella."

One, two, three… it takes three seconds for me to register what she just said. And then I scream.

"OH MY GOD, YOU'RE PREGNANT!"

"I'm pregnant!" she screams back. And then I'm crying. And she's crying. And there's Milo spilling all over our shirts as we hug and cry and laugh.

"When did this happen? How did this happen? Wait, shut up, I know how this happened," I say as she opens her mouth to make some smart-arse comment. "When did you find out?"

"This morning." She wipes tears from her eyes. "It's super, super early. But there was a solid line on the test, and after everything we've gone through, this is our first positive result. I'm so scared, but I'm letting myself celebrate."

"Oh my God. I can't believe it." I squeal again. They have been trying for a baby for over a year and were going to start IVF treatments in a few months. "I'm so happy for you. Definitely let yourself celebrate, even if it's early. I'm sure it's normal to feel nervous and scared. Oh Mills, I'm so happy for you!" I hug her again. "Whatever you need from me, I'll be there to support you. Clay, too."

"Thanks, babe. You're the best friend I could ask for!"

"Likewise."

We spend the rest of the night talking about babies and thinking of ridiculous names Millie can suggest to Clay, purely to get a reaction from him. It's almost midnight before I get home, and when I'm lying in bed with a smile on my face, I'm glad to have something to think about other than my own personal dilemmas.

CHAPTER 33
Xavier

I haven't seen Ella in two weeks and it's killing me. I know it's my fault that I haven't seen her, but I didn't think it would be too difficult to cut back a little. I find myself reaching for my phone throughout the day and hoping she's messaged me, only to remember that we aren't supposed to be talking as much. Not to mention, I'm *so* horny. It seems I've gotten used to a more frequent and consistent sex life. I'm counting down the minutes until I get to see her this afternoon, but not just for the sex. I miss her.

Two hours on a Sunday is all I'm able to offer this week. She was busy this morning, with book shopping and brunch with Millie I believe, and I have work tonight. I hate it, but I guess it works in our favour and goes along with the whole 'spending less time together' arrangement. I'm finishing up with a few bits of housework when my phone rings. I look at the screen and it's my mum.

"Mum, hey," I say as I answer it.

"Hi Xav. How are you, dear?" she asks.

"Yeah good. Just tidying the house before heading out this afternoon. How are you?"

"I'm alright. Hey, listen, I'm calling about your dad."

"Dad? Is he alright?" I ask.

"Yes, yes, he's fine. Well, sort of. He's had a little bit of an accident and has hurt his back."

"Oh shit. What kind of accident?"

She sighs. "He was trying to lift a keg at the pub of course, and he completely threw his back out." I can almost hear her eyes rolling through the phone.

"Of course he was. I've told him so many times he needs to stop. How is he doing?" The man is coming up to 70 and yet he is still determined to try and do everything himself.

"I think his pride is hurt more than anything. You know what he's like." I murmur my agreement. "But he is on bed rest for a while and will require physical therapy for a few weeks to get better."

"Damn, he must have really done something."

"He sure did. Anyway, he wanted to talk to you about something and was hoping you'd be able to swing by the house this afternoon before your shift."

"This afternoon?" I ask. I'm supposed to be seeing Ella this afternoon. I've been looking forward to it all week.

"Yes, he said it was pretty important."

Important. Could this finally be the moment he hands over the reins? Shit. I have to go see him. *Ella is going to be so disappointed.*

"Okay. Yeah, that should be fine. I'll come around at say, 3pm?"

"Perfect, I'll let him know. Thanks, Xav."

"No worries, Mum. I'll see you later."

"Bye!"

I end the call, my mind spinning with possibilities. I'm not going to get my hopes up because this has happened too many times, but this could be the moment. Years of hard work and persistence could finally be paying off. Though there's one thing I have to do first. I pull up Ella's contact details and call her. She picks up after two rings.

"Hey, you," she says as she answers the phone. I can hear a lot of people in the background so she must still be at the bookstore.

"Hey, right back."

"What's up?"

I sigh.

"How mad are you going to be if I have to cancel this afternoon?" I ask.

She's quiet on the other end of the phone for just a moment.

"Has something come up?" she asks quietly.

"Yeah, my dad hurt his back at work. He's fine, on bed rest and needs some physio, but he wants to meet with me before my shift tonight. Mum says it's important and I don't know if I'll have time afterwards to see you before starting work."

"Oh. Well, yeah of course you have to go. I hope he's okay. Do you know what he wants to talk about?"

"She didn't say. I'm hoping today is *the* day. So, keep your fingers crossed for me I guess."

"I will. You'll have to keep me posted."

"Definitely. I'm really sorry for cancelling, I promise I'll make it up to you soon."

"It's fine," she says. I know it's not fine, but she wouldn't admit it. "Maybe you can come over this week sometime if you have a night off."

"Yeah of course, I'll let you know soon what my availability is like." Christ, it sounds like I'm trying to schedule a bloody business meeting.

"Sounds good. Well, I guess I'll have to go and find a book to read this afternoon instead." She chuckles.

"I hope you pick a good one," I tell her.

"I'm sure I will. Give your dad my best wishes. I'll talk to you later."

"Sure thing." I probably won't tell him, mostly because neither Mum nor Dad know about Ella. "Enjoy the rest of your night. Bye."

"Bye."

I breathe out a deep sigh. I know she's disappointed, I could hear it in her voice. I'm disappointed, too. Hopefully our schedules match up this week and I'm able to go and make it up to her.

I have just under two hours until I have to be with my parents, so I whip up a quick lunch and then get to finishing the housework before driving over to their place. It takes about 20 minutes to get there and I'm feeling nervous. I really hope this is it. I pull into the driveway and take a deep, calming breath before getting out of the car and heading up to the front porch. I don't bother knocking; instead I open the door and yell "hello" as I walk in.

Mum comes bounding down the hallway to greet me. I wrap her up in a hug.

"Hi, my son." She reaches up and pats me on the cheek. She's always done that, ever since I was a child.

"Hey, Mum. How's he doing?" I ask.

"Fine, grumbling like the old man he is."

"You're older than him."

"Semantics. You'd think he was on his death bed the way he keeps going on. Typical man baby."

I laugh. My parents have been married for over 40 years and I've never known a couple like them. Still just as in love with each other today as they were when they got married.

"Sounds about right. Is he in bed?" I ask as I nod my head toward their bedroom.

"Yep, go on in, he knows you're coming."

I swallow hard as I walk down the hallway and stop outside their bedroom door. I give myself a quick internal peptalk and walk in. Dad is sitting up in bed, propped up by a few pillows, with his laptop open on a pillow in his lap. The man really doesn't know the meaning of rest.

"Still on your computer, do you even know how to relax and recover?" I ask him.

"If you must know," he says, "I'm actually watching a movie, not working. So, shush." He shows me the screen and I have no idea what the movie is, but I am genuinely shocked.

"Oh, well jokes on me, then. How are you feeling?" I ask.

"Bit sore. And I tell you what, I'm already sick of being in this bed." He grumbles.

"I bet. I can't recall the last time I heard of you being in bed later than 7am."

"Mmm." He groans in reply.

"So," I start, as I sit on the edge of the bed. "What did you want to talk about?"

He sighs and closes his laptop, putting it aside.

"I know you've been at me to retire for a long time," he starts.

"I haven't been *at* you, I've just gently encouraged you."

"Same shit."

I laugh.

"You've been working really hard, and I can see how much the place means to you."

I nod. "I want nothing more than to continue your legacy. Jimmies is my second home."

"I know, mate. I really thought I had a few years left in me, you know? But as soon as I felt my back give out, I knew it was time. Your mother and I have decided it's time."

My heart is pounding so hard I'm surprised he can't hear it.

"Are you telling me… you're retiring?" I ask.

"Yes. It's time for me to hand over the reins. Jimmies is yours, Xav."

I choke out a laugh. Finally, I've been waiting years for this moment. Years of planning and new ideas and possibilities. Years of proving myself and doing everything I can to make him see I'm worthy. *It's really happening.*

"Thank you. I'll make you proud, I promise. I won't let you down." I'm surprised to feel myself choking up and getting emotional.

"I know you will. You're a good man, Xavier. I know you think I haven't been listening to you and your ideas for a while, but I have. I've been keeping a catalogue of everything you've suggested and everything you've done, waiting for the right moment. Selfishly, I just needed to be ready. With the right focus and motivation, which I know you have plenty of, I can see you bringing the place up to a standard I was never able to. I'm excited to see what you're going to do."

My eyes well up and I hastily wipe the tears away.

"This means so much to me, Dad. Truly."

"I'd give you a hug, but it hurts." He laughs and the winces from the pain.

I chuckle and then stand up to plant a big smooch on his slightly wrinkled forehead.

"Rest up. Spend this time in bed to come up with some fun things to do during retirement."

"Yeah, yeah. Oh also, I took the liberty of having your shift covered tonight. Go and celebrate with your friends or something. A lot is going to change from now on, I hope you're ready knuckle down and give it all you've got." He winks at me.

"You know I will. Jimmies is in safe hands. And thanks." I know exactly who I want to celebrate with tonight. "I'll pop in after the lunch shift on Monday and we can talk business," I say.

"Sounds good, I won't be going anywhere." He gestures to the bed.

I smile at him and leave the room, closing the door gently. Mum is standing in the hallway, eyes gleaming and silently clapping with glee.

"Oh, I'm so happy! I've been waiting for this moment for years!" she says as she pulls me into a tight hug.

"Me too, Mum. Me too."

I hastily say my goodbyes and once I'm in my car, I pull out my phone and make a call.

"Hello?" she answers.

"Hey Ell, so it turns out I have the night off…"

CHAPTER 34
Ella

I'm absolutely over the moon for Xavier and his new promotion, but damn I wish he still had a bit more time for me. I know we agreed to talk less and see each other less, but I thought maybe with the new role we'd still see each other somewhat regularly. Despite his new hours supposedly being more 9 to 5, he's working more than ever. Other than a quick dinner nine days ago and a Sunday afternoon hook-up, we haven't spent any time together. I know he has to work hard to establish himself at first, but the little voice in my head keeps whispering to me that this is coming to an end and he's just going to disappear. I know it's my own anxieties causing these feelings and I'm trying to not overthink it and make up scenarios in my head, but old habits are hard to break.

When he came over three weeks ago to tell me his dad had decided to retire, I'd never seen him so happy and so excited. His whole face had lit up and honestly, I think I fell for him even more. *Turns out a man with passion and ambition gets me going, who would have thought?* He had wanted to celebrate, and he did so by worshipping my body for hours. It got to the point where I had to tell him I couldn't handle any more as my body had become so over sensitive, that the slightest whisper of a kiss could have had me shattering. He stayed the night and I had savoured every second in his arms. We did agree to no more sleepovers, but once again we broke our own rule. He had told me the next few months would be difficult, and that he had a lot of work to do, so I knew we would see each other even less. It's not like he didn't warn me. I also told him I'd give him time to sort out all of the other stuff going on in his life, so on top of the new role, I shouldn't be surprised that we have less contact.

It's now Sunday, three weeks since he was handed the job and three weeks since our last proper moment together. He's planned to come over tonight for dinner, so I've decided to go all out and cook us something rather than just get takeaway like we usually would. He always teases me about how much pasta I eat so I've decided to show him why I eat so much by cooking him my favourite pasta dish, roast pumpkin ravioli with burnt butter and sage sauce, complete with homemade garlic bread. I first ate this dish when I travelled to Ireland of all places, and it has been a staple in my diet ever since.

I've gone all out for this dinner. I figured other than our night of passion, we hadn't really had a moment to properly celebrate his news. I've cleared up the dining room table—which is unheard of as I eat almost every meal on the couch—and set it up nicely with matching cutlery. I even lit a candle, but I'm still debating if that's too romantic or not. I bought a bottle of wine that cost more than ten dollars, and I have a tub of *Ben and Jerry's* in the freezer for dessert. I really hope he likes it.

I've finished preparing the garlic bread, I have the oven preheating, and the saucepan on the stove, ready to boil the water for the pasta. I check my phone for the time, it's 6:15pm and he's due to be here at 6:30pm. *Perfect.* I go to my room and do another outfit check, knowing full well he could care less about what I'm wearing, but still, I want to look cute. I've opted for the blue sundress I wore back when we first met. I know how much he liked it and I really want to make an impression on him tonight. I don't know why, maybe I just want to remind him that I'm here.

I head back into the kitchen to put the garlic bread in the oven and put a frying pan on the heat, ready to start making the sauce. I go through the motions, and when I'm sure the sauce is almost ready, I put the pasta in the pot. It only takes a few minutes to cook, so I take that time to turn off the oven and get two plates out for serving. I check the time again, it's 6:35pm. That's fine, he's probably just stuck in traffic.

I get the garlic bread out of the oven and put it on a plate on the table and cover it to keep it hot. I drain the pasta and add it to the pan with the sauce. I spoon it onto the plates and then grate some parmesan cheese over the top, then place them on the table and fill our glasses with wine. I take a photo of my set up and send it to Millie with the caption #wifeme. She laughs in response and tells me to have the best night.

I check the time again, it's now 6:47pm. *Okay, that's odd for Xavier.* He's normally quite punctual. As I'm thinking of an excuse as to why he could be running late, my phone rings in my hand, and it's him.

"Hey! I was just about to message you. Everything okay?" I ask.

"Hey Ell, I'm so sorry. I'm not going to be able to get to your place for a while, I'm running a little late."

"Oh." My heart sinks. "Well… how late do you think you'll be?"

"I'm not sure. I won't make it for dinner, I know that much. But I can probably come over later. I know what I'd like for dessert," he says with a seductive chuckle.

I take a subtle but deep breath to keep my emotions in check. I plan a cute little dinner date and he's now bailing on me, but still expects to come over later in the night to fuck. I know that's literally what this 'friends with benefits' arrangement is supposed to be, but I thought maybe now that he'd gotten the promotion, it would be different. I take a second deep breath.

"Um, well, I had actually planned a celebratory dinner for you tonight."

"Aw really? That's sweet. Can we do a rain check? We can get our usual takeaway the next time I come over."

Breathe in. Breathe out. Don't get emotional.

"No, I mean I—I already cooked dinner. Tonight. For us, for you. It was going to be a surprise," I say. The line is quiet on the other end for a little bit.

"Oh."

"Yeah," I whisper. "But it's fine. You're working, I get it. Really. I should have told you what I was planning. I'll just… have leftovers now for lunch tomorrow. Lucky me!" I try to laugh but it comes out strained.

"Ell, I am really sorry. Things just got busy, and I lost track of time. I can still come over after I'm done but I don't know what time that will be."

"I know. It's fine. Um, maybe we just won't worry about tonight. I should probably have an early night anyway. Gotta work tomorrow," I say. It's getting harder to keep my emotions at bay and a single tear escapes. As much as I want to see him—I *really* want to see him—I don't want him coming here just to fuck me and then leave. *I'm worth more than that. I deserve better than that.*

"Okay," he mumbles. "I'll try and free up some time this week to see you. I'm sorry, again."

"I'll talk to you during the week, then," I say as more tears escape and start streaming down my face. I really hope he can't tell that I'm crying.

"Goodnight, Ella."

"Night."

I hang up the phone and let the tears free fall, just like my therapist told me to. I fall onto my couch and curl up in a blanket to gain some semblance of comfort. I'm not crying loudly, there's no sobbing or heaving. The tears fall silently and trickle down my cheeks and onto my chest. I look at the dining table set for our dinner, the candle still flickering in the dim light, and our dinner still sitting there ready to be eaten. It only sends a fresh wave of tears streaming down my face.

It shouldn't hurt this much. This hurts more than when I got stood up by that douchebag, whose name I can't even remember now. I shouldn't be this upset over a stupid dinner but I am. So what? He got caught up at work, he didn't know I had dinner planned for us. We're only supposed to be physically involved. It's not like he's my boyfriend or husband...

I guess I just thought I meant more to him, especially after we confessed our feelings. I know why this hurts so much—it's because I fucking miss him.

I allow a few more minutes to cry and feel sorry for myself before heading into the bathroom to wash my face. I look at my reflection in the mirror and I just look tired. I take a few more deep breaths and head back out to the kitchen. Then, I scrape the pasta into takeaway containers. I'm not hungry anymore, but at least I do have lunch for work tomorrow. I blow out the candle. Normally I'd make a wish, but honestly, I'm too defeated to even try. I throw everything else in the sink, grab both glasses of wine, and head into my bedroom, ready to do what I always do when a man lets me down; escape into my current fantasy novel to be with fictional men instead. My phone buzzes and it's a message from Xavier.

XAVIER

What did you cook for dinner tonight?

I consider it for a moment before replying with the picture I sent to Millie. The table set for two with the candle flickering and dinner ready for us both. Fuck it. Let him see the effort I put in.

ELLA

My favourite pasta, the one that I told you about.

I put the phone down, take a massive gulp of wine and open my book, gently of course, so as to not crack the spine. After a few moments, my phone starts ringing and surprise, it's Xavier. I stare at it for a moment, before putting it on silent and ignoring the call. I don't have anything else to say tonight, I'm tired. My phone lights up as he tries ringing again, and still, I ignore it. After a few minutes a new message comes through.

XAVIER

I'm so sorry, Ell. It looks amazing.
I wish I could be there.

"Yeah, but you're not. You could be, but you're not." I mutter to myself. I ignore the message, switching my phone 'to do not disturb' mode, and finish the first glass of wine. Finally, I settle into my book, hoping that magic battles and mystical beasts will help me escape the feeling of complete and utter disappointment.

CHAPTER 35
Xavier

God, I'm such an arsehole.

By 9:45pm, I'm finally back home after another gruelling day at the office. I open my phone for the hundredth time and look at the photo Ella sent me again. A lump forms in my throat. She cooked me her favourite meal and set the table with a goddamn candle and everything. I bet she even had dessert. All to celebrate me and my promotion. And I fucking bailed on her because of that promotion. To top it all off, I offered her a late-night booty call instead. *I'm an absolute prick.*

I've tried calling her five times now and I don't get an answer. I don't blame her, to be honest. I wouldn't want to talk to me, either. I really should have called her earlier to let her know I wasn't coming, but I got stuck on a call with the manager of a new brewery that I'm hoping to start stocking, and I lost track of time.

This is exactly the sort of thing I was worried about happening. Having to cancel plans because of work. I have to put the business before anything else—I have to make my dad proud. I don't want to hurt anyone along the way and that's what I've already done.

I close down the message and tilt my head back against the couch, sighing. I don't know how to do this. I need to talk to someone.

I pull up my group chat with the guys and ask if any of them are free tomorrow night for a beer after work. At Jimmies, of course, since I'll likely be working late, but I can take an hour when they get there.

I open up my message thread with Ella and look at the photo once more. I consider calling her again, but I know she won't answer. I need to give her some space, so I settle for a text instead.

XAVIER

I'll call you after work tomorrow.
Sweet dreams, Ell x

She doesn't reply, and again, I'm not shocked. I open the group chat with the guys and by some sort of miracle, they are all free for a beer after work tomorrow. Why is it that when we want to plan a bigger get together, it takes months to coordinate something, but a last-minute knock off works out fine with a day's notice? Weird, but whatever. I'll take the good luck. They all plan to meet me at Jimmies by 5:30pm.

I have a quick shower, my mind wandering to the fact that I could be in Ella's shower with her right now, and I'm pissed at myself even more. I drag myself out of the shower and collapse onto my bed, falling into a fitful sleep because I can't shut off my goddamn brain.

It's right on 5:30pm and all the guys are here. I'm still shocked we were able to orchestrate last minute plans.

"So Xav, what's up? It's not like you to organise a spontaneous catch up," Jake says as a beer is placed in front of each of us. Lena is working tonight, and I don't necessarily want her hearing my conversation, so I move us over to a table in the beer garden towards the back corner.

"I know, I just feel like I need some advice. I've got a bit going on at the moment and… I'm a bit lost," I say.

"Yeah, we thought as much," Ben adds.

"So, what's been happening?" asks Dale.

I launch into the story. First, I talk about the job. They all know I've finally taken over, and I tell them about how much focus it is taking up and about all the stuff I want to achieve. I tell them about Dad's legacy and how I want to make him and the rest of the family proud. I then jump into the Jade stuff—how I feel like I failed her, and our relationship, and I'm scared that I'll do it again.

"Is there a reason you're scared about it happening again, Xav? Like, have you met someone?" asks Jake.

I close my eyes and inhale deeply.

"Yeah." I breathe.

"Ayo, our boy's been holding out on us!" yells Dale. "Give us the details mate, she hot?"

"Jesus, Dale. Of course, he holds out on us if that's the first thing you ask," says Ben.

"What?" Dale shrugs, but then looks at me and sees the look on my face, which can only be read as frustration. He raises his hands in defeat. "Okay, okay. Sorry. Tell us about her."

So, I do. I tell them how I met Ella, how we started out as friends, and then after both of us admitting our attraction to one another, we started a physical relationship. I spared them the details, much to Dale's disappointment, and told them how eventually we both developed feelings.

"And now I'm running Jimmies and have less time to spend with her; I have too much riding on this job to be able to commit to something properly. I'm scared that if I say yes, let's try, I'm just going to break her heart, like I did to Jade. I don't want to lose Ella, and I'm hanging on to her but not giving her what she deserves, which isn't fair on her." As soon as I finish the sentence, I feel a little bit lighter, like even just talking about it a little bit has eased some of the pressure. They're all silent for a while and then both Ben and Dale look at Jake. He is the wisest and most mature of us all, and I almost laugh at the fact we are all looking to him for advice.

"Well… you're certainly a busy boy." He laughs, we all do. "I get why you're stressed, Xav. Ella sounds really great, and I love that you've connected with someone new. I'm really happy for you."

"Why do I hear a 'but' coming?" I ask.

He sighs.

"But… you've been waiting to take over this place for years. You've been preparing, planning, and dreaming, and it's finally yours. You're working overtime to establish yourself quickly, and after everything you just said, it's obvious you're…" he pauses.

"Distracted." Ben finishes.

"Yeah," says Jake. "I think you need to figure out what your priority is right now and make that your focus. You're right, you can't keep Ella waiting and wondering when you'll commit to her, and it's obvious you need to work on overcoming your fear of disappointing people. So, I think—and I hate to tell you this—you need to make a choice as to where you are focusing all of your energy. Is it on Jimmies? Or is it on Ella?" He smiles sadly.

"I hate that plan," I mumble and take a swig of my beer. "I don't want to give her up."

"So, then continue to run this place as it has been when your dad was in charge," Dale says.

"I don't want to do that either."

"Trying to do it all isn't going to work, mate. You'll burn yourself out by trying and to be quite frank, it's selfish of you to keep holding Ella at arm's length when she's ready to give you everything and you're not ready to reciprocate," Ben adds. We all look at him.

"What?" he asks. "Just because I'm quiet, it doesn't mean I can't impart some wisdom."

I huff a laugh, but then really take in what he said. I asked Ella to wait for me to figure things out, but that was before Dad retired, and now I have a huge responsibility to not only my dad, but the community here at Jimmies.

"You're right. I am being selfish. Even before Dad retired, I was selfish in asking her to wait for me. I just…" I trail off.

"You don't want to lose her. I get it," says Jake. "Do you love her?"

I hesitate to give them an answer, which seems to be an answer in itself.

"Damn, Xav," whispers Ben. He looks at me with sympathy.

"I know I give you a lot of shit, mate, but I didn't realise you loved this chick. That's rough, man. I'm sorry," says Dale. He presses his mouth into a thin line and gives me a sad smile.

"If you love her, Xav, you have to give her your all. And if you can't, you need to walk away before she falls even further." Jake pats me on the shoulder.

"I know. I know." I sigh. I look down at my beer, hoping the boys don't catch sight of the tears lining my eyes that are ready to fall.

"Hey man, it'll be okay. We're here for you." I guess Jake saw the tears. He pulls me into a hug, and I allow a few of the tears to fall. It's not that I'm ashamed to cry, I just don't want to cry at work. He holds me for a moment and then he pulls away.

"You got this," he says as he grabs me by the shoulder. I laugh.

"I really don't, but I appreciate the confidence nonetheless."

We finish our beers and I walk them out to their cars, and to my surprise, they all give me a hug this time. Even Dale gives me a proper one. I wave them off and head back inside to my office and sit down in my chair. I lean back and close my eyes. Deep down, I know what I have to do. I really, really don't want to fucking do it, though.

I told Ella I would call her tonight, so I pull out my phone. It rings four times and just when I think she won't answer, she picks up on the last ring.

"Hello," she answers. Already, she sounds flat.

"Hey, Ell. Hope this isn't a bad time to call?"

"No, it's fine. I was just reading."

"Okay. That's good. Uhh..." *I hate this, I hate this, I hate this.* "Are you busy after work tomorrow? I wanna come over, just to talk about stuff." I hope that didn't sound too foreboding. I know for someone with anxiety, telling them you want to talk about something can be incredibly triggering.

"Um, yeah. I'll be free after 7pm."

"Okay, thanks."

"Just make sure you give me a heads up if you're not going to make it."

"Yep, I will. I promise." A fair enough request given how much of a dick I was last night.

"Okay. Well, I just got to a good part in my book, so I'm gonna go. I'll see you tomorrow," she says. *She sounds so… I can't think of the word. Tired? Over it? Sick of my shit?*

"Okay, no problem. Have a good night."

"Bye."

"Bye," I say, but she had already hung up.

CHAPTER 36
Ella

It's 7:05pm and there's a knock on my door. *Well, at least he's shown up tonight.* I've actually been home since 5pm, but I didn't want him here for dinner. I'm still too upset over Sunday night to have him over for a meal. I get up from the couch and walk over to the door. I lift my chin and straighten my spine, trying to make myself appear indifferent. I open the door and there he is, still in his work attire, looking a little dishevelled. He's not leaning on the doorframe this time, and he doesn't greet me with a bright smile like normal. Something tells me this is going to be a difficult conversation.

"Hey."

"Hey. Can I come in?"

"Yeah."

I step aside for him to walk in and close the door behind him, taking a moment to settle myself before turning and facing him. He's staring at me with something that looks very much like guilt in his eyes. I hold his stare for a while before he takes two steps forward and draws me into his arms. He crushes me into him and it's with instinct that I wrap my arms around his waist. I don't know how long we stand there not saying anything, and just holding each other. Eventually, I'm the one to break the hug. I step back and I don't look at him as I walk over to the couch and sit, wrapping myself in my blanket.

"So, what do you want to talk about?" I ask.

He walks over and sits next to me on the couch. He looks like he's about to take my hand, but he hesitates and decides not to. He clears his throat.

"First, I want to say sorry again for the other night. If I had known that you'd gone to all that effort for me, I never would have cancelled on you."

"It's fine. I should have told you what I had planned."

"No, it's not fine, and don't try and blame yourself just because you didn't tell me your plan. I was an arsehole, it's as simple as that. And for me to just assume I could come over later in the night to fuck, after everything you'd done for me? I'm so sorry."

I'm about to say it's fine, but I hold my tongue. He upset me, and so he should know exactly how he made me feel.

"You're right, it's not fine. We hadn't seen each other properly in three weeks, and you ditched me. If you had called earlier, it might have been fine, but I felt like an afterthought. And when you said you could still come over later in the night, it made me feel cheap. Like… I was only worth your time if you got to fuck me."

He looks as though I've just shattered him with my words.

"Ella, that's not how it is at all."

"That may be so," I say, "but it's how you made me feel in the moment, regardless of it not being your intention."

"It wasn't. I never want to make you feel as though I'm only with you for the sex. That's not how I feel about you. You're my friend, first and foremost. You know I think the world of you. But you're right, and I don't want to invalidate your feelings by trying to tell you that you shouldn't feel that way. I can't tell you how sorry I am. Truly."

"I know."

We're quiet for a moment, and when I look at him, he's staring at the floor. He looks defeated.

"That's not all you wanted to talk about, is it?" I ask tentatively.

"No, it's not." He pauses. "I wanted to talk about us."

"Okay. What about us?"

"When we first started this, we promised each other it would be a strictly physical relationship—friends with benefits, if you will. That obviously changed, we both admit that."

"Yeah," I whisper. I don't know where this is going, but my gut is telling me it's not good.

"This all happened before Dad retired. I thought I could do it all, you know? Establish myself in the new role and make my family proud; work hard to make Jimmies the best damn pub around. I also wanted to make you happy and see if we could turn this 'friendship' we have into something more. I thought once I got the job I could do it." His throat bobs.

"But?"

"But I can't. And I've had to think about where I really need to put my focus right now." He looks at me with unshed tears in his eyes.

"And I'm not that focus." I say.

"I can't give you the love and attention you deserve, Ell. I've been waiting for years to take over Jimmies, and it's finally happened. It's my dream. And then you came along at a time where I was faced with all of this extra responsibility and this extra pressure to achieve something great. You deserve someone who can make you their priority. Someone who won't ditch you because they worked too late and can commit to you wholeheartedly. I can't give you that right now. Look at what's happened already, I've barely had time to talk to you or see you, and the first opportunity I have, I bail. I've already hurt you; I can't do it again."

A few tears slide down his cheek and I resist the urge to swipe them away. It's not my job to comfort him, not when my own heart is breaking.

"I understand," I murmur. I can't find any other words to say. I suspected this was coming—I knew, deep down, this would be ending.

"I just really need to focus on the business right now, I can't afford any distractions."

My head snaps up at that.

"Distractions." I repeat. "I'm sorry… are you insinuating that what I am to you is a distraction?" I can feel my anger bubbling to the surface.

"No, I didn't mean it like that—" he backtracks.

"Yes, you did. Trying to give me attention is distracting you from your work. Awesome. It's nice to know that while I'm over here being supportive, encouraging and caring for you more than I have anyone else, you simply see me as a distraction." Tears well in my eyes and fuck, I wish they would go away. I can't cry right now. Words are bubbling to the surface, and I can feel myself losing control.

"Ell, please."

"I love you!" I tell him, tears escaping. "That's probably the worst thing for you to hear right now, but I fucking love you Xavier."

He's gone completely still. He looks at me like a broken man, torn between one dream and another.

"You love me," he whispers.

I nod.

"Yes. I love you. I tried so hard not to fall, I promised you that I wouldn't. I promised myself, because I knew that falling for a man who couldn't love me back was destined to end in disaster."

"Ella… look at me." I shake my head. "Look at me." He places his hand on my cheek and turns my head so he's looking me in the eye.

"I wish I could give you what you want. You know how much you mean to me." He's openly crying now.

"But not enough." I whisper.

He drops his hand and his face crumples, and my heart shatters along with it.

"I can't do it all. I can't lead you on and keep you waiting around for me to sort my shit out. It's not fair. You deserve so much more and it's selfish of me to keep you around, just because I'm desperate to hold on to you."

I turn away from him then.

"I wish things could be different. I wish we'd met in like six months' time and the business had settled, and the timing was perfect." He mumbles.

"The timing is perfect for me." I state.

"I know."

"So… what? We just completely cut contact. No communication at all, never seeing each other again?" I ask.

"I… I don't know." He ponders. "At first, no contact is probably the best."

We sit in silence for a few minutes more and I can't handle it anymore.

"I need to be alone right now, Xavier. Can you go? Please?" I beg.

"Yeah. Of course." He gets up off of the couch, slowly, like this conversation has aged him 30 years. I get up and follow him to the door on shaking legs, my body on the brink of an emotional breakdown.

We get to the door, and he turns to me and pulls me into his arms again, gently this time. I hold on to him because this might just be the last time I do. I inhale his scent, committing it to memory because I never want to forget how comforting the smell of him is. I look up at him, both of us still crying. I memorise every inch of his face. When I can't take anymore, when my heart starts hurting too much, I pull away, wiping the tears from my cheeks.

"Goodbye, Xavier," I whisper.

"Goodbye, Ella. I'm sorry." He doesn't bother to wipe the tears from his face as he turns and walks out the door.

A small sob escapes my lips as I close the door behind him before he can turn around for a final look, not knowing if my heart could handle it. I throw myself back down on the couch and cry, and cry, and cry. Finally, I call Millie.

"Hey, Ell!" she answers.

"Millie…" I sob.

"Oh, fuck. I'll be there in 20 minutes."

CHAPTER 37
Ella

"I really need you to focus, Ella. This has to get done today."

"Yep. Will do," I say through clenched teeth.

"Good. It really should have been done last week, but I guess I'm not surprised. You have been a bit slow lately," my boss says.

"You never gave me a deadline for this task. Sorry for not realising it was such a priority," I say back. I am not in the mood for this today.

"You should have asked. Try and show some initiative in the future," she replies and walks back over to her desk.

"This is above my paygrade," I mutter under my breath.

She's asking me to come up with a presentation for a Year 8 class about their new English text. It's a book I love, and so she decided I could do the presentation instead. Normally I would be excited, but now I know it was just because she couldn't be bothered and palmed it off to me, even though working with classes is not in my job description. She told me two weeks ago there was no rush on it, but now there apparently is, and it's my fault because I didn't ask for a specific date. This is really not the week to be pushing me. I am on edge, and I know it won't take much to send me over.

Four days. It has been four days since I confessed to Xavier that I loved him, and he walked out of my house. Millie came over straight after I called her and listened to me rant and cry until late into the night. I've cried myself to sleep every night since, and every day I wake up feeling miserable.

Unwanted. Not enough.

I wish I was able to take some time off of work to just reset, but it isn't worth the guilt trip I will get for not being here. Plus, the work will pile up, and my boss will complain about how my absence has caused her stress, and the time I spent at home trying to improve my mental state will be wasted. I just need to get through the rest of today and I will have all weekend to do nothing but wallow in self-pity.

I spend the rest of the morning trying to finish this presentation, and finally, it's lunch time. As soon as the school bell rings, I am out of my chair and heading towards the staff room. Millie is in our usual corner, and I plonk myself down on the chair next to her, leaning my head back and taking a deep, steadying breath.

"How's your day going?" Millie asks around a mouthful of pizza.

"Fucking fantastic," I mutter.

"Is she busting your arse again? Want me to fight her?"

I chuckle.

"She is, but it's fine. I'm used to it. I just want to get through today without her lecturing me again and then I can spend my weekend sitting in misery."

"Ell, you shouldn't have to put up with her bullshit. I know you love working here, and I know that's mostly because we get to see each other every day, but I think you should really look at getting a job elsewhere. You've dealt with this long enough. You deserve better."

"I know. I just… I hate change. I hate instability. At least working here, I know what to expect, even though it's not great. Better the devil you know, right?"

"Nope. Sorry babe, I love you, but you have to start doing better for yourself. At least have a look for other jobs. Do it for me? Please? I want to see you happy and thriving, and right now, that just ain't happening. And it won't if you stay here. You know I'm right."

I sigh. I know she is. I haven't been happy here for a long time. But change is scary, and with my anxiety and self-worth at an all-time low right now, the idea of starting somewhere new terrifies me.

"I'll look, I promise. I doubt there's anything out there, though. Do you know how hard it is to find a job in libraries?"

"You never know. I just want to see you happy, Ell."

"Me, too," I tell her.

The rest of my lunch break speeds on and by the time I get back to the library, I am two minutes over my allocated 30-minute window. I look over at my boss as I sit back down at my desk, and she looks at the clock, then her watch, and shakes her head at me. I ignore her and settle into getting my presentation finished.

Half an hour later, she leaves the library with no explanation. I take the opportunity to have a look online at available library jobs. There aren't many, but there is one that looks interesting. It's a Library Manager role, overseeing a small primary school library and one staff member. I don't have to have a teaching degree, just experience in a similar role. It sounds perfect, but I'm still hesitant. I send myself the job listing and then close the tab just as my boss walks back into the library, right over to my desk.

"Ella, how is the presentation going?" she asks.

"I'm almost done, just finishing up the slides."

"Okay. Look, I've just spoken with management about how you're going. There are concerns."

"Concerns about what?"

"Your productivity and commitment to the job."

I stare at her blankly.

"Care to elaborate?" I ask.

"You aren't meeting deadlines, you're late coming back from breaks, you spend a lot of time talking with people. You don't show any initiative and get your back up whenever I ask you to do something. I am just not seeing the effort on your part, and I think perhaps you need to think if this is the right job for you."

My mouth has dropped as I look at her and wonder at the absolute audacity of this woman.

"I'm sorry… are you suggesting I am not fit for this role?" I ask, angrily.

She says nothing and just looks at me, expectantly, like she wants me to agree.

Normally, the people pleaser in me would just sit back and take this 'advice' and get on with the job. But this time, I can't. I am so sick of this woman trying to make me feel like I am not good at what I do. I am sick of her making me feel worthless, and that I am merely the help when really this place wouldn't function without me. I am done with staying quiet when people walk all over me.

"No, you know what? I do everything you ask me to. I do more than is required in my role. I know I am good at this job. If I don't get things done on your timeline, it's because you've failed to give me a deadline. You say I come back late from lunch, but you also know that I often don't get to lunch until 15 minutes have passed because I'm dealing with students. So really, I get 15 minutes to eat my lunch most days. As for the initiative, I have plenty. You just don't let me use it because I am 'just the technician' and need to stay in my lane. Perhaps you should focus more on your management style and less on whether I am fit for this role, because if you look around, everything gets done. I do my job, I do it well. If you can't see that, then that is on you. Not me."

She just stares at me, blinking like she can't believe I am actually standing up for myself. She shakes her head and starts walking back to her desk.

"Just make sure to get the presentation to me by the end of the day."

My chest is rising rapidly as I take in deep breaths. Of course, she is completely ignoring everything I said. I know she's threatened by me. It should be flattering, but I'm over it. I deserve respect, and I know that I will never get it from her. I open up the job listing again and start updating my resumé. Millie was right, I deserve better than this. *It's time for a change.*

CHAPTER 38
Ella

THREE MONTHS LATER

"So, Ella, how have you been since we've last spoken?" Jane asks. It's been three months since I said goodbye to Xavier, and this is my third therapy appointment with her since it happened.

"I've been good—better," I say. "I feel as though I'm finally starting to feel like myself again."

"That's wonderful!" she exclaims. "What have you been doing to help yourself heal?"

Heal. I don't like that word, not in this context. It makes it sound like what I went through was some sort of major traumatic experience. I said that to Jane once, and she said that everyone's pain is subjective. I was hurt and upset, and my heart does need to heal. I tentatively agreed, but I still don't like it. It makes me feel like I'm broken.

"I've been journaling again, that's helped. Any time I feel like reaching out to him I write in my journal instead. I've been spending time with friends more, helping Millie with baby things. I've been reading more. I've even dabbled in writing just to see if I can."

"That's great. And how is the new job going?"

By some miracle, within a week of applying for the Library Manager job, I had a phone call telling me I was successful in gaining the position.

I was ecstatic. Telling my boss I was quitting was one of the best feelings I've ever had. Naturally, she tried to claim the success of my new manager role as her own, claiming to have mentored me into being capable of such a position, and encouraging me to spread my wings and search for better opportunities. I just snorted and walked away.

"It's amazing. It's just me and one other older lady working there, and it's just so much fun. Despite having more responsibility, I feel less stressed or anxious than ever. I can't believe I put up with so much shit from that old place for so long—I don't know how I lived with that feeling every single day for six years."

"I'm so glad to hear, really. I can see for myself the change in you and it's great to see it. Have you heard from Xavier at all?" she asks.

"Not really. Just a couple of messages here and there just checking in. It's nothing more than a 'how are you' and a 'yeah, I'm good, and you?' sort of exchange. I'll admit though, I've been following his progress on Instagram with the pub, and he's done so much work. He's doing really, really well. I'm happy for him."

She waits. I sigh.

"I miss him." I admit.

"I guessed that. And it's completely normal and valid. You're grieving a friendship and you fell in love. Once you do that, it's hard to fall out of it."

"Impossible, is more like it," I mutter. She laughs.

"If he approached you now and said he wanted to be with you and commit to you fully, what would you say?" she asks, tilting her head.

I open my mouth to answer but stop myself. My immediate response is yes, I'd take him back in a heartbeat. I force myself to sit with the question and really think about it, like Jane probably wants me to. She knows what my immediate response would be; her subtle smile tells me that.

What would I do if Xavier showed up on my doorstep and wanted me back? If he promised me commitment and love, and everything I wanted from him the first time. *Could I take him back?* Maybe. I know what I deserve, in life and in love and in everything in between. He would have to prove it one thousand percent that he was ready to commit to me fully.

"If he could prove to me that he was in this for real this time, then maybe. It would take a lot of work on his part to convince me, though," I tell her.

"I thought as much. You've worked hard these last few months to convince yourself of what you truly deserve. Make him work for it," she says with a wink. I love it when she says things like that—it makes me feel like I'm talking to a friend, not a trained professional.

"Oh, he will. But that's if he comes back to me at all. I'm not going to wait around and hope. In fact, I have a date lined up for later in the week. I'm not super excited for it, but I figured I might as well give it a go. It's another set up from Millie and Clay. Not a blind date this time, since I refuse to do that ever again." *No fucking way.*

"That's great, Ella. What's his name?"

"Logan. He seems nice, and I don't have a good reason to not meet up with him. So, we will see how I go."

"When is it?"

"Friday night. He's picking me up from Millie's house and taking me to some up-and-coming bar he's just discovered." I have four days to prepare myself. I still hate dating.

"Well, I look forward to hearing all about it at our next session."

We wrap up the appointment and on my drive home, I think about Xavier. It's a daily struggle to not reach out to him, but he ended things with me, and I really don't want to be that girl. At some of my lower points, I thought about 'accidently' pocket dialling him, so he'd call me back. Or sending him a Snapchat that was intended for 'someone else'. Stupid shit I used to do in my early 20s to get attention from the guys I was seeing. Then I remember I'm in my 30s and I'm not a loser, so I pull my head in and find another distraction.

Distraction. I think that's the hardest thing I've had to overcome. He insinuated that being with me was a distraction. Though he may not have intended it to come across this way, he made me feel as if all of it was my fault. Jane and Millie have done a good job of convincing me that it is not, in fact, my fault. I believe them now, and I also believe he didn't say it to hurt me. I do believe he cared for me, and he was just scared and didn't know what to do. I was the collateral damage of a man who couldn't make up his mind. That's hard to get over, but I'm getting there. Starting with this date on Friday.

CHAPTER 39
Xavier

"Hey, Xavier. Come on in."

"Hey, Brian. Thanks for fitting me in today."

After everything that happened over the last couple of months with Ella and Jimmies, not to mention the last year with Jade, I finally decided it was time I talk to someone. Ella suggested I see a therapist and gave me Brian's number. I'm pretty sure she meant the recommendation as a dig, since "please, go to therapy" was the gist of the conversation, but it works for her, so I thought I'd give it a try.

I follow Brian into his office and take a seat on the navy blue armchair. There's not a whole lot to look at, a circle of armchairs in different shades of blue, a desk in the corner, a few houseplants, a bookshelf full of textbooks, and some others on dogs and music. On the wall above the desk is a framed quote, *'At the end of the day...'* and I ponder over the meaning behind it.

I look at Brian, and if I were to describe him, he gives off teddy bear vibes. He's a bigger guy, with reddish brown hair, a beard, and thin, wireframe glasses. I'd put him in his early 50s. He has gentle eyes, and a calming demeanour. I know some people struggle to connect with a therapist, and I'm really hoping Brian is a good fit for me. This is my third session and so far, so I'm feeling pretty comfortable.

"It's no problem, you were lucky to get a cancellation appointment. What brought you in here today? What's been going on?"

"I've been thinking a lot about what you said last time, about how sometimes we have to be selfish to get to where we want to go in life. I definitely agree with you in the most part, and I know that if I had stayed with Jade, we both would have been miserable in the end. I just… I keep thinking about Ella. I think I made a mistake in ending things."

"Ah, I see. Go on."

"I miss her. I thought I was doing the right thing for everyone, but after a few months apart, I'm realising I should have just tried. She was so willing to try, and I refused to give us the chance."

"So, you're feeling a bit of regret?" he asks.

"Yeah. I know it sounds so shitty, but I didn't realise what I had until I lost it. The business is doing well, and I'm happy with its projection. But what's the point in having this success if at the end of the day I'm going home to an empty house? What's the point if I have no one to celebrate life with?"

"It's not shitty. It's life. Sometimes we have to lose things to learn their value."

"I guess." I toy with my bottom lip. "I just don't know what to do now."

"Do you want to try again with her?"

"Yes. But I have so much guilt. She told me she loved me, and I walked away. How am I supposed to redeem myself after that? How do I make it up to her?"

That's if she even wants to talk to me. I would completely understand if she never wanted to see or speak to me again.

"I can't answer that for you, Xavier. The only thing I can suggest is for you to talk to her. If she refuses to talk to you, that's her prerogative, and you will know where you stand. But if she is willing to talk, you need to be open and honest."

"I think I just worry that I'll end up disappointing her again, like I did with Jade."

"You can't let that fear stop you from trying. Every relationship is different. Just because one thing didn't work out, it doesn't mean the next one will end the same."

"I feel bad though, coming back after only a few months."

"Distance makes the heart grow fonder. It also helps you see things with a different perspective. One thing I always say, hindsight is 20/20. When we look back on situations in the past, we see things more clearly that were not clear to us at the time."

"That is very profound, Brian."

He laughs.

"I know. Makes me sound very wise, I think."

"It does. But it also makes a lot of sense. I just have to figure out what to do next. I'll admit, I'm still scared that what I give won't be enough for her."

"It sounds to me, Xavier, that you don't value yourself very highly."

"Maybe. I think it comes from that feeling of disappointing everyone. Who would want to keep me around after I've let them down?"

"Can I ask, has anyone actually outright said that they were disappointed in you? That you've let them down?" he asks.

I pause and think. I think about when I broke up with Jade—she was upset of course, but she never said she was disappointed in me, and Ella never said anything either. And Dad never said that was the reason for not giving me the business sooner...

"No..."

"So why do you think everyone is disappointed in you?"

"Because I hurt them."

"Hurt doesn't automatically mean they're disappointed. You say you hurt Jade when you broke up, but you remain friends. Do you think she's disappointed in you?"

"I don't know."

"I think you need to have a few conversations, Xavier."

"I think you're right. I just..."

"What is it?"

"I don't know where to start with Ella."

"Start by saying sorry, and then tell her how you feel. Start by trying."

"Okay. I think I can do that."

"I look forward to getting an update in our next session."

I look at the clock and my time is pretty much over.

"Damn." I laugh. "Time really does fly by when you're in here."

"It sure does."

"Can I ask one thing before we finish up?"

"Go for it."

"The quote in the frame, what does it mean?" I ask.

He smiles.

"Every day I ask myself, at the end of the day, what really matters? What is most important to me? This is a hard job, and some days I wonder how I could possibly keep going, but then I think about the people I'm helping, and at the end of the day, that's what matters."

"That's… that's really great. Thanks, Brian."

"Anytime. You've got this, Xavier. I'll see you again in three weeks."

"Perfect. See you then."

CHAPTER 40
Xavier

"Hey, Jade. Just letting you know I'm heading to your place, but I'm gonna be early. Hope that's okay. If not, too bad, you should have answered your phone and told me. See you soon!"

I leave the voicemail on Jade's phone as I'm halfway to her apartment. After speaking to Brian, I'm feeling a little lighter, and a little less guilty for ending the relationship with Jade. I need to have a conversation with her, just to see how she's really doing since the breakup. To see if she's actually disappointed in me. We've talked about it, but it has always been surface level.

I pull up out the front and make my way to the entrance, punching the number of her apartment onto the keypad and I wait for her to buzz me up.

"Xavier, um, hey. You're early."

Jade's voice comes out statically through the intercom. Weird, normally she just buzzes me in.

"Yeah, I called and left a message. Can I come up?" I ask. There's a pause.

"Um. Yeah, yes. See you in a bit."

The speaker buzzes and the door swings open. Jade's acting weird but I can't think about it too much otherwise I'll chicken out of this conversation. I catch the elevator up to her floor and knock on the door. It takes her a minute to answer, and then she's there opening the door, looking a little flustered.

"Hey! Come on in," she says with a smile, albeit a very large one, suspiciously large.

I walk in and close the door behind me.

"Hey, sorry for getting here early, I finished work a little sooner than anticipated—" I stop talking because sitting at Jade's kitchen table is Lena. "Oh, hey, Lena. Sorry, I didn't know you would be here."

"Hey, Xav, it's all good. I wasn't planning on being here by the time you came around but you're early, so…" she trails off and looks at me sheepishly. I check the time and I'm only 20 minutes early. I'm not surprised that Lena is here per se, since she's one of Jade's best friends, I just hoped Jade and I would be alone for this.

"Fair enough." I sit down at the table opposite Lena, and Jade just sort of hovers at the table. I look at her, and I look at Lena. They're both looking at each other, and then to me.

"Okayyyy. You're both being weird. What's going on?" I ask.

They look at each other again and then Jade sits at the table next to Lena.

"Xav, we've been separated for what? Over a year now?" I nod. "I love that after the initial hurt, we've been able to stay friends. There's just something I've been wanting to talk to you about for a while." She's playing with her hands in her lap, a tell-tale sign she's nervous.

"I love it, too. I've also wanted to talk to you about some stuff, and that's why I'm here." I glance over at Lena and frown a little. She doesn't seem to be getting the hint that this should be a conversation between just the two of us.

"Right. Okay. Do you want to go first or should I?" she asks. I gesture for her to go first.

She looks at Lena again.

"Well, I wanted to talk about, like, moving on," she says nervously. I sag with relief.

"That's what I came to talk about too," I tell her.

"Oh, really? That's great! I've wanted to tell you for so long, but I didn't know how you would handle it."

Huh?

"What do you mean? Tell me what?"

She hesitates.

"My… um. My new relationship…"

I go still. *New relationship?*

"Uhh, what new relationship, Jade?"

She looks at Lena again and so, I do too. I look between the two of them and it hits me. Jade smiles at Lena and takes her hand.

"Ohhh," I say, mostly because I have nothing else to say.

"Please don't be mad," Jade whispers.

"Mad? Why would I be mad? I love Lena. She's great," I say, maybe a bit too quickly. Though it is true, I do love Lena. She's not just a great employee, she's a great friend.

"Thanks, Xav," Lena says.

"You're not mad that I'm… dating a woman?" Jade asks hesitantly.

"Oh, no, I'm not mad about that, God. I know you've always been bicurious, Jade. We were together for quite a while, remember?" I smile at her, and I hope it puts her at ease. I have no issues with her dating a woman.

"Yeah, I remember. I'm glad, Xav. I was worried."

"No issues here, I'm happy for you. How long has this been going on?" I ask.

They look at each other.

"Six months," Jade says with a wince.

"Six months!"

"I'm sorry! We really wanted to tell you, but I didn't know how."

"It's fine. I'm not mad. I'm just… I dunno. Frustrated." Six months. I was seeing Ella at the same time as Jade was seeing Lena.

"Why are you frustrated?" Jade asks.

"It's Ella, isn't it?" says Lena. I nod. "What happened there? I thought you two had something?"

"Um. We did. I ruined it, of course."

Jade leans across the table and takes my hand in hers and squeezes.

"Tell us everything."

I swallow hard and take a deep breath.

"We were just friends at first, and then the sexual chemistry just sort of grew naturally, and we decided that perhaps we could start a strictly physical relationship. No emotions or feelings."

Jade snorts and I frown at her.

"Sorry," she says. "Those sorts of arrangements never stay physical."

"Yeah well, I was hopeful. We did have a good thing going for a while, but then feelings got involved."

"Okay, and then what happened?" Lena demands.

"I fucked it up. The whole time I was seeing her I told her I wasn't ready to commit to something new because I was afraid I couldn't give her what she deserved, which was time and effort. And then Dad finally retired, and I took over the business, and it all got too much. Something had to give. I couldn't risk disappointing her like I did to you, Jade, so I ended it."

"How long ago did you end it?" Lena asks.

"About three months ago."

"Hmm, that makes sense. You've been grumpier for around about the same time," she says. Jade smacks her arm.

"Ow! What? It's true. You wouldn't know, you don't have to work with him."

Jade shakes her head and then looks at me.

"Xav, I love you, but you're an idiot."

"Thanks."

"I understand you didn't want to hurt her, I do. But you can't compare how our relationship ended to what could have happened with Ella. We were together for five years and it fizzled, I see that now. I was hurt and upset, but I was never disappointed in you, Xav. I hope you know that. You can't let that fear of disappointing someone hold you back from trying," Jade says.

"I realise that now. I've actually started seeing a therapist, and he said something similar."

"That's so great, Xav. I hope it's helping."

"It is."

"So, did you love her?" Jade asks, smiling softly.

"Yeah, I think I did. Still do, really," I say.

"Aww!" they both say at the same time.

"Oh, shut up." They laugh. "It's too late now anyway. I hurt her, and it's been three months. I've probably lost her."

"How do you know? Have you two spoken since?" asks Jade.

"Not properly. A couple messages here and there—she actually gave me the idea of therapy, but nothing in the last month."

"So, you never know."

"Maybe." I chew on my bottom lip and think everything over, the last three months in particular. Business is booming. Jimmies' social media presence has grown quicker than I anticipated, and because I've started stocking drinks from craft breweries and distilleries, we've drawn a whole new crowd. The place is busier than ever, and I'm so proud.

"What are you pondering?" Lena asks.

"Just thinking about the business," I admit.

"Business is booming." Lena states.

"I know, the place is doing so well. It's just… what's the point of having success if I can't share that with someone?"

They both nod in understanding.

"I wish I could have seen it that way months ago. She was willing to wait, you know?"

"Okay, even though I would never advise a woman to wait around for a man, she sounds like an amazing woman," Jade says.

"She is. Even Meryl loved her."

"Wow. Now I am impressed." The memory brings a smile to my face.

"So, fight for her."

I look up at Jade.

"You said so yourself, she deserves someone who will commit to her wholeheartedly, and will give her everything she deserves. Do you think you could do that now?"

"I want to make it work. I think it'll be hard, but I want to try. I didn't know how good it was until it was gone."

"So, fight for her. Do what you have to, to get her back."

"What if she doesn't want me anymore?"

"You'll never know unless you try. She has every right to turn you down after everything, but she may just miss your stupid head and want you back anyway. It sounded like she really loved you, so you just have to try."

"Thanks. Who would have thought that my ex-girlfriend would be the best person to come to for dating advice." I get up and give her a hug.

"I'm better than those guy friends of yours. They give the worst advice I've ever heard," she mutters into my shirt.

I wince.

"Ahh. Yeah, I may have gone to them looking for advice on this."

Jade pulls back and playfully smacks me on the back of the head.

"Well, no wonder you stuffed things up. Those guys suck! Remember when they half convinced you that I was cheating on you, and that's why our relationship wasn't working?"

"Yeah, I remember."

"Next time you need advice, you come to us. Or your therapist. Understand?"

"Yes, ma'am."

"Good." She gives me another squeeze and pulls away.

"Alright, you should probably go home, because now that I've told you my little secret, a huge weight has lifted off of my shoulders and I would like to ravish my girlfriend to celebrate."

I laugh, a big deep belly laugh that I haven't heard in a long time.

"Okay, yep, I'm out of here." I walk over and give Lena a hug.

"This doesn't change anything between us Lena, you're still my friend. And I'm still your boss."

She chuckles. "I'm glad. See you at work on Friday."

"See you there. Have fun, you two!" I show myself to the door and head downstairs to my car.

I sit there for a while, and I too feel like a huge weight has been lifted off my shoulders. The guilt and the fear, however, is still there. Jade is right. I need to fight for Ella—I need to at least try. *She's worth fighting for.*

CHAPTER 41
Ella

"Deep breaths, Ella. You are a strong, hot, amazing woman and you can do this," I say to myself in the mirror. Logan will be here any minute to pick me up for our date. I'm hiding in Millie's bathroom giving myself a pep talk because deep down, I'm freaking the fuck out.

"You good in there, babe?" Millie asks as she knocks on the door. I take one more deep breath, nod at my reflection in solidarity, and open the door.

"Yep, I'm good." I plaster on my best and most confident smile.

"Yeah… so then why do you look like you're about to eat me?" She eyes me suspiciously.

I tip my head back and laugh, there's no fooling her.

"Just some pre-date nerves. I'm fine. You've definitely vetted this guy, right? We're not about to have a repeat of Old Mate Douchebag?"

Millie cringes.

"I vetted him, trust me. I wouldn't be letting you go out with him if I even suspected it would end like that other one did."

"Good. I wish I knew where we were going."

"He still hasn't told you?"

"Nope. Wants it to be a surprise. Wherever it is, it sounds pretty cool."

"I think it's cute that he wants to surprise you. He wants to impress!" Millie bounces a little on her toes. She's just as nervous as me, I think.

There's a knock on the door and both our eyes widen in excitement and nerves. Millie squeals a little bit and I grab her for a quick hug. I bend down to her little baby bump and give it a gentle pat.

"Wish Auntie Ell good luck, she needs it!"

Millie laughs and bats me away.

"Get out of here, you. Have fun and text me later. If you're comfortable enough having him drop you off at home, let me know, otherwise he can drop you back here. Love you!"

"Love you, too. See you later!"

I rush to the front door and grab my bag on the way. I steady myself, put on my best but more subtle smile and open the door.

"Hey, Logan."

He's tall and blond. Clean shaven. Muscular, but not over the top. He's exactly my type. Or, what my type used to be… before Xavier.

"Hey, Ella. You look nice. Ready to go?"

"Yep! Lead the way." He gestures towards the road where his car is parked, and I follow him out.

It's a reasonably quiet drive filled with simple conversation about how each other's week has been. He works in marketing, so I don't really know much about what he's talking about, but I try to seem interested and ask questions when needed. I don't really pay attention to our surroundings as he pulls us into a car park.

"So, I hope you like this place! Apparently it's been around for a while, but it's under new management, and everyone's talking about it."

My stomach bottoms out and I'm instantly nauseous as I look out of the window of the car and see that we have pulled up out the front of Jimmies.

"Oh, shit," I whisper, quietly enough he doesn't hear me.

"Have you been here before?" he asks.

"Um. Yeah, a few times." *I sucked off the owner in his office.* "But not since the management changed."

Shit, shit, shit. I can't be here. What if Xavier's working? I can't see him for the first time in three months on a goddamn date!

"Oh, cool," Logan says. "You're in for a treat. Their whole vibe has changed in the last few months. It's awesome."

He unbuckles his seatbelt and goes to open his door, but I am frozen in my seat.

"You okay?" he asks.

"Yeah. Yep, all good." I shake myself out of it and swallow my anxiety. I can't get out of this without explaining to Logan why I don't want to be here, and I really don't feel like explaining to him that the new owner is the metropolitan lumberjack that I may or may not still be in love with.

I undo my seatbelt and get out of the car on shaking legs. Maybe he's not working tonight. Now that he's in charge, he shouldn't be working nights anymore. I cross my fingers and toes that he has already gone for the day.

Logan leads the way and I pretend I have no idea where I'm going. I feel like I'm going to be sick, but I swallow it down because this guy really does deserve a chance. I'm going to try and not ruin it by acting like a nervous wreck.

The changes to the bar are subtle, but they have definitely made a difference. Some of the older furniture has been replaced with some modern pieces. Gone are the old wooden tables and chairs, and the colour scheme has changed from an old-timey pub to a modern, industrial looking bar. The music that was playing has gone from classic '80s hits to acoustic renditions of current popular songs. The bar is well stocked with craft beers and gins and the glassware has been updated. It still has touches of the same Jimmies charm I've always loved, just with Xavier's modern take on it. I love it. The place is packed with a younger crowd, and I feel so proud of the work Xav has put in. His dream is coming true.

We approach the bar and Lena is there. I'm nervous to see her again but there's literally nothing I can do about it. She smiles at us and does a double take when she sees me.

"Ella! Hey! It's been a while. How are you?" she asks. Looking just as gorgeous as always.

"Hey, Lena. I'm good. The place looks great!" I gesture to the space.

"It does, doesn't it? He's done so well." We both know who she's referring to, and all I can do is offer a smile and nod. It's then she looks at Logan who is practically drooling at the sight of Lena and I refrain from rolling my eyes.

I mean I get it, but he could be a bit more subtle.

"And who is this?" she asks, giving me a side eye. I swallow a lump in my throat.

"This is… um… Logan.."

"I'm Logan. You are?" Logan says it at the same time as me and thrusts his hand towards Lena for a handshake. This time I *do* roll my eyes. This guy is on a date with me for crying out loud. Not going great so far.

"I'm Lena. Friend of Ella." Lena looks pointedly at him and gives his hand a limp shake before brushing him off and facing me once again.

"So, are you two on a date or something?" she asks. I swallow again.

"Yeah, we are. First date." I say, avoiding her eyes.

She hums under her breath before returning her attention to Logan.

"Well Logan, what can I get for you? I already know what she likes." She nods in my direction.

He orders a pint of some craft beer I've never heard of, and I take the moment to scan the room.

"Looking for someone?" she asks with a knowing smirk.

"Nope. Just taking in the… ambience." She shakes her head as she pours Logan's beer from the tap and then moves onto making my amaretto sour. I'm a little shocked that she remembers my favourite cocktail, but I guess it is her job.

Logan pays for our drinks which was nice. I must thank Lena for making me a cocktail which ended up costing him a little bit more, especially when I was just going to order a cheap glass of wine. We're about to head out into the beer garden to grab a table when I see him.

He's walking out of the corridor that leads to his office, laptop bag on his shoulder, and he's heading straight for the bar. I'm frozen on the spot, and I can't look away from him. He's on his phone, probably reading an email or something, and he walks straight past me without noticing. I turn to watch him, and he goes behind the bar to speak to Lena.

"Hey, Lena. I'm off for the night. Have a good weekend—*oomph*. Ow. What was that for?" I look at Lena and she is clearly elbowing him in the ribs to get off his phone. I should turn and run, but my feet have decided now is a good time to just stop working completely and I'm stuck there, watching.

Lena is pointing her head in my direction in a not-so-subtle way and muttering something under her breath.

"What, Lena? I can't hear you. He looks around to the direction she's pointing her head towards, and he scans the area, scanning over me once and doing not a double take, but a triple take when he sees me.

"Oh." He mouths.

"Yep," Lena confirms.

We both stare at each other for a long while before I'm shaken out of my stupor by Logan. He gently places his hand on the middle of my back and starts to guide me towards the beer garden. I think he's saying something, but I can't hear anything over the roaring in my ears. I finally break eye contact with Xavier, who seems just as shocked as I am, and turn to Logan who's looking at me expectantly.

"I'm sorry, did you say something?" I ask.

"Yeah, I asked if you were okay. You look like you've seen a ghost," he says into my ear, a little closer than necessary, but I'll put that down to it being loud in here.

I look back at Xavier and his eyes are darting between me, Logan, and Logan's hand on my back. Even from here, I can see his jaw tick.

"No, not a ghost, just thought I saw someone I used to know."

"Oh, okay. Are you good to still go outside?" he asks, and I nod. I force myself to turn away from Xavier once again and this time I don't look behind me as I walk outside with Logan and find a table. By pure fucking coincidence, it's the same table I sat at on my date with Jed, the night I met Xavier. The universe is a prankster.

We start talking about the usual stuff you talk about on a first date, career, family, hobbies, travel. I want to give this my full attention, but I can't, knowing that Xavier could still be inside, watching me on a date. My ears perked up when Logan asked me if I read.

"Yeah, I love to read. I mean, I'm a librarian, so it would be weird if I didn't." He laughs at that. "Do you read?" I ask.

"Yeah, I do every now and then."

"Oh cool. What sort of books do you like to read?"

"Non-fiction mostly. I'm really into those self-help type books at the moment. I've been working on myself a bit and they've really opened my eyes to a lot of things."

I stifle the urge to groan.

"Do you have a favourite book or author?" Please say something half decent or I may just walk out on this date.

"Umm, let me think. Oh yeah, I can't remember the title but there was this one by some famous guy, his name starts with a J… Jordan someone?"

I know exactly who he is talking about, and I now have a major red flag.

"What about you?" he continues. "What do you like to read?"

"Fantasy and romance, mostly."

He laughs. This man actually tips his head back and laughs.

"Aw, that's cute. Is it like fairies and stuff? With little magic spells?"

"Um. Sort of. Not like a Tinkerbell type fairy."

"Uh huh. Sure," he says patronisingly. "And romance novels, do you read them often?"

"Fairly often, I switch between those two genres quite consistently." He ponders this for a moment. "Why?" I ask.

"Well, I just don't know how comfortable I would feel about the woman I'm dating frequently reading romance novels."

I don't think my jaw could have dropped open any further. *What the fuck?*

"And why wouldn't you be comfortable with that?"

"It gives women unrealistic standards of what to expect in a relationship," he says nonchalantly.

I stare at this guy in disbelief. I had heard that these sorts of guys existed out there, but this is my first time experiencing one in the wild. I have the biggest ick to have ever icked right now. I think of Xavier, and how he read my favourite books and was always asking me for recommendations. We even tried some of the moves he read about in bed!

I'm done, I can't keep going. I need to get out of this date. Like, now.

"Right. Hey, I just have to go to the toilet, are you good to wait here?" I ask, standing up from the table with my bag.

"Sure thing." He leans back in his chair as I walk away from the table. I notice his eyes drift towards the bar, and I bet my left kidney that he will try and sneak over to chat to Lena while I'm gone.

I escape into the bathroom and call Millie. She answers almost immediately.

"Uh oh. Not even an hour in and you're calling me. This can't be good," she says.

"Oooft. So bad, Millie. Firstly, he's brought me to fucking Jimmies of all places."

"NO."

"Yes. And secondly, he just told me he wouldn't want his girlfriend reading romance novels because it would give her unrealistic expectations in a relationship!" I'm whisper-screaming at this point.

"Put him in the bin!" Yells a drunk voice from one of the cubicles. *I love women.*

"I agree with drunk girl," says Millie. "He's trash. I'm sorry Ell, I really thought this guy would be better."

"It's fine, you didn't know." I sigh. "I just have to get out of here, like ASAP."

"Okay, get an Uber to our place and we can debrief over a Milo."

"Perfect. I'll message you when I'm on my way."

"Be safe! Oh, and Ell…"

"Yeah?"

"Was he there?"

"Yeah." I breathe.

"Shit. Was it weird?"

"Yep. I froze, he froze. We couldn't stop staring at each other. I think I went deaf at one point."

"Whoa."

"Yeah."

"Okay, hurry up and get home to me so we can debrief properly. I may just have a Milo while I wait for you as well."

I laugh. "Okay, see you soon."

I hang up the phone and open up the Uber app, I'm so focused on the screen that I walk straight into someone. Strong hands grab me and steady me, hands that I know all too well. I look up, and there he is.

CHAPTER 42
Xavier

"Hi," she says, it comes out all breathy and squeaky, and it's the cutest sound I've ever heard.

"Hi," I say back with a smirk. One that pops my dimple that I know she loves, and yep, her eyes dart right to it.

I realise that I'm still holding onto her, and I let go. She immediately steps back and half stumbles again, so I grab hold of her once more.

"You all good?" I ask. I rub my thumb gently on her upper arm, not sure if I'm overstepping, but she doesn't yank out of my grip so that's a good sign.

"Mhmm. I'm great. Was just peeing." I laugh and she looks horrified at herself that she just told me that. "I mean, I was just in the bathroom and then you were here, and then you're still here holding me, and um… what?"

I laugh again. I think flustered Ella is probably one of my favourite versions of her. She has no idea what's coming out of her mouth and it's fucking adorable.

"Why are you laughing?" she demands, but there's a slight smile on her lips.

"No reason. How… how are you?"

"I'm fine, I'll be better once I escape and get back to Millie's."

"Oh?"

"I'm on a date." She cringes.

"Yeah, I kind of assumed." I felt sick the moment I saw that guy put his hand on her back. I wanted to rush over there and claim her as my own. Lena talked me off the ledge. "How long have you been seeing this guy?" I have to know if it's a thing.

"Oh, I'm not seeing him. This is the first date. I hadn't met him before tonight." I almost collapse at the relief I feel.

"And given that you told me you want to escape, can I assume it's not going well?" I ask.

She scrunches up her whole face.

"Awful. Like there were a few subtle red flags when we got here but I decided to just give him the benefit of the doubt. But he just said something that made me immediately go NOPE. I'm done."

"What did he say?" I'll kick him out of the bar for life if he insulted her.

"He said he doesn't like women reading romance novels because it gives them unrealistic expectations."

My jaw drops.

"That was my exact reaction!" she says.

"What a douchebag. Does he not know how incredibly helpful those books can be? I mean we…" I trail off. I can't bring up our past, that's not fair, so I clear my throat. "He doesn't know what he's missing, I mean."

She blushes and God, I want to just take her face in my hands and kiss her.

"Exactly. He has no idea. But I can't spend another minute talking to him. I need some sort of excuse to get out of the date."

I tap my finger on my chin like I'm seriously pondering a solution for her. She laughs a little.

"Given what you've just told me, I bet if you told him you just got your period unexpectedly, he will end the date straight away."

Her smile spreads until it's a full-blown grin, and I swear my heart stops beating. *She is exquisite.* That dick bag has no idea what he's missing.

"Brilliant. That'll definitely work. Thank you."

"Anytime. I'll walk with you to the garden."

"Sure."

We walk towards the doors but then Ella stops short and chuckles.

"I called it," she says, mostly to herself.

I follow her line of sight and I see Logan leaning against the bar, very obviously trying to hit on Lena. She's making drinks and remaining polite, but is very clearly giving him zero reason to think she's into him.

"Called it?" I ask Ella.

"Oh, I made a bet with myself that he would try and chat Lena up while I was in the bathroom. He was practically drooling over her when we first got here."

I chuckle, but then I take in what she's really saying. That this guy would rather try and pick up Lena tonight and not her.

"I mean, I can't blame him really. Lena is gorgeous," she continues.

"So are you."

She looks at me again and that blush creeps back up her cheeks. I've missed making her blush so badly it hurts.

"Thanks." She looks down at her feet. The urge to lift her chin and kiss her is so overwhelming that I have to ball my hands into fists to stop myself from doing something stupid.

"I guess there's no need to give him some excuse to get out of here, he doesn't look like he will be going anywhere any time soon."

"Very true. Guess I should order my Uber before he realises." She unlocks her phone and opens up the app.

"I could take you home if you need a lift," I blurt out.

She stops what she's doing and looks at me.

"If you want to, you know, save money or whatever. I can drop you off."

"I'm staying at Millie's tonight."

I wave a hand. "That's fine, it's no trouble."

"It's half an hour in the opposite direction of your house," she points out.

"I want to make sure you get home safe."

She chews on her bottom lip for a minute and thinks about it. She looks down at her phone and frowns.

"Fine. But only because this Uber would have cost nearly $40, and I'm a cheapskate."

"Great. I'll just say goodbye to Lena. Wait here."

I walk over to the bar and pull Lena aside.

"Hey, I'm taking Ella to her friend's place. That Logan guy is a fucking loser. I'll let security know to stick around once your shift is done to make sure he's not hanging out waiting for you."

"Thanks, Xav, appreciate it. I can handle him. Good luck." She pats me on the shoulder and gets back to work. Logan acts like she hadn't even just walked away from him mid conversation. I roll my eyes and walk back over to Ella who's waiting patiently but fidgeting.

"Ready?" I ask.

"Yep."

We walk outside and around the side of the building to where my ute is parked. She walks around the passenger side, and I follow so I can open the door for her. She smiles shyly up at me and thanks me before sliding into the seat. I close the door behind her and all but skip around to the driver's side. I turn the car on and, almost instantly, music starts blaring out of the speakers. I rush to turn it down, but it's too late. She heard it.

"All Too Well? Really, Xav?" She's trying so hard not to laugh.

"10-minute version. It's a good song," I mumble.

"Oh, don't worry, I know. I just didn't pick you to be a Swiftie."

"I never used to be," I admit.

Her mouth pops open just a little but then she catches herself. I look at her and smile and then focus on the road ahead. But not before I turn the music up just a little bit so we can appreciate it in the background. I see her smile to herself out of the corner of my eye.

We sit in silence for most of the drive, only breaking it when Ella gives me directions to Millie and Clay's house. When we get there, I turn off the ignition and we sit in the awkwardness. Neither of us are sure what to say. Eventually, Ella clears her throat and takes off her seatbelt.

"Well, thanks for the ride, Xav." She goes to open the door.

"Wait."

She stops.

"Are you busy tomorrow?"

"Um, not really. Just housework and stuff."

I swallow my nerves.

"Can I bring you a coffee in the morning? Just to talk and you know, catch up on things."

"I don't know, Xav…"

"Just one coffee. For half an hour. 10 minutes even. Please?" I'll beg if I have to. I just need to talk to her.

She sighs deeply and looks at me. I think she can read the desperation on my face because her posture softens a bit.

"Okay. One coffee."

"Done. I'll be there at 10am?"

"That's fine. See you in the morning."

"Goodnight."

I watch her to make sure she gets inside safely. Millie opens the door and they both look over at me and give a little wave. I wave back and they close the door.

I drive home with the biggest smile I've had on my face in three months.

CHAPTER 43
Ella

I feel like I'm going to be sick.

Xavier is due to show up any minute now. I couldn't sleep last night—I felt too nervous to eat breakfast and now my stomach is protesting. Currently, I'm on the couch, staring at my front door waiting for the inevitable knock. My knees are bouncing, and my bottom lip is hurting because I've been biting it all morning.

I've been repeatedly giving myself a pep talk, making sure to remember all that I've learnt these last three months about what I deserve and what I won't settle for. He might not even be coming here to want to get back with me.

"Oh God, what if he's met someone else?" I whisper to no one.

I shake my head. No, he wouldn't do that to me. *I hope.*

"Stop letting old insecurities get the better of you," I tell myself.

I drink some water to try and cool myself down as I'm feeling flushed, but all it does is set off a wave of stomach rumbling. I really should eat. I'm about to get a muesli bar from the cupboard when there's a knock on the door. I check the time, 10am on the dot.

"Okay, okay, okay. Be cool. Be calm. Don't take shit," I whisper. I pull my shoulders back and hold my head up high, then I walk to the door and open it. I almost instantly melt into a puddle the moment I see him, because the man is dressed in a goddamn flannel shirt and is wearing glasses.

GLASSES. And to top it off, a backwards fucking cap. He's holding two coffees. One of them is an iced latte and my stupid little heart warms at the sight of him remembering my coffee order.

"Hey, may I come in?" He smirks.

I realise I've just been staring at him in awkward silence. I just nod like a fool and let him inside.

"Thanks." He chuckles.

I close the door behind him and motion to the dining table. I figured we needed a more formal setting for whatever conversation we are about to have, so I'm avoiding the couch. Not to mention the last conversation we had on the couch ended with him leaving. So yeah, the dining table is the best choice.

"Iced oat latte, right?" he hands me my coffee. Again, I just nod. "Have you gone mute since last night? Or am I just so hot that you've been stunned into silence?"

My head whips around to him and I narrow my eyes.

"No fair. You did it on purpose," I say.

"Did what?" he asks innocently.

I gesture to him and wave my hand up and down.

"All of… this. You know I'm a sucker for a flannel. And when the hell did you get glasses? Are they even real?"

He laughs. "Yes, they are real. I had my eyes tested and it turns out I don't have perfect vision. So, you like them then?"

"Nope."

"Sure." He laughs again.

I take a big drink of my coffee and sigh. It's so good and my stomach is grateful to have something in it, despite it only being coffee and milk.

"So, how's business going?" I ask.

He tells me about all of the changes he's made and how it's drawn in a younger patronage, which is what he planned all along. He's figuring out the social media stuff but seems to be doing really well so far. Everything seems to be working out exactly as he had dreamed it.

"That's amazing, Xav. I'm so proud of you," I say. And I mean it.

"Thanks. How's work going for you?" he asks.

"Pretty great actually, I quit."

"No way! That's amazing. What are you doing now?"

"I'm managing a small primary school library now. I'm so happy there."

"I'm happy for you, you deserved so much more than that shit hole."

I laugh softly. "Absolutely I did. I won't let anyone make me feel worthless and incapable ever again."

"Good."

We sit in silence for a minute, and I stir the ice around in my drink.

"So, why are you here, Xavier?" I ask bluntly. Might as well rip off the band aid.

He sighs and sets down his coffee.

"I'm here because I'm an idiot," he admits.

"Oh?"

"I messed things up with us, badly. I hurt you. I haven't stopped thinking about you since I left, and I realise now I may have made a mistake."

"Really?" My heart is hammering in my chest.

"Yes. I spoke to Jade and—oh wait, did you know her and Lena have been seeing each other for like six months?"

Now that is news to me, and the surprise of it must show on my face.

"I know, that was my exact reaction. I'm happy for them obviously, but I was so surprised."

"I bet! That's great though."

"Yeah. Anyway, I talked to Jade, and I have also been talking to that therapist you suggested."

"Oh! You started therapy? I didn't think you actually would."

"Well, it seemed to help you, so I thought I'd try it. It's helped a lot. And I've also made some realisations."

"Okay…"

"I was scared. I still am. Like I told you once, I didn't want to let you down or disappoint you. I didn't want to disappoint my dad or my family either. I put so much pressure on myself and I was so scared of failing you that I never gave us a chance. It was better to end things before they got too serious, but instead I hurt you, hurt myself, and ruined a perfect opportunity for happiness."

"So… what does that mean now? Obviously, we can't change the past, and you still have the business to run. Let's not forget that was the main reason for you leaving me. Distraction, remember?" I ask, pointing to myself.

"You were never a distraction. I was just lost, and I know that's not an excuse. With the business, the hardest part is done. I still have a lot of work to do, but already my hours are settling and I'm home more. But when I am home, I'm alone. And I've realised, after talking with Jade and Lena, that there's no point in celebrating my success with Jimmies if I have no one to celebrate with."

"I would have supported you. I could have been there," I say.

"I know you would have. At the time I didn't think I could do it all—commit to you and run the place. But now that things have settled, and I've had time to think things over, I have a new perspective."

"And that is?" *Honestly, how can he not hear my heart pounding from where he's sitting?*

"That you don't realise how good something is until you lose it. I want you by my side. I miss you so fucking much, Ell."

I swallow the automatic response that was going to come out of my mouth and just look at him. I need more than that, and he knows it.

"I didn't even try to make it work back then, but I want to try now. You deserve everything and I want to give it to you. No more half arsed promises, no more maybes. I'm ready to commit to you, fully. I want you to be mine and I want to be yours."

Don't cry. Don't cry. Don't cry.

"I don't know, Xav. I was devastated when you left, Millie can tell you that. But I've also grown from it, I know my worth and I know what I deserve. I won't settle for anything less. How can you guarantee that you won't leave me in the lurch again?"

"And you shouldn't. You should never settle for less. And if you kick me to the curb right now, I would completely understand. I can't promise it will be easy and that we won't hit any bumps along the way. I just want a chance to prove to you…" His throat bobs. "I just want to prove to you how much I love you. I do love you, Ella. I want to give you the world if you'll let me."

Well, now I'm crying. I look away from him for just a moment and squeeze my eyes shut. I take a second to calm my racing heart and process what he's just said. *He loves me.* Can I give him this chance? He may be ready to commit to me now, but am I ready? Ready to risk my heart again after everything?

Of course, I am. With conditions, obviously. Does that make me an idiot? Maybe. But I'm still hopelessly in love with him and there's only one way to find out if it will work. The risk of heartbreak is there, but I will forever regret not trying.

I say nothing as I get up out of my chair and crawl into his lap, linking my arms behind his neck. His body relaxes under me, and I can see the relief in his eyes.

"I love you too, Xavier. Of course I love you. I never stopped."

His entire face lights up and he leans in to kiss me. I put a finger to his lips and stop him.

"Hold on. I'm not done." He kisses my finger and I roll my eyes.

"There will be conditions. We can't just jump straight back to how we were, okay? We need to start from the beginning. Which means… no sex. Not for a little while, at least."

The man pouts like a toddler scorned.

"I'm serious. I want us to date properly this time. If we just jump straight into bed, then we go back to how we were before, and I don't want there to be any confusion as to what we are. There also won't be any more second chances, okay? I can't keep going through all of this, so if you stuff me around or hurt me again, we are done. For good this time."

He nods. "Okay. We can do that. And yep, totally fair. I won't waste my second chance, I promise. Anything else?"

I think for a second.

"No more hiding what we are to each other. I want to be with someone who is proud to call me his. You don't necessarily have to scream it from the rooftops, but I refuse to be a secret again."

"Absolutely. And I *will* scream it from the rooftops. There will never be a moment where you doubt how I feel about you, and our friends won't doubt it either."

"Okay." I smile shyly at him.

"Anything else?" he asks.

"Um, no. I think that's all for now." He tucks a stray lock of hair behind my ear and wipes away an errant tear from earlier.

"So, can I kiss you now?"

"Yes, Xavier. You can kiss me now."

The words are barely out of my mouth before his lips are on mine. It's the softest and sweetest kiss we've shared, as though he's trying to convey all of his feelings into this one kiss. All I can feel right now is love.

EPILOGUE
Ella

"HAPPY BIRTHDAY, LOVERRRRR!"

"HAPPY BIRTHDAY, BITCH!"

It's Millie's and my birthday and we've just arrived at our party destination. We decided to do a double date for our birthday this year, mostly because Millie and Clay only have a babysitter for the twins until a certain time and they're too tired to do much else these days. We've settled for Korean BBQ for dinner followed by karaoke, much to the dismay of Clay and Xavier.

I rush over to the table where Millie is waiting for me and give her the biggest hug.

"You literally saw each other two days ago," Xavier says behind me.

"So what? I hug you every day when you come home from work. What's the difference?" I ask.

"Okay, you've got me there. Happy birthday, Millie." He pulls Millie into a hug of his own.

"Thanks, Xav!"

Xavier then greets Clay with a hug and sits down next to him. Millie and I beam at each other. The guys have sparked up quite the bromance since Xavier and I officially became a couple and I love it. My boyfriend being best friends with my best friends' husband? It's a dream come true.

"Alright," Millie starts, "we've got a babysitter until 11pm, so let's make the most of this night! Soju for everyone!"

She orders us all a round and we order our food. It's been so long since I've had Korean BBQ and I'm so excited my mouth is watering. It all arrives on the table and Clay and Xavier take over the cooking—*men and their BBQs*. We dig right in and eat our weights worth of meat and kimchi pancake, to the point of having to undo my pants at the dinner table.

"That was so good, but I think you guys are going to have to roll me out of here," I say to the group.

"Same."

"Me too."

"I feel fine," says Xavier.

"Weird, normally you're the one grumbling the most," I say.

"I guess I controlled myself tonight for a change." He smirks.

After that day when Xavier came over and asked me to give him another chance, we've been pretty much inseparable. He truly meant it when he said he would give it everything he had. He planned date nights, and when he wasn't at my house, or I wasn't at his, he would call me most nights just before bed. He held my hand in public and any time he introduced me to someone as his girlfriend, he said it with such a sense of pride. I know that sounds like the absolute bare fucking minimum, but given my history it was so refreshing to not have to ask for an ounce of affection or acknowledgement. We did settle into a proper routine eventually, and after six months, he asked me to move in with him. I said yes, as long as he built me a library. With a rolling ladder.

He did.

So, we've been living together for a year, we've travelled all around the country, and are planning our first overseas holiday together later this year. I'm so excited. I'm finally going to Italy!

I'm still seeing Jane every two months, but most of the time it's just to give a progress report and ask her advice on menial things. Since leaving my toxic job, my anxiety is so much more manageable, and Xavier and I are going strong, so I rarely need to talk to her about him anymore. I feel better than I have in years and it's a wonderful feeling.

As for Xavier, Jimmies was named one of Adelaide's top five establishments last year, all because of what he's done with the place. I'm so proud of him; his parents are too. He's done such a great job and I'm so happy that his hard work has been recognised. It was all worth it, in the end.

"So, are you too full to go to karaoke?" Xavier asks.

"Absolutely not!" Millie and I say at the exact same time. The guys groan.

"Hey, don't complain," I say. "We promise to not JUST sing Taylor Swift songs this time."

"Bullshit," says Clay.

"I second that," Xavier chirps.

I poke my tongue at them.

"Too bad. It's our birthday so we can do what we want!" I say.

"Exactly. Let's go!" says Millie as she stands from the table.

We pay the bill and make our way to the karaoke bar which is only a few blocks away. Honestly, the walk is probably helping us digest all the food we just ate.

We check into the venue and book out our private karaoke room. Millie and I spend 10 minutes curating our playlist as the boys go and get us drinks.

"This is so great, Mills. I love sharing my birthday with you," I say.

"Me too. I know we haven't been able to see each other as often since the twins came along, but tonight is our night, and we are going to make the most of it!" She hugs me again.

When Millie and Clay found out they were having twins, they were both equal parts ecstatic and terrified, but they couldn't be better parents if they tried. They ended up with a boy and a girl, Lola and Patrick. They are the cutest little cherubs, and I am so proud to be their auntie. Our weekly milo catch ups are less frequent but nothing else has changed in our friendship. We're still the same old Ella and Millie.

"Alright ladies, drink up. Have you picked the songs?" Clay asks as he brings in a tray of drinks for us all.

"We sure have!" I tell him.

"Let's get this over with then."

For the next 40 minutes, we torture and entertain the boys with the most pitchy renditions of Taylor Swift and every other girly pop artist we could find. We gave them a couple of songs to perform, too, and they provided us with the most pathetic attempts at karaoke I've ever seen in my life. We also tried a few couples' duets, and that just ended with us in fits of laughter.

Eventually one of the workers pops their head into the room to tell us we only have 20 minutes left of our booking.

"Okay, how about Clay and I pick the last few songs for you guys to sing. Just to keep you on your toes."

Millie and I look at each other and shrug.

"Okay."

They kick us out of the room so that the songs are a surprise and call us back in after a few minutes. The first two songs they pick are God awful songs from the '70s that neither of us had heard of, and so our performance was subpar.

"We decided to be nice for the last song and play you one that we know you love," Clay says, as 'Love Story' by Taylor starts playing.

"Eeeeeeee!" Millie and I squeal and situate ourselves right at the front of the room in front of the screen,

As we get to the final chorus, the door of the room opens again and it's one of the karaoke staff. In his hands is a huge cake, full of sparklers. In the dimness of the room, they give off a soft, sparkly glow and it sets up the perfect backdrop for us to belt out the final lyrics of the song. The staff member heads back out of the room and closes the door, the music trails off, and the guys start singing happy birthday. Millie and I hold each other and sway along to the sound. It's always an awkward thing, when people sing happy birthday to you. You never know what to do or who to look at.

"Hip hip, hooray! Hip hip, hooray! Hip hip, hooray!"

"Close your eyes and make a wish, my love," says Xavier.

"Xavier, they are sparklers, not candles."

"Humour me."

I roll my eyes but do as he says. I take a second to think of a wish. I think of everything that I have right now, and really there isn't anything else I could ask for in this moment. Except... maybe one thing...

I make my wish and blow on the sparklers and as to be expected, they don't blow out.

"See, they don't blow out!" I say, and I look at Millie. She's wide eyed, looking behind me with her mouth dropped open.

I turn to look at what's gotten her so shocked and there is Xavier, on one knee, with a ring in his hand.

"Marry me, Ella."

There are tears in his eyes as he holds the ring up to me with shaking hands.

I am frozen to the spot for a few seconds and then it hits me. I collapse onto the floor in front of him and I am sobbing. My hands cover my face as my shoulders shake and tears stream down my face. I look up at him again and he's also crying, but also smiling. The brightest smile I've ever seen.

"I don't know what it is you wished for, but this is my wish. For you, for us. So, will you, my love? Will you marry me?" he asks again.

I nod frantically.

"Yes. Of course I'll marry you!" I sob.

He stands up, pulling me with him, and slides the ring on my finger. He kisses me deeply and I can honestly say that this moment right here is the most joy and happiness I've ever felt in my life.

After a while, when the rest of the world comes back into focus, I then hear the absolute wails of delight from Millie, who is clinging to Clay and sobbing just as much as I am. Clay, the cheeky bugger, has filmed the whole thing. Millie breaks from Clay and pulls me into a hug, jumping up and down, and of course that makes me sob even harder.

"Did you guys know?" I demand.

"I had no idea!" cries Millie. "I can't believe it, Ell. I'm so happy for you. Oh my God, you're engaged!"

"I knew," Clay says proudly.

"How could you not tell me!" Millie demands.

He just waves his hand up and down at her.

"For this exact reason. You would not have been able to keep it together, admit it."

"I mean… okay, fair. There is no way I would have been able to act normal if I knew."

I laugh and hug her again, and then hug Clay. I couldn't be happier to have shared this moment with them.

"Alright, Mills. Let's give these two a moment. We'll meet you guys out front." They leave the room and I just look at Xavier and smile.

"Holy shit." I breathe.

He walks over to me and kisses me again.

"So, what did you actually wish for?" he asks, curiously.

"To spend the night in a bookstore with unlimited spending money."

He throws his head back and laughs, pulling me close to him, and resting his chin atop my head. I wrap my arms around him.

"Are you happy?" He asks.

"I've never been happier." I tell him.

I look down at my new ring and smile. It's so beautiful, a simple gold band with an oval diamond. It's crazy to believe that two years ago, I was promising this man that I wouldn't fall for him. And now, we're about to promise to love each other for the rest of our lives.

And unlike that promise two years ago, this is a promise I will keep. Forever.

ACKNOWLEDGEMENTS

I don't even know where to begin. I can't believe I wrote a whole freakin book and its published! Is this real life?!

I started writing this book at a pretty low point in my life. I lost my dad in March 2023, and needed an escape, one that was new to me and could keep me preoccupied. This journey has helped ground me in a time when I felt like my world was being flipped upside down.

What I wanted to achieve with this book was to encapsulate how frustrating and disappointing the dating world is right now. I was in it for nearly eight years and it SUCKED. If you felt confused or frustrated by the characters actions and choices, that was the point. If you wanted to throttle Xavier for treating Ella like his girlfriend but not wanting to commit to her, welcome to situationships! I wanted readers to feel as confused and frustrated as women in the dating world feel, and I hope I was able to accurately represent what a lot of women go through.

Firstly, I want to thank my bookstagram community. You guys have been cheering me on since the moment I mentioned I was thinking of writing a book. Without the constant encouragement and enthusiasm from this community, I probably would have given up. I want to especially highlight my fellow indie authors on booksta. Thank you for guiding me on this journey with your own experiences and giving me the very best advice.

In particular, I want to thank my girls Jess and Etta. Jess, over a year ago I was sitting on your couch, telling you stories of my dating experiences. We laughed, we cried, and then you looked at me and said, "you should write a book." I created a group chat with you and Etta, called it "Em's writing a book" and from that moment, it was on. You girls have been there right from the beginning and I couldn't have asked for a better cheer squad. I love you both immensely. Thank you for your continuous support. Even from you Etta, my token non-romance bestie. Thanks for putting up with my cringe!

To my Beta team, thank you all for your inciteful feedback and assistance in making my book as good as it can be. Your comments were keeping me fed. I appreciate the constructive comments and hype you gave, absolute angels the lot of you and I wouldn't have been able to do it without you.

To Kaitlan, we had barely spoken at all until you reached out to give me advice on commas (lol). Since then, you have been such a big help, providing me with industry knowledge and advice that I normally wouldn't have a clue about. You have been instrumental in my publishing journey, and I can't thank you enough.

To my marketing queen Britt. You, my girl, are a power house. Thank you for the late-night zoom meetings, endless messages back and forth and all of your help in getting my book out into the world. My website? Stunning. You did that. I love you for it.

To my partner, Matt. Thank you for supporting my dream so wholeheartedly. Your love and encouragement means to world to me. I knew I loved you when you revealed you had been reading all of my favourite books. Thank you for being my inspiration for Ella's revelation.

To my editor Elaelah, you're an angel. Thank you for your kind words and generosity and the work you put in to make this book as polished as can be.

To my family and friends, particularly those who don't read, thank you for supporting me and cheering me on despite having no clue at all about books and writing and bookstagram.

And a big thank you to you, the reader. Thank you for giving my silly little romance book a chance. It's not literary masterpiece, but it is a part of me and who I am, and I will be forever grateful that you gave me just a moment of your time.

ABOUT THE AUTHOR

Fuelled by her passion for storytelling, a strong cup of coffee and a good laugh, Emily Nicole is a new voice in the world of Australian romance. Her love for reading began at a young age, and as she reached adulthood, resulted in a dream career as a librarian. She is constantly surrounded by books. When she's not at work, reading, or writing, she's busy listening to Taylor Swift, reviewing books on her Bookstagram account and interacting with fellow book lovers.

www.ingramcontent.com/pod-product-compliance
Lightning Source LLC
Chambersburg PA
CBHW061154210726
48294CB00006B/1668